LORD
SUNDAY

For a full list of titles and more information, go to:
www.garthnix.co.uk

LORD SUNDAY

GARTH NIX

ILLUSTRATED BY TIM STEVENS

HarperCollins *Children's Books*

First published in the USA by Scholastic Inc 2010
First published in Great Britain by HarperCollins *Children's Books* 2010
HarperCollins *Children's Books* is a division of HarperCollins*Publishers* Ltd
77–85 Fulham Palace Road, Hammersmith, London, W6 8JB

www.harpercollins.co.uk
www.garthnix.co.uk

This production 2013

ISBN 978 0 00 793264 1

Typeset in Stempel Garamond by Palimpsest Book Production Limited,
Grangemouth, Stirlingshire
Printed and bound in Great Britain by
Clays Ltd, St Ives plc

To all my very patient readers, editors, family and friends;
and to two writers of science fiction and fantasy who
particularly inspired me to write this series and lit my path
ahead. Thank you, Philip José Farmer and Roger Zelazny.

CHAPTER ONE

Arthur fell.

The air rushed past him, stinging his eyes and ripping at his hair and clothes. He had already fallen through the hole made by Saturday's assault ram, past the grasping roots and tendrils of the underside of the Incomparable Gardens. Now he was plummeting through the clouds, and a small part of him knew that if he didn't do something really soon he was going to smash into Saturday's tower and in all likelihood be so badly broken that even with his newly reshaped Denizen body he would die – or wish he was dead.

But Arthur didn't do anything, at least not in those first few, vital seconds. He knew it was an illusion, but it felt like the wind was holding him up, rather than rushing past. In his left hand he held the small mirror that was the Fifth Key, and in his right he clutched the quill pen that was the Sixth Key, which he had wrested from Saturday and taken with him over the edge. Because of this, Arthur felt powerful, triumphant and not at all afraid.

He looked down at the tower below him and laughed – a deep, sarcastic laugh that was not at all like his normal laughter. He was about to laugh again when Part Six of the Will, in its raven form, caught up with him, its claws latching on to his hair and digging into his scalp.

"Wings!" croaked the raven urgently. It hung on to his head for a second, then lost its grip and spun off, calling out, "Fly! Fly!" as it tried desperately to keep up.

Instantly, Arthur lost his sense of euphoric invincibility and came back to his senses. He properly took in the speed of his descent for the first time and saw that he was going to hit the tower very, very soon.

This is all wrong, he thought. *Where are my wings?!*

He frantically searched his coat, even as he remembered that his grease monkey wings were still in the rain mantle that he'd exchanged for his current disguise as a Sorcerous Supernumerary – the disguise he'd used to infiltrate the assault ram... too successfully perhaps, for he'd gone with the ram when it broke through into the Incomparable Gardens. While he had then got close enough to Superior Saturday to claim the Sixth Key, he'd fallen back through the hole in the ceiling of the Upper House.

Now he was falling a very, very long way down.

Even starting from such a height, Arthur had fallen far faster than he'd thought possible. He was going to miss the actual peak, he saw, and crash into the main part, some fifteen levels below.

No wings, thought Arthur. *No wings!*

His mind halted in panic and all he could do was stare at the tower, tears streaming from his eyes because the wind was rushing by so fast. He found himself flapping his arms as if somehow that might help, and he was screaming, and then—

He crashed into a flying Internal Auditor, who screamed as well. Together they tumbled through the air, the Denizen's wings thrashing wildly. Arthur tried to rip the wings from the Auditor, but he didn't want to let go of the Fifth and Sixth Keys, so he couldn't get a proper grip. He tried to transfer the Sixth Key so as to hold both Keys in his left hand, but in that vital moment the Denizen kicked free and dived away, his wings folded back.

Arthur fell again, but the collision had checked his speed. He had a few seconds to take action and his brain finally got back to work on problem-solving, instead of gloating over the Sixth Key or cowering in fear. He knew there was no way to avoid colliding with the tower – unless he never actually arrived there...

A hundred feet from impact, Arthur somersaulted into a swan dive. Stretching his arms out below his body, he drew several steps in the air with the Sixth Key. The pen left glowing trails of light, which instantly took on the appearance of solid white marble steps.

Arthur hit hard, immediately tucking himself into a ball to roll down the Improbable Stair. As he bounced and tumbled over each step, he knew he had to get his speed under control. Even when he stuck out his leg, he only tumbled sideways – and kept falling. Climbing up the Improbable Stair was bad enough, with the chance of coming out on some random Landing anywhere in time or space. Falling down it – completely out of control – was even worse.

Arthur remembered the Old One's caution, the words now echoing inside his head, in between thuds, bangs and the jangling pain of new bruises.

It is possible to end up somewhere you particularly do not wish to be, the Old One had said. *It is even likely, for that is part of the Stair's nature.*

He tried again to stop, but since he was still clutching the Keys, he couldn't even grab on to the edge of a step. It was more like falling down a slide than a staircase, much more so than could be normal or natural. The Stair itself was working against him, accelerating his fall, leading him somewhere he doubted he'd want to be.

Thoughts of really terrible places in history began to flash through Arthur's mind, thoughts made more awful because he knew that if he focused on any one place for too long, the Stair would take him there.

He tried to turn on his stomach and stop the endless slide with his elbows, but this didn't work either, though it hurt a lot. Arthur grimaced as his funny bones were repeatedly jarred. Before his transformation from a mortal boy into a Denizen or whatever he had become, he would have been screaming with pain, and his arms would have broken like sticks. But the Keys, and his use of them, had changed his bones, skin and blood beyond anything a doctor would recognise as human.

Arthur was afraid there were other changes too, changes inside him that removed him even further from humanity, things that went beyond his new size, strength and durability. But this was a distant, nagging fear that was currently overwhelmed by his current panic.

I have to stop, he thought. *I have to get off the Stair!*

He rolled on to his back, gasping as the front edge of each step smacked him in the backbone. He put the Sixth Key in his mouth, so he would have a hand free. Then he raised the mirror of the Fifth Key, held it in front of his face and tried to focus on it as he continued his juddering descent.

The mirror had been blocked by Saturday's sorcerers inside the Upper House and it might not work inside the Stair either, but Arthur had to take any chance he could to get out. First, though, he had to find a way to hold the mirror steady and he had to keep the picture of Sir Thursday's bedroom in his head. This was very hard to do. He tried to visualise it, but he kept thinking of places he didn't want to go, like the plague-ridden London of Suzy Turquoise Blue's time, or the island in the middle of a sun where he'd found Part Two of the Will. Even as a Denizen, Arthur knew he couldn't survive if he came out of the Stair into the heart of a star.

He also wouldn't survive an emergence into Nothing. Which meant he also had to stop thinking about Doorstop Hill or any parts of the House that he knew had already been consumed by Nothing. So much of it was gone already, as the Void spread into the House, destroying everything in its path. Arthur shivered inside as he remembered the great wave of Nothing that he had fled a moment before it destroyed Monday's Dayroom—

No! Arthur yelled to himself. *Think of somewhere safe. Somewhere easy. Home. But even home might not be safe – I've got to just stop and think—*

But he couldn't steady the mirror, or get his

mind to focus on somewhere safe. Instead he rolled over again and grabbed at the next step with his free hand, his fingernails raking across the marble, down one... two... three steps. His arm almost came out of its shoulder socket as his slide was arrested, and he nearly dropped the Sixth Key when he couldn't help but groan at this new and sudden pain.

But he stopped.

Arthur sighed and dropped the Sixth Key from his mouth to his bloodied hand. He slowly stood and set his foot on the next step. It was time to start climbing back up, while thinking hard about where to come out.

He was just about to start doing this when the Stair disappeared in a flash of bright white light. Arthur's foot met no resistance. He fell forward into a hole full of evil-smelling mud. The Stair, as it always tried to do, had thrown him out on to some random Landing, which could be anywhere in the Secondary Realms, and could also be at any time in the past.

Arthur almost went face-first into the mud, but he recovered his balance in just enough time to stagger forward and crash into a sandbagged earth wall instead. He bounced off that, went back into the hole and windmilled his arms desperately for a second, before ending up planted backside-first in about a foot of yellow, stinking mud.

He sat there long enough to make a face, then slowly got back to his feet, the mud making a popping sound as he rose. There were other stranger noises too, distant high-pitched electronic squeals that hurt his ears.

Arthur looked around. For a moment he thought he'd come out in a World War One trench, back in the history of his own Earth. But that thought only lasted for a moment. He was in a trench all right, but the mud was a lurid, unearthly yellow and stank of sulphur. The sandbags, now that he looked at them properly, were pale blue.

He tapped one, and his knuckles sank in a little bit and then bounced back.

Foam, thought Arthur. *The sandbags are filled with something like packing foam.*

The zinging noises were getting closer. Arthur didn't know what was making them, and he had no intention of hanging around to find out. The only question was whether the Fifth Key would work if the Improbable Stair had dumped him off somewhere back in time, as well as into the Secondary Realms. If he couldn't use the mirror, he'd have to use the Stair, and that meant getting back on to it as quickly as possible. Theoretically, as he had two Keys, he could enter the Improbable Stair pretty much anywhere, but he knew in practice it was bound to be more difficult, and there was a very good chance that his next trip on the Stair would take him somewhere worse than this.

Quickly, he put the quill pen inside his silver bag, along with his yellow elephant and the medallion he'd been given by the Mariner. Then he replaced the bag safely inside the pouch of his utility belt. He kept the Sorcerous Supernumerary's large coat on, over the top of his coveralls. Even though the yellow mud looked like it was boiling, it felt cold – and if Arthur felt it, that meant it was very cold indeed.

This was confirmed by his breath, which wasn't just fogging out, it was freezing in the air. In only a few minutes, he developed a long, thin beard of ice crystals that sparkled from his chin down to his chest. The sunlight, though very bright, was more red than yellow, and he could feel no noticeable heat from it on his face or hands.

Wherever he was, it wasn't Earth, and Arthur suspected it wasn't somewhere a normal human could survive for a second. He was thankful that he could, but it also sent a pang through him, another reminder of what he had become and what he no longer was.

He raised the mirror and was about to visualise Sir Thursday's chamber when he glimpsed a reflection from behind him. He spun round just as something jumped down from above the trench. It was a flash of movement and it took a moment for Arthur to process that at its heart was a seven-foot-tall armoured stick insect, holding a tube in its first lot of spiked forearms and pointing it at Arthur. Before he could react, he heard the squealing noise up close for the first time and felt a savage pain as golden blood suddenly boiled out of a hole that went straight through the bicep of his left arm.

Arthur turned the mirror and directed his will. The Fifth Key caught the red sunlight, gathered it up and concentrated it a millionfold before projecting it at Arthur's enemy in a tightly focused beam.

The insect was cut cleanly in two. But the top half continued to scrabble towards Arthur, and the forearms tried to aim the tube again. Arthur, furious and in pain, directed his anger through the mirror. This time the Fifth Key conjured up a roaring column of fire that stretched from the ground up into the stratosphere and completely incinerated everything in the trench in front of Arthur for at least a hundred yards.

As the fiery column slowly sank back to the ground, Arthur spun around again, checking behind him. He listened for the squealing noises and, though he couldn't hear them, he heard something else: a clicking noise, getting louder and closer. Arthur knew what it was – the sound the insect soldier's limbs had made when it had moved, but magnified a thousand times.

He jumped up on the trench's firing step and looked out on to the yellow mud no-man's-land of this alien war. Thousands of stick-insect soldiers were marching towards him, all perfectly in step, all holding those squealing tubes.

I could kill them all from here, thought Arthur. He felt a feral grin begin to spread across his face, before he pushed it away. He had the power, it was true, but he knew he didn't have the right. They weren't even really enemies; they knew nothing of the struggles in the House. They might look like giant stick insects, but obviously they were sentient beings, as technologically advanced as humans, perhaps even more so.

So what? thought Arthur. *I'm no longer human. I am Lord Arthur, Rightful Heir to the Architect. I could kill ten thousand humans as easily as ten thousand alien insects.*

He began to raise the mirror, visualising an even bigger, more awesome column of fire, one that stretched from horizon to horizon, saving only him from the inferno.

"No," whispered Arthur. He forced his self-righteous pride and anger back. "I am *me*... I'm not *Lord* Arthur and this is wrong. All I have to do is leave."

He swung the mirror round and looked into it, trying to think of Sir Thursday's chamber and not all the destructive things he could do to anyone or anything that opposed him.

But he couldn't focus – it was all he could do to keep his rage in check. He really wanted to destroy the insect soldiers, and every time he almost had a mental picture of Thursday's room, it was replaced by images of fire and destruction.

As Arthur struggled with his thoughts, the mirror remained constant. He saw only his reflection, the now all-too-perfect face, so handsome that even a beard of frost could not lessen his unearthly beauty.

Arthur groaned and put the mirror back in his pouch. The horde of insect warriors was approaching at a steady pace and had neither slowed nor speeded its advance. The forward ranks hadn't aimed their weapons either, but he suspected he was probably in range. Arthur looked at the hole in his arm. It was neatly cauterised, but he could see right through from one side to the other. Only his sorcerously altered body allowed him to cope with such a wound. It felt about as painful as a paper cut to him now.

But he knew he could not survive a hundred – or a thousand – such wounds. He also knew that the rage he was barely keeping inside him would come out long before then, and that he would use the Keys to wreak destruction such as even these warring aliens had never imagined.

I have to get out of here, thought Arthur. *Before I do something terrible...*

He jumped back down and tried to visualise the Improbable Stair. That could be its first step there, the pale blue sandbag that was the firing step of the trench. It just had to turn white and luminous, and that would be the way in.

"White and luminous," said Arthur. "The way into the Improbable Stair."

Ahead of him, the clicking noise suddenly increased in volume and tempo. The soldier insects were beginning their charge.

"White! Luminous! Stair!" shouted Arthur.

A squealing *zing* went over his head, but he didn't turn or look. All his attention was on that one pale blue sandbag, which was slowly, ever so slowly, beginning to turn white.

CHAPTER TWO

Suzy Turquoise Blue, sometime Ink-Filler Sixth Class, Monday's Tierce and General of the Army of Lord Arthur, waggled her left foot just enough to start her spinning in an anticlockwise direction. She'd been slowly turning clockwise for the past hour and she felt like a change. She could introduce that motion with only a slight movement of her foot, which was fortunate since it was the only part of her that wasn't tightly wrapped in the inch-thick scarlet rope that suspended her from a crane that had been swung out some 16,000 feet up on the eastern side of Superior Saturday's tower.

"Stop that!" called a Sorcerous Supernumerary, who sat at the base of the crane. He was reading a large leatherbound book and dangling his legs over the edge of the tower. "Prisoners are not to spin anticlockwise!"

"Sez who?" asked Suzy.

"The manual says so," replied the Supernumerary rather stiffly, tapping the book he held. "I just read that bit. *Prisoners are not to spin anticlockwise, for the prevention of sorcerous eddies.*"

"Better wind me in then," said Suzy. "Else I'll keep spinning."

She had been hanging there for more than six hours, ever since being captured by the Artful Loungers near the Rain Reservoir, where Arthur had gone down the plughole in search of Part Six of the Will. Since being a prisoner was a definite improvement over being dead, which was what she thought was going to happen when the Loungers had attacked, Suzy was quite cheerful.

"It says here, *Prisoners are to be left dangling in the wind and rain at all times, unless ordered otherwise by Suitable Authority,*" said the Supernumerary.

"It's stopped raining," said Suzy. "It's not all that

windy either. It's quite nice in fact. Besides, aren't you a Suitable Authority?"

"Don't make me laugh," grumbled the Supernumerary. "You know quite well I wouldn't be here if everyone else wasn't up top, fighting Sunday. Or down below, fighting the Piper."

And that's only the half of it, thought Suzy with a smile that would have annoyed the Supernumerary if he'd seen it. *Superior Saturday is fighting Lord Sunday up above in the Incomparable Gardens; the Piper is fighting Superior Saturday's forces in the lower portions of the Upper House; Dame Primus is trying to hold back the Nothing that is eroding the House, while also preparing to attack Superior Saturday; Arthur hopefully by now has got Part Six of the Will and will be trying to obtain the Sixth Key...*

It's all like a very complicated game, thought Suzy as she spun back towards the Supernumerary. *I wonder if anyone really knows what's going on.*

Thinking about games gave her an idea. Artful Loungers were too crazed and dangerous to try to trick, but this Sorcerous Supernumerary was more like a normal Denizen.

"You know, if you wind me in, we could play

chess," said Suzy. She pointed her toe at the chess set that was on top of the closer desk. It looked to be a very fine one, with ivory pieces that had ruby-chip eyes.

"That's one of Noon's sets," said the Supernumerary. "We can't touch that! Besides, I failed chess."

"We could play draughts. We oughter play something until my rescuers show up and chuck you off the building," said Suzy.

"What?" asked the Supernumerary. He looked around nervously. Unlike most of Saturday's tower, the prison section at level 61620 (that was really floor 1620, which was quite high enough) was a solid buttress attached to the main building, rather like a shelf that was put on as an afterthought. It was not made up of open iron-framed office cubes, but was a broad and elegant veranda of teak decking that ran alongside the tower for a hundred feet. The outer edge was lined with a dozen cranes that were mounted so that they could pivot and swing their hooks out over the edge, to suspend prisoners some 16,000 feet above the ground.

Currently, only one of the cranes had a dangling prisoner. The Internal Auditors who usually ran the prison level had all left to join Saturday's assault upon the Incomparable Gardens and had presumably dispatched all their prisoners before their departure. Now only Suzy was there, guarded by two Sorcerous Supernumeraries. One was reading the manual, and another was prowling back and forth in front of the single, large leather-padded door that led back into the tower proper. As she paced, she muttered to herself about awesome responsibilities and the inevitability of things going wrong. This Supernumerary had not once looked over at Suzy, almost as if she wanted to deny the existence of her prisoner.

"What do you mean, rescuers?" the Supernumerary with the manual asked. "And why would they chuck me off the tower?"

"I'm a Piper's child, right?" asked Suzy. "Who's attacking the tower?"

"The Piper," said the Supernumerary. "Oh... I see. But he'll never get this far."

"Dunno about that," said Suzy. "I mean, Saturday's nicked off with all the best fighters, ain't she? I mean, *she's* all right, *she'll* be living it up in the Incomparable Gardens, with her Artful Loungers and Internal Auditors and all. It's you poor blokes I feel sorry for."

"We always get the worst jobs," admitted the Sorcerous Supernumerary. "You know what the higher-ups call us? *Maggots*, that's what. At least that's what one called me once... "

"Wot's your actual name then?" asked Suzy. "I'm Suzy Turquoise Blue."

"Giac," replied the Supernumerary. He looked over the edge and sighed. "I was enjoying being up this high till you said I might get chucked off."

"Course, you might not get thrown off," Suzy said thoughtfully.

"I bet I would," said Giac. "Bound to be. Just my luck."

"They might just cut your head off," said Suzy. "The Newniths, I mean. The Piper's soldiers. Big, ugly brutes they are, with charged battle-axes and the like. I'm glad I'm on the same side as them, is all I can say."

"They'll never get this far," repeated Giac uneasily.

"Might as well 'ave a bit of fun before whatever happens happens," said Suzy. "Tell you what – why don't you bring me in, we'll play draughts, and then when the Newniths show up, I'll get them to just take you prisoner. Instead of cutting your head off."

"I have to do what the manual says," replied Giac gloomily. "Besides, one of the Internal Auditors might come back. They'd do worse than cut my head off."

"Worse?" asked Suzy. "Like what?"

"Encystment," said Giac with a shudder. He turned a page in the manual and stared at it, then sighed and shut the book.

"It's so nice up here," he said. "Particularly without the rain. I really do think ten thousand years of rain is a bit much. My socks might even dry if it stays fine."

"Be even better with a game of draughts," said Suzy. "You don't have to untie me. Just swing me in and I'll call out the moves. Then, if one of your lot shows up, you can swing me out again and they'll be none the wiser."

"I suppose I could..." Giac put the book down and peered at the workings of the crane. "I wonder if it's this wheel... or perhaps this lever?"

"No! Not the lever!" shouted Suzy.

Giac withdrew his hand, which had been just about to pull the lever that would release the hook and send Suzy plummeting down to certain death.

"Must be the wheel, then," he said. He started to turn it and the crane responded, rotating on its pivot until Suzy was brought back to dangle above the floor of the veranda.

"Good work," said Suzy. "I s'pose you still don't want to touch Noon's set?"

Giac nodded.

"Well, get a piece of paper and draw us up a draughtboard."

As Giac got some paper and a quill pen out of the closer desk, Suzy spun herself slightly away from the Denizen so that he couldn't see her as she wriggled two fingers under the rope around her waist, feeling inside one of the pockets of her utility belt. She could only reach one pocket and she knew there was nothing as useful as a knife in there. Still, ever optimistic, she thought there might be something. It was an effort, but she did manage to get a grip on a cake of best-quality waterless soap. Slowly she drew it up into her hand.

Bloomin' soap, she thought. *What am I going to do with that?*

"This will serve," said Giac. He set out a sheet of thick paper on the floor near Suzy's feet and quickly drew up the board. "I'll rip up some more paper to make the draughts. Do you want to be blue or white?"

"Blue," said Suzy. As she rotated around again she manoeuvred her hand so that she could push the soap between two strands of rope. Being waterless soap, it was quite slippery and she thought she might be able to make it shoot out, if she could just get a good grip and snap her fingers in the right way. "What's your friend doing?"

"Hmmm? Aranj?" asked Giac. He looked around at the other Sorcerous Supernumerary, who had stopped pacing by the door and was now sitting down with her legs pulled up and her face on her knees, appearing rather like a crushed black spider. "She's gone into a slough of despond. It couldn't have helped to have you talking about our heads getting cut off."

"What's a sluff of despond?" asked Suzy.

"Acute misery," replied Giac as he tore up a

blue sheet of paper, "resulting in withdrawal from the world. Happens to a lot of us Sorcerous Supernumeraries. Had a bout of it myself a thousand years ago. Not too serious, mind – it only lasted twenty or thirty years. I suppose I should be suffering now, but you were right about the draughts. I'm looking forward to our—"

At that moment, Suzy forced her fingers together with a snap and the soap shot out. It struck Giac in the side of the head, but with very little force.

"Ow!" he said. He looked around wildly, but Suzy was still all tied up and slowly spinning in place. "Who did that?"

"Dunno," said Suzy. "It just came out of nowhere."

Giac picked up the soap and looked at it.

"Grease monkey soap," he said. "Probably thought it was funny to drop this over the side, somewhere up top. Oh, well. Let's get started."

"You can go first," said Suzy.

Giac nodded and set out the paper draughts on the makeshift board. He'd only just laid them all down when a breeze blew in, picked them up and lofted them over the edge of the veranda to spin and twinkle away.

"We'd better use Noon's board and the pawns for draughts," said Suzy. "Tell you what – if you don't want to touch it, how about you cut me down and I'll do all the moves? That way you can say you never went near it."

"I don't know..." said Giac. He looked longingly at the board. "I would so love to play a game. It's been such a long time since I played anything."

"You get me down and we'll play draughts until someone shows up. If it's your lot, you just say I escaped a minute ago. If it's the Piper's Newniths, you can change sides."

"Change sides?" asked Giac. "Um, how could I do that?"

"Well, you just stop obeying Superior Saturday and start obeying the Piper... or someone else. Lord Arthur, for example."

"Just like that?" asked Giac wonderingly. "And it would work?"

"Well, I s'pose it would," said Suzy. "As long as you didn't run into Saturday herself. Or one of her superior Denizens, like Noon."

"But they've gone up top," said Giac, pointing. "Invading the Incomparable Gardens. I could change sides *now*."

"First things first," said Suzy. "It's one thing to change sides; it's something else to have the other side accept you."

The half smile that had begun to form on Giac's face crumpled. "I knew it couldn't be easy as that."

"Course you *will* get accepted if you let me go," said Suzy. "That's the first thing. So it's still pretty easy."

"You mentioned Lord Arthur," said Giac. "How many sides are there again? I mean, besides Saturday's?"

"It's a bit complicated," said Suzy quickly. "I'll explain when you get me down. I can draw a diagram."

"I like diagrams," said Giac.

"Good!" said Suzy. "Get me down and I'll draw one. Quickly!"

"All right," replied Giac, and something like a small smile flitted across his face. It was the first time Suzy had ever seen a Sorcerous Supernumerary look even remotely happy.

Giac pulled the lever and Suzy dropped to the

floor of the veranda. The Denizen strode over and began to undo the knots.

"I'm a rebel," Giac said happily. "Do you think I'll get a uniform? Something brightly coloured? I rather fancy a red—"

Before he could say anything further, something large and black streaked in from the open air and struck him in the back of the head, sending him sprawling across Suzy. As Giac hadn't properly undone any knots, Suzy was still trapped. All she could do was wriggle out from under his unconscious form.

"Suzy Turquoise Blue?" asked the black object, which was reforming itself from a kind of bowling ball made of tiny swirling letters into a raven made up of tiny swirling letters.

"Yes," said Suzy. "Let me guess – Part Six of the Will, right?"

"At your service," said the raven. "In a manner of speaking. I've come to rescue you, as Lord Arthur instructed."

Suzy sniffed. "I don't need no rescuing," she said. "Had it all organised, didn't I? 'Cept you've just knocked out the Denizen wot was untying me. Where's Arthur?"

"Mmm... not entirely... mmm... sure," said the raven as it pulled at a knot with its beak. "There – slither out."

Suzy slithered out of the loosened bonds and checked Giac. He was unconscious, but the faint smile was still on his face, suggesting that he might be dreaming of a colourful uniform. She looked over at Aranj too, but the other Denizen hadn't even looked up and was still crouched down, totally rejecting the world around her.

"'Ow do you knock out a Denizen?" asked Suzy. "I tried it myself once or twice, but just hitting them never works."

"It is not the force of the blow, but the authority with which it is delivered," quoth the raven.

"Hmmph," said Suzy. She sidled over to the chess set and looked back at Part Six of the Will over her shoulder. "Now, what's Arthur up to?"

"After releasing me and securing the Sixth Key, Lord Arthur went into the Improbable Stair, to a destination or destinations unknown," reported the raven. "Which means that until he returns, it is up to us to secure his position here."

"So he got the Key," said Suzy with satisfaction.

"I told 'im he would. 'Ow do we go about securing the position then?"

As she talked, she picked up the solid-gold queen from Noon's chess set and idly slipped it into one of the pockets of her utility belt.

"We must open an elevator shaft to the Great Maze," said the raven, "make contact with my other parts, and bring in troops to secure this tower and the entry into the Incomparable Gardens."

"Right," said Suzy. "That can't be too difficult. Where do we go to open an elevator shaft?"

"The sorcerers assigned to blocking the elevators are on Levels 6860 to 6879. We merely need to access a desk on one of those levels."

"What if they're still full of sorcerers? Or been taken over by the Piper's lot?"

"The Piper's forces have not advanced beyond the lower levels," said the raven. "Or at least they hadn't when I last looked. There are still a great number of Saturday's lesser troops down there."

"Right, then," said Suzy. She walked back over to Giac, sat him up and lightly slapped him on the cheek. "Come on, Giac! Ups-a-daisy!"

"What are you doing?" asked the raven. "You'll wake him up."

"I know," said Suzy. "He might come in handy and he's on our side now. Ain't you, Giac?"

Giac looked at her woozily.

"Yes," he mumbled. "I think so. Which side was that again? Did you draw me a diagram?"

"I'll draw you up one later," said Suzy. "Now, where's an elevator at? Or the Big Chain? Lead on, Giac!"

CHAPTER THREE

The Improbable Stair became real and Arthur sprang on to its first step. Even as he left the alien world behind, hundreds of energy beams crisscrossed the air where he'd been – and one of them struck the side of his head. Even Arthur's magically transformed flesh and bones could not withstand such a forceful strike. He felt it like an ice pick to the brain, an intensely cold and numbing blow that made him black out for a second. He stumbled on the Stair and almost lost his balance, before some primal instinct separate from any intelligence forced him to stagger up the steps.

Golden blood streamed down his cheek and dripped upon the Stair. Arthur wiped it away and inadvertently felt what had to be a gaping hole in the side of his head, above where his ear used to be.

My ear's gone, thought Arthur, shock beginning to leapfrog through his body. *I'm going to die... but I can't die...*

He staggered up another few steps. There was golden blood in his eyes now, and a terrible chill was spreading through the right side of his head and down his right arm and leg. It was becoming harder to move; he had to step up with his left foot and then drag his right leg after him. If it got any worse, he would fall for sure, down the Improbable Stair to some even deadlier place...

I have to get somewhere safe, somewhere I can recover, thought Arthur. He tried to visualise Thursday's chamber, but he couldn't. Just as a hurt animal desires only its own den, all he could think of was his own bed, his own room, back on Earth.

But I shouldn't go there... It will restart time, and the Army is going to nuke the hospital, and I'm in no state to do anything. It's been so long since I lay on my bed... so long... my bed...

The Improbable Stair vanished and Arthur fell into his very own bed.

He lay there, stunned, for what felt like a very long time. He couldn't move and after a little while he realised that he could only see out of his left eye. He was also unable to move his head, so he lay there on his side, his one good eye slowly scanning his bedroom.

It was just barely light outside the window, the sky showing the faint glow that precedes the dawn. His desk lamp was on, casting its fairly ineffectual circle of light. The clock on the wall said half past ten, which was clearly wrong, given the light outside. Arthur watched the minute hand for a while and saw that the clock had stopped, perhaps days ago.

Apart from the stopped clock, the room looked exactly as it had always looked, which he supposed was a good sign. Even the stopped clock might be a positive, because time itself might still be frozen, temporarily halted by the power of the Fifth Key. Arthur had done that because the Army, temporarily controlled by Saturday's minion Pravuil, in the guise of a General, had been about to destroy East Area Hospital with micronukes, supposedly in order to eradicate the Sleepy Plague, Greyspot, and other viruses that were concentrated at the hospital.

Arthur hoped it was still a few minutes before midnight on Friday, and that he'd come back in time to properly stop the nuclear attack.

But when he'd stopped time, there had been a strange red tinge to the light. Arthur couldn't see that now. And what's more, Arthur had come back from the Incomparable Gardens, albeit indirectly. Returning from the seventh demesne of the House would mean returning to Earth on a Sunday – and in order for it to be a Sunday, time must have passed since he'd frozen it on Friday.

Which meant it was probably more than a day since the Army had nuked the hospital, and the only reason everything seemed OK was that the house was far enough away not to be destroyed by the blast.

Though it would still be affected by radiation, Arthur thought, and that led him to attempt to get up. If any of his family was at home, he had to help them. He hoped his mother would be there, but in his heart he knew that wasn't going to happen, since he knew she hadn't been on Earth since before he defeated Lady Friday, and was probably a prisoner of either Superior Saturday, Lord Sunday or even the Piper.

At least his father was safely far away, on tour with his band, The Ratz. His oldest brother, Erazmuz, was in the Army, in fact with the clean-up operation that would follow the nuclear attack. Staria, Patrick and Suzanne, like Erazmuz, were much older and all lived in other cities.

That left Arthur's sister Michaeli and his brother Eric, who normally lived at home, or at least theoretically did, since both spent a lot of time with friends. But they could be here, and in danger. He had to get up and see.

But when he tried to move, he felt the pain in his head increase, and the cold paralysis that affected his entire right side grew stronger.

Arthur shut his good eye. Slowly, with a hand that felt ridiculously weak, he felt into the pouch and closed his bloodied fingers on the Fifth Key. Using sorcery here on Earth was bad, since it would affect the world in a negative way, but he didn't really have a choice, other than to use only one of the two Keys, to limit the side effects on the world around him. He couldn't wait for his body to heal itself, though he knew it probably would in time. He had to use sorcery to accelerate his healing.

He tried not to think of the hole he'd felt in his head, and how in this case "healing" probably meant regrowing part of his brain.

Arthur gripped the mirror harder, concentrated his mind on what he wanted to happen and muttered fiercely, "Fifth Key! Heal me, make me good as new, as quickly as you can!"

A terrible, explosive pain shot up Arthur's fingers. He cried out, and then began to sob as his body was twisted from side to side, and the bones in his spine cracked and screeched. He felt his skull knitting back together and the skin stretching across, all of it accompanied by almost unbearable agony.

Then it was over. Arthur felt limp and tired, but otherwise all right. Gingerly he opened his right eye. He could see perfectly well through it, but just to test it out he read the titles on the spines of the books in the shelf above his desk, pleased to note that even in the dim light from the lamp, he could read the smallest type.

Arthur was just about to look away when he saw the small book on the far end of the shelf, a book that shed a soft and rippling blue light. He opened both eyes to make sure of what he was seeing. Certain, he jumped up and snatched it off the shelf, sitting back down with the slim, green-bound notebook held fast in his right hand.

A Compleat Atlas of the House and Immediate Environs was back in Arthur's possession.

Arthur patted the cover, then put the Atlas carefully away in the silver pouch. As he straightened up from doing that, he caught a glimpse of himself in the mirror on the back of the door, the mirror that his mother had insisted on putting there so he would remember to comb his hair before he came down in the morning.

Arthur looked at the reflection for a few seconds, then moved closer to the mirror to study what he had become. He had been healed, true enough. But he had also been changed again. His hair had become spun gold, all perfectly arranged and shining. His skin had become a deep red-bronze, smooth and poreless. There was no white in his eyes, just a soft golden glow around an utterly black pupil and iris.

I look like some kind of android, thought Arthur bitterly. *Or a statue that's stepped off its stand.*

He stared for a moment longer, before looking down at the crocodile ring on his finger. It was now entirely gold. Not even a glimmer of silver remained to show that some last vestige of humanity remained in his blood and bones. His body was one hundred per cent Denizen. Or perhaps even something more, as the gold shimmered with its own soft light and its colour varied from a rose gold to the butter yellow of the pure metal.

Arthur shut his eyes for a moment and shook his head, trying to cast away the feelings of self-pity that were rising inside him.

"I don't... I don't care," he said softly to his reflection. "I have a job to do. It doesn't matter what I have become. It doesn't matter what I look like."

He pushed open the door and softly trod downstairs.

I hope no one is home, he couldn't help thinking. *I hope they're safe somewhere else. And that they don't have to see me this way.*

The house was very quiet. Arthur slipped quietly down the stairs, pausing to listen every four or five steps. He had learned to be cautious. He was also wondering what he should do. He couldn't stay – that was for sure. He had to get back to the House as soon as he could. But before he did that, he might need to stop time again. Or perhaps try to clean up whatever had happened...

At the landing just before the living room, Arthur stopped and took a deep, unfettered breath. He still found it amazing that he could take such a breath, one that went to the very bottom of his lungs, and that he could breathe out again without wheezing or difficulty. His asthma, like his old body and even his old face, was apparently gone forever.

After taking that breath, Arthur walked into the living room – and stopped as if he'd hit a wall. There was his *mother*, who was sitting on the sofa and reading a medical journal, as if she had never disappeared, as if the world outside was normal, as if all the things that had happened to Arthur, his family and the city had never occurred.

Arthur took a step forward, ready to hurl himself upon her and hug her as tightly as he could, to recapture that sense of safety that he had always felt in her embrace.

But after that first step, Arthur hesitated. He had changed so much, he was so different to look at. Emily might not even recognise him. Or she might be afraid of what he had become.

Either situation was too awful to contemplate. Arthur's hesitation turned into a terrible fear and he began to back away. As he did so, Emily put the journal down and turned her head, so that she was looking directly at him. Arthur's eyes met Emily's, but he saw neither recognition nor fear in her gaze. In fact she looked right through him.

"Mum," Arthur said, his voice weak and uncertain.

Emily didn't respond. She yawned, looked away from Arthur and picked up the journal again, touching the screen to bring up a different article.

"Mum?" Arthur walked right up to her and stood behind her chair. "Mum!"

Emily didn't respond. Arthur reached out to touch her shoulder, but stopped an inch away. He could feel a strange electric tingle in his fingers, and his knuckles pulsed with the ache of sorcery. Slowly he pulled his hand back. He didn't want to accidentally set off a spell that might hurt – or even kill – her. Instead he held his hand out to cover the screen of her journal. But she kept reading, as if his hand was simply not there.

The article was about the Sleepy Plague, Arthur saw. It was entitled "First Analysis and Exploration of Somnovirus F/201/Z, 'Sleepy Plague'" and was written by Dr Emily Penhaligon. The Sleepy Plague had been the first of the viruses that had been spawned by the presence of the First Key and other intrusions from the House. Though swept away by the Nightsweeper that Arthur had brought back from the Lower House, other viruses had been created by powers of the House that should not have been on Earth. Emily was a pre-eminent medical researcher, but even she could have had no idea of the real reason the new viruses had suddenly appeared.

Arthur took his hand away and went to sit on the other chair in the room. He had felt so relieved to see his mother, because he'd thought she had somehow returned safely to their home. Now that relief was gone. He couldn't be sure it even was

Emily sitting opposite him, or that this was in fact his home.

"I'd better have a look round," said Arthur. He spoke loudly, but Emily didn't react. He watched her for a few seconds more, then got up and went downstairs to the kitchen.

The screen on the refrigerator, which Arthur had hoped would be active so he could check the time, date and any news, was blank.

Arthur turned away to head over to his father's studio and the computer there, but first he noticed something unusual through the kitchen window. He should have been able to see the dawn light coming through, but it was blocked by something green that was pressed right up against the glass.

Arthur went closer. There was a bushy tree or perhaps a hedge growing right next to the window, its foliage so thick that he couldn't see through it. But there hadn't been a tree there before, and in fact there should have been nothing but bare earth outside the kitchen because Bob hadn't got around to doing the landscaping yet.

Arthur went to the kitchen door and opened it. The door opened inward, which was just as well because there was a solid expanse of spiky green hedge outside. It was so thick Arthur couldn't see through any part of it, or get any idea of how far it extended.

One thing was clear. The area around his home had been transformed, and it added to Arthur's growing suspicion that this wasn't really his house at all.

He sat down at the kitchen table and took out *A Compleat Atlas of the House*. It looked like the real thing and Dame Primus had told him it would probably reappear somewhere near him, that he should check out bookshelves. There was only one way to find out, and to check exactly where he was and what was going on.

Arthur laid the Atlas on the table and said, "I need to know where I am."

He was about to reach for his Keys to use their power to activate the Atlas, but he didn't need them. His touch was sorcerous enough. The Atlas flipped open and grew until it was the size of a glossy magazine.

The double-page spread it had opened to was blank at first, then writing began to appear on the left-hand page, much slower than when Arthur had looked at it before. It was as if the invisible hand was being opposed or held back in some way, for the letters were not only slow to appear, they were in an almost illegible scrawl rather than the beautiful copperplate writing the Atlas usually used.

Arthur guessed what the Atlas was going to say before the first word was complete.

Incompa...

"But how can this be the Incomparable Gardens?" asked Arthur as soon as the words were finished, a long minute later. "And why are my house and my mother in it?"

Can't answer... opposed by the Seventh Key... came the ever-so-slow reply. The last word was almost unreadable, the final letter not much more than a blob of ink with a downstroke.

"Is that really Emily upstairs?" Arthur asked. He focused his mind more strongly upon the Atlas, and slipped his hands into his pouch to hold and draw on the power of both the Fifth and Sixth Keys, the mirror in his left hand and the pen in his right. He could feel something fighting back, some power opposing his attempt to use the Atlas. It was like an unseen presence pressing on his face, trying to push him back from the table and the open book.

Arthur fought against it, though he remembered Dame Primus saying the Seventh Key was paramount, the most powerful of all, and like all the Keys, it was even stronger in its own demesne. But surely, he thought, having two Keys would enable him to have some chance against it?

The Atlas slowly wrote a single, misshapen letter. Arthur couldn't quite figure it out for a moment, till he turned his head slightly and saw it was a *Y* that was partly rotated, followed very slowly by two more letters.

"Yes," read Arthur aloud.

But the Atlas kept writing. Another word appeared, each letter painstakingly spelled out over several seconds.

"And," read Arthur, and then, "no."

"Yes and no? How can it be yes and no?" Arthur asked angrily. He felt rage build up inside him. How dare this ineffectual Atlas be so slow and so inexact!

"I must have the answer!" shouted Arthur.

He thumped the table with the Keys and thought furiously at the Atlas. *What do you mean, "yes and no"?*

But the Atlas wrote no more and Arthur felt the power that opposed him grow stronger. It kept pushing at his face and he found himself turning his head, unable to keep looking at the Atlas, no matter how hard he tried. Then, with a crack, his head snapped round past his left shoulder, and with a snap that was almost as loud, the Atlas shut itself and returned to its normal size.

Arthur growled. His vision was washed with red, a red that pulsed with his rapidly beating heart. He lost conscious thought. In one second he was sitting at the table, the rage building inside him. In what felt like the next second he found himself standing above the wreckage of the table, his hands balled into fists, with splinters of wood sticking out from his knuckles.

The Atlas, undamaged, lay on top of the broken pile of wood.

Arthur stared at it and the splintered timber. He was shocked by what he had done, for the table had been old and immensely solid, and could not have been smashed by even the strongest of men without a sledgehammer. He was even more shocked by the fact that he had done it involuntarily, that the rage had been so strong he had lashed out without his conscious mind even being aware of it.

The anger was still there, smouldering away like a fire that needed only the merest breath to make it blaze again. It scared him, because it came out of nowhere and was so powerful. He had never been like this before. He was not an angry person. Or at least, he had not been before he became the Rightful Heir. Once again, as he had thought so often, he wished he had not been chosen by the Will to be the Heir, even though it had told him he would otherwise have died from an asthma attack. That was the only reason he'd been chosen, or so the Will had said. It had wanted a mortal, and one who was about to die.

Arthur shivered and forced himself to take a long, slow breath. He counted to six as he breathed in, and to six as he exhaled. As he did so, he felt the rage diminish. He tried to visualise it being forced back into a small, locked box from which it could not emerge without him consciously releasing it.

After a few minutes, he felt slightly calmer again and was able to think about what was going on.

OK, I'm in some part of the Incomparable Gardens. I need to get out, get back to the Great Maze, and rally the Army of the Architect to invade the Upper House.

Arthur stopped in mid-thought. That was what Part Six of the Will had suggested, but perhaps that wasn't the best course of action. Dame Primus and Sir Thursday's Marshals could get the Army organised without him, and whatever might be the outcome of any battle, he would still need to find Part Seven of the Will and release it. Then, with its help, he could force Sunday to give up the Seventh Key. With that in his possession, it wouldn't matter if Saturday or the Piper conquered the Incomparable Gardens. With all Seven Keys, Arthur could defeat any opposition. And, more important, he could stop the tide of Nothing that was destroying the House.

All I have to do is find the Will, thought Arthur with sudden clarity. *I've done it before. I can do it here. I'm attuned to the Will. I am in the Incomparable Gardens and it is supposed to be here somewhere. I'll just focus my mind on it and it will tell me where it is.*

While this was the most prominent thought in

Arthur's mind, another small part was not so sure. As he tried to focus his thoughts on where Part Seven of the Will might be, a good portion of his subconscious was also trying to tell him that this might not be a good idea, that it might even alert Lord Sunday to his presence, and that despite the two Keys he held, and the overconfidence they had engendered in him, Lord Sunday and the Seventh Key would probably make very short work of Arthur, especially an Arthur who was without allies of any kind.

But the angry, triumphant Arthur was more powerful. He bent his mind on reaching Part Seven of the Will. He was just thinking he felt some feeble touch from it when the green hedge suddenly shivered and split apart. A boy – a Piper's child – stepped through the gap and, without a word of warning, lunged at Arthur with a six-foot-long, three-tined gardening fork, each of the tines red-hot, the air around them blurred from the intense heat they radiated.

CHAPTER FOUR

Leaf adjusted the surgical mask she was wearing to keep the radioactive dust out of her lungs. She had a white doctor's coat on as well, surgical gloves and a floral plastic shower cap on her head. Once upon a time, the other people in the line might have laughed at her, but now they all wore strange combinations of hats and headscarves and raincoats and rubber gloves – anything to avoid breathing the radioactive dust and to keep it off their skin.

She'd been waiting in the line for water, food and antiradiation drugs since soon after dawn that Sunday morning. The Army had fired their micronukes at East Area Hospital a little over twenty-eight hours before, at one minute past midnight on Saturday morning, initiating a hellish twenty-four hours for Leaf and Martine and all the sleepers at Friday's private hospital.

It would have been bad enough for Leaf on her own, without the added responsibility of looking after all the people who had been put to sleep by Lady Friday, who had wanted to harvest their memories. After Friday's defeat, Leaf had shepherded the sleepers back from Friday's otherworldly lair, only to learn of the impending nuclear strike, and then as Arthur's time stop had begun to wear off, she'd had to make a frantic and not entirely successful attempt to move everyone to the underground level.

Though Friday's building was less than a mile from East Area Hospital, there was a slight hill between them, and it had also been shielded by a taller, very solid warehouse building, so it had not been badly damaged by the explosive force of the micronukes. However, there had been small fires all around the outside and everything was contaminated by radiation – though no one knew how bad the contamination was and Leaf hadn't been able to find out. To make the situation even more difficult, all the sleepers had woken up over the course of the Saturday morning, and were badly disoriented and often wanted to just get up and get out. This was double trouble, because all the doors needed to be kept shut to keep radioactive particles out as much as the sleepers inside.

An hour or so after the nuclear strike, special fire trucks had rumbled in and put out the spot fires with their water and foam cannons, though no fire-fighters got out of the vehicles. They were followed by armoured personnel carriers that drove up and down the streets, their external bullhorns loudly crackling with instructions to civilians to stay inside, keep doors and windows sealed, and stand by for further orders.

Those further orders had come on Saturday night, with designated aid stations to be opened the next morning to issue water, food and medication. Every household had been told to send one member, and warnings were issued about wearing gloves, a face mask of some kind and a coat that could be discarded before going back inside.

Leaf had come out to get help for the sleepers, who included her Aunt Mango. Lady Friday had never intended that her private hospital would actually cater to live patients, so there was very little food or medicine, and the only water they knew was not contaminated came from a single water cooler barrel that had been in the front office, and that had only been enough for the merest sip when shared among so many people.

Leaf ran her tongue around the inside of her dry mouth as she thought of that water barrel. She could see people ahead of her in the line coming back carrying big, sealed containers of water and Army-issue backpacks that were presumably stuffed with food and medicine.

She'd tried to explain to one of the soldiers standing guard that she wasn't from a normal house and needed more help, but he'd refused to listen and told her to join the queue. She'd tried to argue, but he had levelled his assault rifle at her and told her again to get in line. His voice through his gas mask had sounded nervous, so she'd backed off.

It had meant an hour's wait, but she was almost

up to the desk where two more soldiers, bulky and strange in their biohazard suits, were checking people off before they got their hand-out. Two more soldiers stood nearby, with their assault rifles ready, and an armoured personnel carrier was parked so that its turret-mounted gun was aligned with the long queue of people that stretched behind Leaf. In some ways it looked like they were in enemy territory, not on a relief expedition in their own country, but then Leaf supposed the soldiers were nervous that some people would attack them because, after all, they had destroyed the hospital and irradiated the surrounding region, supposedly in order to sterilise it against further viral infection.

"Name?" asked the soldier when Leaf got to the desk. Even through the mask, she sounded kinder than the soldier Leaf had spoken to first. "How many in the family? Anyone sick?"

"My name's Leaf, but I'm not here for my family. I'm from Friday's private hospital three blocks away. We've got more than a thousand patients... and we need help."

"Uh... a thousand patients?" asked the soldier.

Leaf couldn't see her face behind the mask, not even her eyes, as the Army masks had tinted lenses – but she sounded shocked. "A private hospital?"

"I think it's one thousand and seven," said Leaf. "Mostly pretty old, so quite a few are sick. I mean, not from the radiation, or not yet, but just because they were sick to start with. Or just old."

"Um, I'm gonna have to check up on this one," said the soldier. "Stand over there and wait, please."

Leaf stood to one side as the soldier flicked a switch on the side of her mask and spoke on her radio. Her mask muffled her voice, but Leaf could hear a few words.

"Private hospital... thousand or more... not listed... No, sir... map..."

Leaf missed the next few words. Then the soldier was silent, listening to a reply that Leaf couldn't hear at all. This went on for at least a minute, then the soldier turned towards Leaf and said, "OK, Major Penhaligon is coming to see you. Wait there until he arrives."

Major Penhaligon? thought Leaf. *That must be Arthur's brother, who warned him about the nuclear strike.*

She looked around while she waited. East Area Hospital was still sort of visible, about two miles away, though it was only a shell with one high wall still standing. A lot of the buildings around it had also been flattened and there were still some of the sealed fire trucks plying their water cannons on smouldering wreckage. There were also thirty or more orange armoured personnel carriers with the big black Q for *Quarantine* on their sides, lined up along the road that went to the hospital. The closest one had its back doors open and Leaf saw it had four shelves on each side, each holding several long orange bags. It took her a moment to comprehend that these were body bags.

Leaf got a terrible sick feeling in her stomach, looking at those body bags. As far as she knew, her parents and her brother, Ed, had left the hospital in the week when she was unconscious from the Greyspot disease, but she hadn't been able to confirm that. She'd tried to get in touch with them at home, which was several miles away and so at least a bit safer, but all communications were down.

They must be OK, thought Leaf. *They have to be*

all right. I've got to try not to think about them. I have a job to do.

She looked away from the body bags, but the sight of the people in the line was no more encouraging. Though she could only see their eyes, everyone looked frightened.

I'm frightened too, thought Leaf. *Maybe we're all going to die from the radiation. Look at the soldiers – they're in complete protective gear with proper gas masks and everything. But then, if Arthur can't stop the House and the entire Universe from getting destroyed, we're all going to die anyway.*

"Miss?"

A voice behind her made her turn round. Two soldiers stood there. They had no rank badges, but they did have name tags on their suits. One read PENHALIGON and the other read CHEN.

"I'm Major Penhaligon and this is Sergeant Chen," said the shorter figure. "I understand you're from a private hospital closer towards East Area?"

"Yes," said Leaf. "I was kind of there by accident on Friday night. I know one of the... nurses, but there's no other staff there and about a thousand old people—"

"We have no information on this hospital," said the Major. "It's not listed at all, anywhere, so this had better not be some sort of crazy—"

"It *is* there!" protested Leaf. "Come with me and I'll show you. Then if you find out it's not true, you can shoot me or blow me up or whatever else you're all so good at. You're not much good at helping people!"

A ripple of applause answered this loud speech. Leaf looked over her shoulder and saw most of the closer people in the queue were clapping, and one man was even shaking his fist in the air. A woman called out, "You tell 'em, girl! We want help, not bombs!"

"All right," said Major Penhaligon. He clicked a switch under his chin so that his mask amplified his voice, making it loud enough for the people in the line to hear him. "We're going to look into it. Keep in line and stay calm."

He turned the amplification off when he spoke to Leaf. "Where is this hospital?"

"The main entrance is that way, on the corner of Grand Avenue," said Leaf. "I'll show you."

"That's on the edge of the kill zone," said

Sergeant Chen. She was considerably taller and broader than Major Penhaligon, so until Leaf heard her voice, she'd thought it was a male soldier inside the suit. "Were you inside when the strike happened, miss?"

"Yes," answered Leaf. "Underground, with some of the patients. But a lot of them were on the ground floor. What do you mean, the 'kill zone'?"

"If you were underground you'll probably be OK," said Major Penhaligon. He hesitated, then added, "The initial burst of radiation would be lethal anywhere within five hundred metres of the target point, and if there is a hospital there it would be on the edge of that. I suppose we'd better go and take a look. Chen, you better give Miss... uh, Miss..."

"My name is Leaf," said Leaf.

"Give Miss Leaf a shot of CBL505."

"This is an antiradiation drug," said Chen as she slapped an auto-injector against Leaf's neck. She felt the sting of the needle before she could flinch away. "Same as in the take-home packs we're giving out. Uh, sir, if we're heading closer to ground zero we should put Miss Leaf in a suit."

"OK," said Major Penhaligon. "You double back

to... Decontamination Four is for female personnel, isn't it? Get her cleaned and suited up and then call me. I've got to go take care of something anyway."

"Yes, sir," said Chen. She took Leaf by the arm and started to lead her away.

"Thanks," said Leaf. Then, because she was wondering about Arthur and where he was, she added, "Are you related to Arthur Penhaligon, by the way?"

Major Penhaligon swung round. "He's my little brother. Do you know him? Do you know where he is?"

"He's a friend of mine," said Leaf. "But I don't know where he is."

"When did you last see him?" asked Major Penhaligon.

"Er... sometime last week," hedged Leaf.

"Did he mention anything strange?"

"What do you mean?" asked Leaf. She tried to keep her face from showing anything. By any definition, everything Arthur had been involved with in recent times was strange.

"Dad's house is gone," said Major Penhaligon. "Not destroyed. Just plain gone. I've tracked down

Michaeli and Eric – they're with friends, they're OK – but I can't find Arthur or Emily."

"A lot of weird stuff has happened around here," offered Leaf.

"That's for sure," said Major Penhaligon. "Where did you see Arthur?"

"In the hospital," said Leaf. She hadn't been ready for the sudden question. "Friday's hospital, I mean. With the old people. But he left."

"Where was he going?"

Leaf shook her head. "I don't know."

"When was this?"

"Friday night. Uh, after you called him."

"After I called him?" asked Major Penhaligon. "But I called him on the home number! He wouldn't have had time to get anywhere near here from home and according to the neighbours the house was already gone..."

"The phone was switched through," said Leaf, which was true. She just couldn't say that it was switched through to a telephone that materialised out of nowhere.

"I guess that kind of explains how the house could be gone, but I still spoke to Arthur." Major Penhaligon shook his head. "This just gets weirder and weirder. I don't see how there can be an entire hospital full of patients that's not on any database or map either. I'll see you at Decon Four in fifteen minutes, Sergeant Chen, Miss Leaf."

He turned around and strode away. Chen pulled lightly on Leaf's arm, directing her towards one of the side streets.

"This way," said the soldier. "It's not far."

"OK," said Leaf. She was quiet for the first few steps, just thinking about Arthur, and her family, and all the sleepers back at the hospital. There was so much to do. For a moment she wondered why she was bothering, since it seemed the whole Universe might get snuffed out by Nothing anyway.

But the Universe might not end, Leaf thought. *And then where would you be? Better to do something, because it might just work out.*

"What other weird stuff is happening?" she asked Chen.

"Plenty," the soldier replied, but she didn't elaborate. They walked another twenty yards or so, around the next street corner. Leaf saw that the whole avenue ahead was full of dozens of Army and Federal

Biocontrol Authority vehicles. The car parks for the shops and buildings on either side of the avenue were occupied by five huge pressurised tents, soon to be joined by three entire prefab structures the size of Leaf's house, which were in the process of being off-loaded from oversize semitrailers.

Ominously, the prefab buildings had large red crosses on them, and Leaf noted that beyond the Army vehicles, there were at least twenty big, six-wheeled hazardous environment ambulances.

Everyone working wore full protective suits with masks. The whole place added up to an expectation by the authorities that they would have to deal with a very large number of dead and dying people. Chen pointed to the closest pressurised tent, which was pitched in a supermarket car park. The tent had a newly painted sign in front of it, staked into the pavement. The sign had a cartoon picture of a smiling fat man scrubbing himself in a bubble bath, and read: 11TH CBRN BATTALION PRESENTS DECONTAMINATION STATION FOUR.

"Got to have a sense of humour," Sergeant Chen said with a sigh as soon as she saw the sign.

"Why?" asked Leaf.

"You'll see," said Chen. "I guess a small laugh helps everyone cope with the serious stuff. Come on."

As they walked over and Chen waved to the soldier on guard outside the big tent, Leaf asked, "You know the weird stuff... does it involve anyone with... uh... wings?"

Chen stopped and gripped Leaf hard. "Who told you about the General?"

"No one!" said Leaf. "But I've seen... uh... winged people."

Chen released Leaf. "General Pravuil, who was in charge of this operation, disappeared at midnight last night. The sentries outside said they saw people with wings fly him out of an upstairs window and disappear into thin air. Where did you see them?"

"Above the private hospital," said Leaf. "On Friday."

"If you see them again tell the nearest soldier," said Chen. "Or the FBA or whoever. There's a theory going around that they're terrorists utilising some sort of advanced genetically engineered flying system."

"Right," said Leaf. She couldn't see any point in telling Chen that they were Denizens. She wondered if Pravuil, who Arthur had said worked for Saturday, had simply left, or if he'd been taken away by forces working for Dame Primus, or perhaps the Piper. "What do I do now?"

"Go in there," said Chen, pointing to the air-lock entrance of Decon Station Four. "They'll take care of you. I'll wait."

Leaf went up to the door. The soldier outside keyed the outer door, which slid open. Leaf walked in and the door shut behind her. She was in a small, featureless white room.

"Close your eyes and mouth, and stay completely still," said a woman's tinny, amplified voice.

Leaf obeyed. A second later, she gasped as a high-pressure shower came on, the water hitting her hard, like tiny needles pricking her everywhere, even through her doctor's coat. This lasted for about ten seconds then suddenly stopped.

"Open your eyes," said the voice. "Remove all your clothing and place it in the receptacle to your left."

Leaf slowly opened her eyes. There was a faint

hiss of compressed air and a panel slid open in the wall to her left, revealing what looked like a dustbin.

Leaf took off her clothes, but left her underwear on.

"All clothing must be removed, as it may be irradiated," said the woman's voice. "New clothing will be issued. This is normal procedure."

Leaf obeyed and stood there shivering. The panel shut as soon as all her clothes were inside.

"Close your eyes and mouth," said the voice. "Be aware there will be scrubbing, and it may be painful. Keep your mouth and eyes closed."

The needle-jet shower came on again. It was even more painful without any clothes on. Thankfully the pressure eased off after twenty seconds, but there was no real respite as Leaf felt herself suddenly buffeted by what felt like enormous hairbrushes, which mechanically ran up and down her whole body.

"Extend your arms," said the voice.

Leaf bit her lip as the brushes ran over her arms. It wasn't so much the pain, it was humiliating being washed and scrubbed, even if it was being done remotely. She felt like some sort of test animal.

"Stand by for more shower," said the voice.

This third time the shower came on even more strongly than ever. Leaf crouched under the stinging water and fought back a sob.

I was a ship's boy on the Flying Mantis, she told herself fiercely. *I've been through storms at sea and battles with pirates. I can handle this. I've fought Denizens and murderous plants, I can handle this—*

The shower stopped. There was a pinging noise like a microwave finishing and a panel slid open on the right-hand wall.

"Put on the clothing from the right-hand receptacle," said the voice.

The clothing in the right-hand receptacle was just a robe made of something like soft blue paper. Leaf put it on.

"Walk through," said the voice. The inner door opened, revealing a larger room, but one that was as equally bare and white, except for a small folding table. There was a pair of scissors on the table, a portable diagnostic unit and a medical case. A soldier stood behind the table. She was wearing a protective suit like the soldiers outside, but instead of a gas mask she wore a visored helmet like an astronaut's, with an air tube that ran to a small backpack.

"Hi," said the soldier. "My name's Ellen. Leaf, isn't it?"

"Yeah."

"I'm afraid I'm going to have to cut off most of your hair. We'll be doing some quick tests as well."

"Great," said Leaf. "Better get it over and done with."

"That's the way," said Ellen. "You're just getting in ahead of everyone else. We'll be decontaminating everyone in the fallout area, once we get completely set up."

"Everyone who's still alive, you mean," said Leaf.

"Yes," said Ellen quietly. "We'll save everyone we can. Stand on this square, would you, and we can begin."

CHAPTER FIVE

Arthur grabbed the flaming garden fork around the central tine, ignoring the heat and the flames, and ripped it from the grasp of the boy, who fell over backwards and collided with the pantry door, smashing it in. While the boy was still trying to get up, Arthur flipped the fork so he could hold it by the haft and raised it over his head, ready to strike. He was just about to furiously drive it into the boy when he stopped.

He's only a boy, just like me... just like I was, Arthur thought through the red mist of rage. *What am I doing?*

"Don't kill me!" the boy shrieked.

"Why were you trying to kill *me*?" Arthur asked. He didn't lower the flaming garden fork.

"You're s'posed to be a weed," said the boy. Now that Arthur had a good look at the intruder, he was sure he was a Piper's child. He was wearing green boots made from something like rubber; muddy tartan trousers; a short-tailed tan coat over a mustard-coloured waistcoat and green shirt with a frilled front; and a large cloth cap that overhung his face.

"A weed?" asked Arthur. "But I'm inside a *house*. And I'm clearly not a plant."

"I'm s'posed to find a weed that's got into the Garden," said the boy. He reached into a waistcoat pocket and pulled out a grubby piece of paper that had been folded several times. "Look, I got the work order. A mix-up, I guess. They never said someone high up was going to do the weeding—"

"Shut up," ordered Arthur. He leaned the flaming garden fork against the bench and added, "And you, go out."

The fire on the fork snuffed out. The Piper's child stared at it and whispered, "Blimey!"

Arthur took the paper and unfolded it. Despite

a muddy stain across the middle, it was easy to read the fine copperplate handwriting.

Weed Intrusion. Bed 27. Pot 5. Dispatch gardener.

"You're a gardener?" asked Arthur.

"Second Assistant Sub-Gardener's Aide Fourth Class Once Removed Phineas Dirtdigger," said the boy. "Sir."

"Are there a lot of Piper's children in the Incomparable Gardens?" asked Arthur.

"Dunno, sir," said Phineas. "It's a big garden. I only work this bed... well, pots one to fifty. Are... are you Sunday's Reaper, sir?"

"Sunday's Reaper?" asked Arthur. "Who's that?"

"You know, sir. The Sower, the Grower and the Reaper. I did always think they were green, but I've never seen them, not in person, like."

"I suppose they must be names for Sunday's Dawn, Noon and Dusk," mused Arthur. "Now tell me, you called this place a pot. But it's a house, with a woman in it upstairs."

"Oh, yes, sir, she's what we call an exhibit," said Phineas eagerly. "This part of the Incomparable

Gardens is the Zoological Gardens, with people and animals and such like that Lord Sunday has collected. He always takes their home as well, so they're displayed properly."

"Why couldn't she see me?" asked Arthur.

"Oh, sir, the human exhibits would be distressed if they saw us," said Phineas. "They're looped, to keep them safe."

"What do you mean, looped?" asked Arthur.

Phineas scratched his head. "Looped. That's when their time goes round and round, and they're separate from everything. They just do the same things over and over again."

"What would happen if I went up and tapped her on the shoulder?" asked Arthur.

"Oh, you couldn't even touch her, sir," said Phineas. He frowned then added, "Least, I couldn't. You're powerful, so maybe you'd bring her into our time, but that wouldn't be good."

"I suppose not," said Arthur thoughtfully. He was wondering if he could make Emily fall asleep and then synchronise her with House time and take her home... except the house would still be here.

Perhaps if I just took Mum back to somewhere she knows well, Arthur thought. *Even if our place has disappeared, it would be better to get her back to Earth—*

"Who are you, sir?" interrupted Phineas. "Are you... are you Lord Sunday?"

"No," said Arthur. He stood up to his full height, towering above the boy. "I am Lord Arthur, Rightful Heir to the Architect."

"Oh," said Phineas. "Um, am I supposed to know what that means?"

"You haven't heard of me?" asked Arthur. "How I have defeated six of the seven treacherous Trustees of the Architect and taken their Keys of power?"

"No..." said Phineas. "I don't really get to talk to anyone but my boss, the Second Assistant Sub-Gardener for Bed Twenty-seven. His name is Karkwhal and he doesn't talk, not really, so I never know what's going on, even in the rest of the Gardens, let alone the House. It's quite good to talk, I must say. So you're Lord Arthur?"

"Yes. Sworn enemy of Lord Sunday."

"Oh, right." Phineas scratched his nose. "I wonder if I'm supposed to do something – I mean, tell someone you're here or something."

"No," said Arthur. "You don't want to do that."

"Fine by me," said Phineas. "Well, I s'pose I'd better go back to the shed and see what else needs doing. Can I have my flaming fork back?"

"That depends," said Arthur. "Do you know where Part Seven of the Will is?"

"Don't think so," said Phineas. He scratched the side of his nose again and his forehead wrinkled in deep thought. "Nope. Is it rare and valuable?"

"Yes."

"Hmmm... could be in the Arbour... or the Gazebo... or the Elysium. Most likely the Elysium, I should think..."

"Where are these places?" asked Arthur. "Are they part of the Incomparable Gardens?"

"Yes, indeed. Not that the likes of me have been there. But I know where they are, theoretically speaking."

"Why would the Will be in the Elysium?"

"That's Sunday's favourite bit," said Phineas. "Everyone knows that. He keeps all the rarest exhibits there. The perfect place. I'd love to work there, not that I expect they have a weed problem in the Elysium—"

"Ah, the weeds," said Arthur. "What are they exactly?"

"Oh, Nithlings of one kind or another," said Phineas. "When Lord Sunday brings in a new exhibit, sometimes a few weeds come in with them and, if you don't get to them quickly, they spread. Why, there was this one ship thing Lord Sunday brought in that was *covered* in weeds. There were lots of us on that job, and a Sub-Gardener First Class in charge. But I didn't get to do much; they made me hang back and watch for any getting away. Only none did get away. And no one talked to me."

"Why does Sunday collect people and living things for the Garden?" asked Arthur. He remembered that Grim Tuesday had liked to collect valuables, things that people had made, but not living creatures or plants.

"Dunno," said Phineas. "He just does. We have to look after them carefully though – the boss is always going on about that. Weeding, for example. Can't let a Nithling interfere with any of the exhibits."

"Could you show me how to get to the Elysium?" asked Arthur. "Is it far away?"

"I s'pose," said Phineas. He scratched the bridge of his nose. "We'd have to cut between the hedges here, get on to the Garden Path... pick up a dragon—"

"A dragon?"

"Dragon*fly*," said Phineas. "Big ones, fitted for riding. Only I've never ridden one, though I s'pect they'd do what you tell them. Anyhow, we get on a dragon and fly towards the sunset – have to wait for it, of course, cos Lord Sunday moves the sun around, but the Elysium always faces the setting sun."

"If he likes it so much, there must be a good chance Lord Sunday will be there himself," Arthur guessed.

"I dunno," said Phineas. "There's a lot of Garden. You could sort him out though, couldn't you? What with being... what did you say?... the Rightful Heir and all that."

Yes, I could, thought the angry, boastful part of Arthur. But his more sensible side said quite the opposite, remembering what he had been told about the Keys, and how the Seventh Key was paramount over all.

I'd have to find the Will quickly enough to get its

help to force Lord Sunday to relinquish the Seventh Key, thought Arthur. *But if I run into Lord Sunday first, I'll be toast. Perhaps I should get help first, like Part Six of the Will said...*

"I wouldn't mind seeing you and Lord Sunday have a punch-up," remarked Phineas eagerly. "That'd be right promising, I reckon."

"You'd probably get killed just watching," said Arthur bleakly, remembering the Keys being used in battle back in the Great Maze, and when Saturday had first broached the Gardens.

He shook his head and took out the Fifth Key.

"I have to go somewhere," he said. "Don't tell anyone I was here, all right? And make sure this house... this Garden bed stays weed free."

Phineas nodded, but his dark eyes were fixed on the mirror, intent on what Arthur was going to do.

Arthur held the mirror up, looked into it and tried once more to visualise Thursday's room. At first he saw only his reflection, but that wavered and he felt a surge of relief as the now-familiar carpet with its battle-scene motif slowly coalesced into a solid view, with the rest of the room shimmering into focus around it. But just as it was about to become entirely crisp and real, the mirror shook in his hand and the vision wavered. Arthur frowned and gripped his wrist with his left hand to steady it, but the mirror continued to shake and twist, as if someone else was trying to take it away from him.

"Steady!" hissed Arthur, exerting his willpower to keep the mirror still and the scene in view. But just as he had with the Atlas, he felt an opposing force, one that grew stronger and stronger, until the Fifth Key flew from his grasp and clattered on to the floor.

Arthur clenched his fist, but seeing Phineas watching him so intently, he managed to contain his anger. Instead of punching the walls, he knelt down and picked up the mirror, slipping it back into his pouch.

"Maybe I won't be going after all," he said. "How do we get out of here?"

"Through the hedge," said Phineas. "It'll open for me, being a Gardener and all. Just stay close behind."

He touched the hedge that blocked the kitchen door and a boy-sized hole opened in the greenery.

"Come on, bigger than that!" said Phineas. The hole grew large enough for Arthur. Phineas put one leg through it, then hopped back again. "My fork! Can I have it back, please, sir?"

"Yes," said Arthur. "Do you want it lit?"

"Oh, that's all right," said Phineas. "I'll swap it for another one. I just have to have one to hand in."

He climbed through the hole.

Arthur looked around the kitchen and glanced up at the ceiling, to the room above where his mother was trapped in a small circuit of time.

At least I know where Mum is, he thought heavily, then stepped through the hedge.

He found himself in a cool green alley between two hedges that were at least fifty feet tall. Above them he could see a perfect blue sky with a faint touch of white clouds – it looked like it might have been painted by some old master, and possibly was. He couldn't see a sun, but there was a source of illumination somewhere above for the sky was very light. Probably the sun moved along a track, just like the suns in other parts of the House, though Arthur guessed that the one here would be more impressive and move more smoothly than in any other demesne.

"Which way?" asked Arthur. "Left or right?"

"Oh, this way," said Phineas, pointing with his fork. "Four hedge junctions this way, then we take a left, go three junctions, take a right, two junctions, left again, straight on past four junctions, and then through another hedge and we'll be at the Garden Path, which the dragonflies fly along all the time and sometimes the guard beetles run along, though *you* wouldn't be scared of them."

Arthur thought of the beetles he'd seen fighting Lady Friday's forces. He'd almost been bitten in half by one himself.

"How many beetles, and how often do they go along this path?"

"Oh, half a dozen at a time, I guess," said Phineas. He started walking along the alley, idly thwacking the hedges on either side with his fork. "But you don't see them around that often."

They walked in silence for a while after that. It was pleasantly cool between the hedges, with the dappled green light and the beautiful blue sky above. They combined to almost lull Arthur into a sense of peacefulness, but he knew it was only an illusion. He was thinking hard about what he could and should do.

"Are there telephones here?" he asked as they approached the first junction, where two hedge-bordered alleys crossed at a broad, paved plaza. Arthur stayed close to the hedge, keeping in its shadow.

"Telephones?" asked Phineas. "Sure. There's one in Karkwhal's shed. That's how he gets the weeding orders."

"Where is this shed?" asked Arthur. He didn't look at Phineas as the boy replied, but stared around and looked up and along the hedges. He had the unpleasant feeling that he was being watched and there was a slight sick-making ache in his bones, a sign that sorcery was being practised somewhere nearby.

"Karkwhal's shed?" asked Phineas. "That's back the other way. It's closer than the Garden Path, if you want to go there. Don't know why you would, with only old Karkwhal and me there—"

"Quiet!" ordered Arthur. He reached into his pouch and drew out the Fifth and Sixth Keys. "I can hear something."

"What?" whispered Phineas, not very quietly.

Arthur held up his hand to silence Phineas again,

then listened. There *was* something – a rustle in the hedge, as if a large rat was wriggling through the tight-packed greenery. But he couldn't see anything and the sound stopped as he slowly turned his head, trying to fix the position of the noise.

"It's gone." Arthur hesitated, returned the Keys to his pouch and turned round to follow Phineas.

At that moment, two enormous, green-skinned Denizens burst out of the greenery, as if the hedge itself had come to life. They grabbed Arthur's arms and began to twist them behind his back.

Arthur shouted in fury and tried to throw them forward, but they held on tight, and their long, gnarled toes dug into the earth like tree roots, to hold him fast.

"Keys!" roared Arthur, and flexed his fingers. His pouch flew open, and the mirror and the pen flew up towards his hands.

But the Keys never reached Arthur's waiting grasp. They were caught in midair by a bright silver net – a net wielded by Phineas the Second Assistant Sub-Gardener's Aide Fourth Class Once Removed. Only he no longer looked like a Piper's child. In that same instant the tall green Denizens had erupted from the hedge, Phineas had grown and changed. He was now a commanding figure some ten feet tall. He stood above Arthur, holding the writhing Keys in the net with his left hand, while his right was held tight around a small object that he wore on a chain around his neck.

The only thing that was not altered was the intense darkness of his eyes.

"Bind him with the chains," instructed Lord Sunday. "Be careful. He is very strong."

CHAPTER SIX

"Are you sure this is safe?" asked Giac. He was holding on nervously to Suzy's shoulder as they descended on the South-West Big Chain. While the grease monkeys regularly used the various moving chains to go between floors of the tower, Sorcerous Supernumeraries usually took the elevator, so this was a new experience for Giac.

The South-West Big Chain was like a greatly oversize motorcycle chain that ran the thousands of feet from the unseen nether regions of Saturday's tower to a vast bronze guide wheel that was situated near the top. The Chain ran in a broad shaft, going up one side and down the other. Each link was six feet tall and six feet wide, and had a flat space in the middle where the grease monkeys stood, sat or even slept as the Chain rattled up or down.

"Course it's safe," said Suzy. "Provided you don't fall off."

"Oh," said Giac. He peered a little towards the edge and gulped. "Where are we going? And whose side am I on again?"

"We're going to the elevator control floors," said Suzy. "And you're on Lord Arthur's side. Unless we meet up with the Piper's forces first. Then we tell 'em that we're on the Piper's side, though we'll still really be on Arthur's side. It'd be a thingummy, a rose of war."

"A subterfuge," suggested Part Six of the Will, who was lurking inside Giac's partially furled umbrella so that only the top part of his beak was visible, and that only on close inspection. "A legitimate ruse."

"But will Lord Arthur want me?" asked Giac anxiously. "You said that I can decide to change sides, but the other side has to take me on. Will Lord Arthur take me on?"

"As it 'appens, I am Arthur's right-hand man," said Suzy. "Or left-hand girl, I can't remember where I stood last time. Anyhow, me and Arthur is like two fingers of a gauntlet. Or at least the thumb and the little finger. I mean, I'm his top General and all. So if I say you're in, you're in."

"Thank you, ma'am," said Giac.

"None of that," admonished Suzy. "Call me Suzy."

"As you command, Lady Suzy," said Giac. "Oh, the floor below is manned!"

They had been passing floor after empty floor as the Chain descended, the desks abandoned by sorcerers who had been drafted to fight the Piper below or join the invasion of the Incomparable Gardens above. Suzy had begun to think they might be lucky and find that the floor they needed, where the desks that controlled the elevators were located, was also abandoned. But they were now passing floors that were still fully staffed with thousands of sorcerers at their desks, their blue umbrellas now furled at their sides since the ten-thousand-year rain had stopped. Fortunately they were intent on their work, and the few that glanced across did not find the sight of what appeared to be a grease monkey and a Sorcerous Supernumerary on the passing Chain to be of any interest.

"Do you have a plan, Lady Suzy?" asked the Will. "As to how we will activate the elevators?"

"Course I do," snorted Suzy.

"Good," said the Will.

There was silence as they descended several more floors, then the raven poked its head out of Giac's umbrella a little more, so that one sharp eye stared up at Suzy.

"As we will shortly arrive at our destination, would you like to share this plan?" the Will asked.

"I'm thinking," said Suzy. She certainly looked thoughtful, staring at each passing floor and hardly blinking. "Will, I've seen you turn into a ball – can you turn into anything else?"

"Within certain limits, I can change my outward form."

"Could you turn into a message capsule?" asked Suzy. "What colour umbrellas do they have on floor 6879?"

"Green," said Giac.

"And if they got promoted to the next level?"

"Blue," said Giac dreamily. "Beautiful shades and patterns of blue. We're going past the blue floors now."

"So you'll need to be a blue capsule," Suzy told the Will. "I'll come out and say there's going to be a mass promotion of a bunch of sorcerers and I've come to check out the offices for such a big move. They'll all be looking at me... and you, who'll be the message capsule. I'll walk around measuring and so on, and then... and then... I'll put you down on a desk, Will, and when they're not looking at you, you slither down and use the desk to open an elevator—"

"That's not much of a plan," interrupted the Will. "Even I could do better than that."

"I couldn't," said Giac. "What do I do?"

"You follow me around," said Suzy. "Like the Sorcerous Supernumeraries always follow the grease monkeys. Maybe if we need a distraction, you do something."

"We're almost there," said the Will. "And I really think this is a rotten plan..."

"Three floors to go," Giac announced.

"Rotten!" exclaimed the Will, but nonetheless it flew to Suzy's hand and transformed into a blue message capsule. Only close examination would show that it was made of tiny squirming letters of blue type rather than the usual glazed bronze.

"Two floors."

"Get ready to step off the Chain," Suzy said. She took Giac's hand, ready to drag him off if he faltered.

A foot above the next floor, she stepped down off the Chain. Giac followed, but got his umbrella caught in his legs and almost knocked both of them over. They staggered forward, Suzy brandishing the blue message capsule above her head.

All the nearer sorcerers looked across from their desks, their eyes intent on the capsule. Some kept up their two-handed writing, but most stopped. A second later, whispers began to cross the floor, and Suzy saw a ripple of movement spread out from the Chain shaft through the open offices as sorcerers all the way to the far western side of the tower turned to look.

"Grease monkey..."

"Blue capsule..."

"Promotion..."

"*Promotion...*"

"*Promotion...*"

"Mass promotion message!" shouted Suzy. "A dozen sorcerers going up to blue, special wartime rules. I've got twelve gangs coming up in fifteen minutes, but first I need to measure where the offices are going up."

She raised the blue capsule above her head and waved it around a few times, then sauntered through the closest offices. The sorcerers there stared at her, the mirrors they were supposed to watch forgotten, the spells they were meant to be inscribing temporarily abandoned.

Suzy walked further in, towards the nearest bank of elevators. She could see the iron grille doors of the closest elevator, but there was only empty space behind it, rather than the usual wood and glass door of a House elevator.

As Suzy and Giac passed by the closer desks, the muttering behind them changed. The whispers grew louder and sounded angry.

"*Not me...*"

"*Where's the brat going?*"

"*It can't be them...*"

Suzy sped up a little and drew the message capsule

close so she could whisper. "I forgot to ask... Will any desk do?"

"Close to the elevators," replied the Will very softly. "As soon as I'm done, we'll have to run."

Suzy changed direction, the movement eliciting a gasp of expectation from the sorcerers ahead of her, and a groan of disappointment from the ones behind.

"They're getting ready to throw things at the chosen ones," muttered Giac, looming close behind Suzy's shoulder. "And at us, of course."

Suzy didn't answer. She'd fixed her eye on a desk immediately in front of the closest elevator. The sorcerer there was watching her, like all the others, but she thought he looked just a shade shorter than his neighbours, which probably meant he had been recently promoted to the green levels. Choosing him for another promotion would likely create the biggest possible uproar.

As she got closer, the noise behind her increased and the tone of it sounded considerably uglier. Suzy ignored it and stopped in front of the desk with the slightly shorter Denizen. He looked up at her, his eyebrows arched in surprise.

"Yes?"

"You are Mmmph Bltthh?" asked Suzy, turning her head so as to make her garbled words even harder to figure out. As she spoke, she put the message capsule on the desk.

"I am Sorcerer Seventh Class Xagis," said the Denizen.

"Right," said Suzy. "Then it's you and two more desks in that direction and three in that direction."

"I'm getting promoted?" asked Xagis in disbelief. "Again?"

"Yep," said Suzy. "You are— *Ow!*"

A flying inkwell bounced off her shoulder. Suzy ducked a more deadly letter-opener and ran around to the far side of the desk. Xagis was already crouching underneath it. Giac, on the other hand, was capering up and down and pointing out towards the exterior of the building.

"Invaders!" he shouted. "Newniths!"

Suzy grinned at him and gave him the thumbs-up, thinking he was making a diversion. She glanced over the top of the desk, was almost hit by a small tin of chalk that exploded open and powdered Xagis with chalk dust, and saw that the Will had grown little legs and scurried into a drawer of the desk, where it was working away at something.

"Lots of Newniths!" shrieked Giac.

"Prepare to repel the enemy!" shouted someone else. The missiles stopped hitting the desk. Suzy took another look and saw the Denizens were all getting out from behind their desks and grabbing their umbrellas. Giac was still jumping up and down and pointing. Suzy looked where he indicated and saw that his diversion was not just a thing of words and invention. There *were* Newniths coming on to the floor – leather-winged Newniths, flying in on the western side of the tower. They wore flexible plates of dull red armour on their arms and legs, breastplates of the same metal, and closed golden helmets that had narrow eyeslits and crosshatched mouth-holes. Wielding electrically charged two-handed swords, they were more warlike and threatening than any Newniths Suzy had seen before, more than living up to her threatening description of them to Giac.

Xagis took his umbrella and rushed to join the ranks of sorcerers that were forming to oppose the Newniths. There were at least fifty of the invaders already on the western edge of the tower and they had hacked off the heads of the closest sorcerers, who had not been quick enough to get out from their desks or grab their umbrellas. But the Denizens were beginning to fight back, bolts of fire from their umbrellas sizzling across the Newniths' armour. Suzy saw winged Denizens appear behind the attackers too, swooping down at the hovering Newniths that were waiting their turn to come in, an aerial battle commencing.

Suzy looked across at the elevator bank. There was still no sign of an actual elevator behind the grille door.

"How long?" she whispered to the desk. Part Six of the Will had disappeared completely into the drawer and she couldn't see it.

There was no answer.

"How long?" Suzy repeated, much louder this time. There was a lot of noise now, with the Newniths and Denizens shouting and screaming, the *zing* of fire bolts, the squeal of umbrella spikes on armour, the clash and thud of the two-handed swords striking through desks, umbrellas and Denizens.

"Done," said the Will. It came out of the drawer and jumped to her shoulder, becoming a raven once more. Which was unfortunate, as Xagis and a couple of the nearer Denizens happened to be looking back at that moment.

"Treachery!" shouted Xagis. He raised his umbrella, which spat a bolt of fire at Suzy. She dodged, but it would have hit her if Giac hadn't sprung forward and opened his own black umbrella, the fire bolt splashing harmlessly across the stretched fabric.

"To the elevator!" shouted the Will. It launched itself off Suzy's shoulder, bounced off the ceiling and ricocheted into Xagis, turning into something resembling a bowling ball just before it hit.

Suzy and Giac slowly walked backwards towards the elevator, with Giac holding his umbrella open in front of them both. The Will bounced off the floor and ceiling to cover their retreat, knocking more Denizens over like bowling pins. But there were many more rushing over to the elevators, hundreds of sorcerers baying, "Treachery!" with those closest and with a clear line of sight shooting out fire bolts from their umbrellas.

Suzy and Giac got to the grille door at the same time the Sorcerous Supernumerary's umbrella collapsed, burning shreds of material hanging from its steel and ivory bones. Suzy wrenched open the grille and the door behind, but a fire bolt caught both of them as they dived in, and they rolled around on the floor, shrieking and smoking, until the Will flew in, slammed the door shut and turned itself into a blanket that smothered the flames.

"Ow! Ow! Double ow!" said Suzy as she slowly got to her feet. She was about to add another "ow" when the door shook, and through the window she saw the face of a Denizen who was trying to slide the outer grille door open again.

"Where's the operator?" shouted Suzy. She looked round wildly, but apart from herself, Giac and Part Six of the Will, the elevator was empty. There was no operator and the small bandstand in the corner was also vacant.

Suzy looked at the tall panel of buttons to the right of the door. There were hundreds of small brass buttons arranged in rows of twelve that stretched from the floor to the ceiling, some four or five feet above Suzy's head. From Suzy's waist down, these brass buttons were green, blackened and covered in a rather nasty-looking verdigris. Some of the buttons in the middle were also affected by this blight and were generally dull. Only the top rows, above Suzy's head, were bright and shiny, the way they were meant to be.

"Giac, hold the door shut!" ordered Suzy. She looked up at the Will, who was flapping near the ceiling. "Which button's for the Great Maze?"

"This one," said the raven, hitting a button a foot above Suzy's head with its beak. "I hope," it added as the elevator fell away and the window in the door instantly clouded over, becoming uniformly grey.

CHAPTER SEVEN

After her decontamination, Leaf was given new clothes to put on. Scratchy underwear and a desert-patterned camouflage tracksuit weren't what she would have chosen, but it didn't really matter, since she was going to wear a protective suit over the top. Unlike the military or FBA suits, it was bright yellow and had EVACUEE printed on the front and back. Ellen showed her how to put the suit on, which was to step backwards into the connected overboots and then pull up the front inner toothless zip and pull down the outer zip, before folding over the big

Velcro tabs. The gas mask was next. It was a simpler version of the military ones, without a radio or other electronics, and it smelled rubbery and disgusting. Ellen demonstrated how to put it on and clear it, closing the intake valves and breathing out hard.

Leaf was trying it for herself for the third time when Ellen got a call from outside.

"Roger," said Ellen. Then to Leaf, "OK, you're good to go. Major Penhaligon is waiting for you outside."

Leaf turned to go back out the way she had come in, but Ellen tapped her on the shoulder and pointed to another air-lock-style door. "One way in, one way out," she said. "I'll probably see you later for your next decontamination."

"Ugh." Leaf grimaced at the thought of being scrubbed again.

"At least your hair is cut now," said Ellen. "And you might have to wait next time as I expect we'll be busy getting refugees ready to ship out very soon. I bet you'll be happy to get out of that suit by then. Even decontamination will be welcome."

"I guess," said Leaf. Her own voice sounded

strange and dull, heard through the suit's hood and the side panels of the mask. "Thanks, Ellen."

"Just doing my job," said the woman. "Good luck."

Leaf waved and went into the air lock. She had to wait while it buzzed and hummed, before the outer door opened to let her into a pressurised tunnel of clear plastic that led to another portable air-lock structure. This one took several minutes to cycle through, the progress of pressure equalisation and door opening being indicated by a row of tiny LEDs that slowly changed from red to green, a process that Leaf found weirdly mesmerising.

Major Penhaligon was waiting outside the final air lock. Chen was with him, and another soldier whose name tag read WILLIAMS, who was carrying a large medical backpack marked with a red cross.

"Miss Leaf?" asked Major Penhaligon.

"Yes."

"We have a vehicle waiting. Follow me, please."

Leaf followed the three soldiers down the road to a waiting personnel carrier. The back ramp was down, and they trudged up and sat on the benches inside, the soldiers on the left and Leaf on the right. She felt a bit like it was an audition.

The ramp closed after them, and the personnel carrier rumbled off. Leaf couldn't see the driver as the front compartment was separate and sealed.

"Your supposed hospital is here, right?" asked Major Penhaligon. He stretched out to show a folded map to Leaf. It was a detailed aerial and satellite composite map, and Leaf was easily able to pick out the large white building that was Friday's hospital. It had been circled in red pencil with a question mark, and unlike nearly all the other buildings did not have its name or other information printed on the map.

Ominously, there was also a shaded circle drawn on the map. Centred on East Area Hospital, it was labelled INITIAL KILL ZONE and its outer circumference ran across the front of Friday's building.

"That's it," confirmed Leaf, tapping the map.

Major Penhaligon nodded and sat back.

Leaf looked out through the small, very thick armour glass window. It made everything look blurry and it was initially hard to work out exactly where they were, but she soon recognised a building and got her bearings. Only a few minutes later, they pulled up in front of Friday's hospital.

There were no signs outside that indicated the building was a hospital of any kind. It looked just like the other low-rise oldish office buildings on the street, sharing with them the hallmarks of the micronuke attack, as all the windows facing East Area Hospital were shattered and there were burn marks across the facade. There had been some trees out in front as well, but they were now only blackened stumps.

Leaf felt a momentary doubt as she climbed out the back of the personnel carrier. What if all the sleepers were gone, transported back to the House by yet another machination of a Trustee? Then Major Penhaligon would think she was a nutcase or a real troublemaker—

She was thinking about that when Martine suddenly burst out through the front doors. Though she was wearing a scarf over her head and a surgical mask, it was easy to tell just from her staring eyes that she was absolutely terrified.

"Help!" she screamed. She almost fell down the wheelchair ramp, towards Sergeant Chen, who rushed forward to catch her. "There's a thing – it's come from the—"

Martine didn't have the breath to get out what she wanted to say, but Leaf at least was certain she knew. A thing from the House.

"What?" asked Major Penhaligon. "A *what*?"

Martine just pointed back behind her, her arm shaking. "It... it came out of the pool."

"I don't believe this!" snapped Major Penhaligon. "Williams! Take care of this woman."

He brushed past Martine and stormed up to the front doors of the hospital. Leaf hurried after him, calling out, "Be careful! There's... uh... weird stuff going on."

Sergeant Chen, who was striding up the ramp next to Leaf, turned her masked head to the girl. "Weird, like winged guys?"

"Weirder," said Leaf.

"Uh-huh." Chen drew her pistol and racked the slide. "Wait up, Major! Could be real trouble."

Major Penhaligon, who had been about to open the door, hesitated. Then he stepped back and readied his own pistol.

"This seems ridiculous," he said. "But I suppose

it could be the Greyspot virus or something, making someone go crazy. Chen, stay close. Miss Leaf, you wait here."

He pushed open the door and went in slowly, turning his head so that he could scan the corridor despite the limited field of vision imposed by his mask. Chen followed, and Leaf, despite being told not to, followed Chen.

The lobby and administrative offices were empty, but as Major Penhaligon and Sergeant Chen advanced down the central corridor, with Leaf tagging along some distance behind, they heard someone screaming ahead, near where the ramp went down to the lower level.

A sleeper staggered out of the top of the ramp, took several steps and then was horrifyingly gripped by a long green tentacle. It wrapped around the old man, yanked him off his feet and dragged him back out of sight. There was another scream, and then silence.

"You see that?" asked Major Penhaligon unnecessarily.

"Sure did," said Chen. "Twenty feet long at least, and as thick as my arm. I don't want to see whatever it's attached to—"

The tentacle reappeared as she spoke, questing around the corner. It was followed by another, and another, and then the main body of the creature rounded the corner. It was the size and shape of a small car, with dimpled, tough-looking hide that was bright green. It had hundreds of foot-long legs under this central torso, and three big tentacles in total, each of which was easily thirty feet long.

On top and in the middle of its main body, there was another shorter limb, perhaps a neck, about three feet long, which supported a sensory organ that resembled a daisy, hundreds of pale yellow anemone-like tendrils swirling around a central, darker yellow orb. As Major Penhaligon took a step forward, these anemone tendrils all turned towards him, as if it could sense his movement. He stopped, but most of the tendrils continued to point stiffly at him, with only a few still fluttering on the sides, as if they were watching for other potential enemies.

"Watch it, but hold your fire," said Major Penhaligon. He then muttered something into his radio, which Leaf couldn't catch.

"I don't reckon shooting that with anything less

than a fifty cal would be worthwhile," said Chen, but she kept her pistol trained on the creature.

"It's got a collar," said Leaf, pointing to a thin band that was wound around the neck-limb. There was a slim braided lead attached to the collar, and the lead stretched back around the corner.

"You said weird and you were *so* right," said Chen.

"I wonder who's holding the lead," said Leaf.

She was answered a moment later when a humanoid figure stepped out from behind the creature. He was green-skinned, seven feet tall, and wore a tailed coat made of autumn leaves and breeches apparently of green turf. Because he wasn't wearing any shoes, Leaf had a clear view of his long, yellow-brown toes, which closely resembled the taproots of a willow.

In his right hand he held a scythe, the butt planted upon the ground. The staff of the scythe was at least nine feet long, and the curving blade stretched behind him, from shoulder to shoulder. It was made from some dark metal that did not reflect the light.

"I have come for the girl called Leaf," said this

figure, clearly a Denizen. He waved one negligent hand. Leaf noticed that his thumbnails were a darker green than his skin, so dark they were almost black. "You others may go."

"What... Who are you?" replied Major Penhaligon.

"I am commonly called the Reaper, and that will suffice," replied the Denizen. "Leaf-girl, your presence is required by my Master. Come to me."

"Your Master?" asked Leaf. Major Penhaligon was whispering on his radio again, and Chen had moved her aim to the green Denizen. "Would that be Saturday or Sunday?"

"It is not needful that I tell you. Walk to me, child, ere I set the beastwort upon your companions."

"Get ready to run," whispered Chen, so low Leaf almost couldn't hear her.

"Run!" shouted Major Penhaligon. As he shouted, he and Chen started shooting at the beastwort. Leaf turned and sprinted as fast as she could for the doors, the booming shots echoing around her, followed by the clomp of boots as Penhaligon and Chen caught up with her. Chen picked her up under one huge arm as they crashed through the doors, Major

Penhaligon turning around to fire several times into the leading tentacle as it almost grasped his leg. While the bullets hit, they appeared to do little if any damage.

"To the carrier!" shouted Major Penhaligon. The vehicle had turned so that its turret machine gun was facing the door of the hospital, and its back ramp was open. Chen took Leaf out one side, with Major Penhaligon close behind, and as they ran for the ramp, the machine gun started to fire deafeningly over their heads.

Williams and Martine were already inside. They scurried back as Chen, Leaf and Major Penhaligon hurtled in, and then Chen pulled the lever to close the rear ramp. It whined and slowly began to rise, even as one of the beastwort's tentacles slithered around the corner and gripped the edge.

Outside, the heavy chatter of the turret machine gun stopped, and over the internal speaker the driver's panicked voice shouted, "It's not stopping. I can't—"

The vehicle shook with a sudden impact, knocking Leaf to the floor. As she scrambled up, another tentacle came in the other side of the ramp.

Chen hacked at it with her combat knife, but its flesh was like a rubbery sponge. The knife simply rebounded off, no matter how much force Chen applied.

Then the tentacles fastened themselves completely around the ramp and ripped it off, the heavy armour plate torn in half as easily as a stick of licorice. The door went flying through the air to crash into a burned-out car across the street, and the beastwort slithered into view.

Chen and Major Penhaligon tried to push Leaf back behind them, as if they could somehow shield her from the monster, but Leaf resisted.

"No!" she said. It took all her courage to get out the next few words, but she managed. "It's no good. I'll go... I'll go with them. If I do, they'll probably leave everyone else alone."

"That is so," said the Reaper, who stood suddenly in the doorway. "Come. There is little time."

"No!" said Major Penhaligon. He grabbed Leaf's arm as she scrambled towards the rear of the carrier. "There must be something we can—"

"There isn't," said Leaf quietly. She shook off Major Penhaligon's light grip and stepped out of the carrier. She stopped to look back and added, "There's nothing any of us can do. I just... I just hope Arthur can save me... save us all..."

"Arthur?" asked Major Penhaligon. Even distorted by the mask, the surprise and shock in his voice was evident. "My little brother?"

"Yes," said Leaf.

"Enough!" said the Denizen. He reached out and gripped Leaf's shoulder. She flinched under his touch, and felt a wave of fear so intense that she almost fell. But she fought against it and remained upright. She didn't want the Denizen – or Chen and Penhaligon – to see how scared she was. It was lucky the mask covered her face or they'd know, since she couldn't stop the tears that were welling up uncontrollably, or even wipe them away.

"Come!"

"Look after the sleepers!" Leaf shouted before she was pushed away, back towards the doors of Friday's hospital. Only, through the rainbow prism of her tears, she saw they were not the doors of the hospital. They had become one tall arched door, decorated with a thousand swirling patterns and shapes, pictures of things that had happened and things that might yet come to pass, a confusing kaleidoscope of colours and movement that Leaf knew she must not keep looking at, lest she be so drawn in she lost her senses.

In other words, it was the Front Door of the House.

Chapter eight

The two Denizens clamped Arthur's wrists with manacles that shone with their own intense blue light. He had seen that sorcerous steel before, binding the Old One to his clock, so he struggled even harder. But the Denizens were too strong, and they were aided by the unseen power that Arthur felt pressing down upon him, the power that he knew emanated from the Seventh Key that Lord Sunday must be holding in his hand.

As one of the Denizens fastened a chain to the manacle on his right hand, Arthur summoned up all his strength. Wrenching his arm free, he held out his hand, pointed it directly at Sunday and shouted, "I, Arthur, anointed Heir to the Kingdom, claim the Seventh Key—"

Lord Sunday's eyes narrowed. He made a slight gesture with the Key that lay hidden in his cupped hand. Arthur immediately lost his voice, his next few words croaking away into unintelligibility.

"You cannot claim the Key without the aid of Part Seven of the Will," said Lord Sunday. "And I do not wish to listen to your blatherings."

The Denizens finished fastening the chains, drawing Arthur's hands up behind his back. He could feel the sorcery in the manacles. It felt like a terribly cold current in the metal, eternally running anti-clockwise around his wrists. They felt so strong he doubted whether he could break them even if he managed to get back the Fifth and Sixth Keys, which seemed unlikely. They were still jumping and flying about inside the silver net, which Sunday was holding at arm's length in his left hand, while his right held the Seventh Key. Arthur wished he could see what that Key was, but it was entirely hidden. Whatever it was, it had to be small – though it might grow and change, Arthur thought, as Sunday had changed himself.

Lord Sunday looked up and Arthur followed the direction of his gaze. There was something above them, a black dot against that beautiful blue sky with its whispery clouds. The dot grew larger and larger, swooping down towards them from some great height, and Arthur saw it was a huge dragonfly. It descended very quickly to hover up above them, its wings almost touching the tops of the hedges on either side.

It was a *very* big dragonfly. Its body was about sixty feet long and each of its multipart, buzzing wings was easily twice that length. Arthur couldn't see clearly from below, but there was something on its back, a kind of cabin or deckhouse, with stained-glass windows and a roof of wooden shingles.

A Denizen, wearing a one-piece coverall of soft tan leather and a kind of hunting hat with a feather, threw a long rope ladder down from the tail of the dragonfly. The ladder unrolled itself as it fell, ending near Lord Sunday, who quickly began to climb up it, effortlessly taking three or four rungs at once.

While Lord Sunday was climbing up, the Denizen

on the dragonfly went further back along the creature's body and threw down a rope that ended in a large hook. The Denizens holding Arthur looped his chain around the hook, the Denizen above waved to some other unseen crew and the rope was hauled up, leaving Arthur dangling some thirty feet below the dragonfly. It was a very painful position, with his arms twisted behind his back and the manacles on his wrists supporting his entire weight. Arthur knew that prior to his transformation he would have been screaming in pain as his arms were dislocated at the shoulder. Now, though it hurt a lot, he merely grimaced and contained his pain, the anger inside him still stronger than any other feeling.

Part of that anger was addressed to himself.

How could I have been so stupid? Arthur thought. *I should have got out of here somehow, as soon as I knew it was the Incomparable Gardens. I never should have been so careless with an unknown Piper's child...*

The two tall, green-skinned Denizens shinned up the rope ladder and it was drawn up. Arthur heard a whistle above him, and the thrum of the dragonfly's wings increased in tempo and pitch. Its legs, which had been dangling just above Arthur, retracted against the vast abdomen.

The dragonfly zoomed up and jinked sharply to the right in a move that sent Arthur swinging on his chain, jerking his arms enough to make him let out a small gasp. His arms might be dislocation-proof now, but some part of his brain hadn't worked that out and was still sending *intense pain – do something* signals.

Arthur forced the pain back down. Then, with a Herculean effort, he leaned forward till he was head down, hooked his feet through his linked arms and swung through so that his manacled wrists were now in front and above him, and he could hold on to the chains rather than having his whole weight supported by the manacles and his wrists. He was still suspended by chains under a fast-moving giant dragonfly, but at least his wrists and shoulders didn't hurt as much.

With the lessening of the pain, Arthur found he could concentrate on other things, like looking around. The dragonfly had settled into level flight at about a thousand feet up, Arthur guessed, giving him a panoramic view of the Incomparable Gardens.

In other circumstances, it would have been a wonderful vista. Below him was a patchwork of hundreds or possibly thousands of different gardens, all separated by corridors of tall green hedges like the one in which he had been ambushed. There were gardens that were small and green and tidy; gardens of russet and tan that sprawled across many acres; there were deserts and low rolling hills and swamps, and even several beaches that bordered portions of ocean no more than a hundred yards long and wide. A small proportion of the gardens had buildings, varying from garden sheds to minarets and modern buildings that would not have looked out of place in Arthur's home town.

Amid the patchwork of gardens, there were several other locations that occupied much larger areas. One, some distance away on Arthur's right, was a green area that was at least a mile wide and several miles long, with a dry pond or muddy pit at its centre. A moment later, Arthur recognised this as the point where Saturday's assault ram had broken through and, as he peered more closely he saw that there were tiny figures moving around the hole, and across the green lawn towards the ridge of wildflowers, where many more little dots moved. But he was several miles away, with the dragonfly climbing higher, so he couldn't tell if the tiny figures were Sunday's insect soldiers or Saturday's Denizens.

Not that it really matters, thought Arthur. He needed to concentrate on what he was going to do, instead of wondering about what was happening in the battle between Saturday and Sunday – or, for that matter, the battle in the Upper House below them, between the Piper and Saturday.

He looked up at the manacles on his wrists. As far as he could see, with the wind in his eyes and the constant swinging back and forth as the dragonfly changed course, the manacles were all one piece of sorcerous steel. They had no keyholes or bolts or any other obvious fasteners, and the chain ran through protruding eyelets that were half an inch thick and seemed as much part of the manacle as the main band, with no signs of welds or any weakness that might be exploited.

It was likely that they could only be unfastened by the Seventh Key or some similar power. Perhaps Arthur, with all the other six Keys, might be able to command his release if he was not opposed by Lord Sunday. But he didn't have even one Key now.

He brought his wrists together and tried to get the fingers of his right hand under the left manacle, to see if he could bend or break it with his now otherworldly strength. But the manacles were too tight, and in his heart he knew there was no chance that they could be opened by any physical act. Made with sorcery, they could only be undone by sorcery.

Next, Arthur tried to summon a telephone, as he had done in other parts of the House. But whether he asked for one aloud or simply tried to will a telephone into existence, nothing happened.

After that, he tried to call the First, Second, Third and Fourth Keys to him, as he had done in the Middle House. But that didn't work either, no matter how he shouted and raged, his voice hoarse from whatever Sunday had done to him, made worse by the constant rush of wind.

Always, he felt the unseen pressure of the Seventh Key working against him. It was clear that he could not prevail against it.

Despite that, after a bit of a rest, or as much of

a rest as it was possible to have while swinging on chains under a giant dragonfly moving at full speed, Arthur tried again. But all he managed to do was give himself a raging headache, to add to the pain in his wrists and shoulders.

Eventually he just let himself swing by his chains and tried to think. He was in a desperate situation, Arthur knew that much. While he now was very hard to kill, Lord Sunday certainly had the power to slay him if he wanted to, though if he did want to, he presumably would have already done so.

Arthur thought about that a little more. Sunday had been able to catch and hold the Fifth and Sixth Keys while Arthur was being bound, but perhaps if he'd tried to kill Arthur, the Keys would have defended him more strongly. Also, if he did kill Arthur, then Sunday could never take the other Keys. They had to be handed over willingly.

It was possible that Lord Sunday might not even want the other Keys. Arthur had no idea what Sunday really wanted. After all, it was Saturday who had set the fall of the House in motion, and Saturday who had invaded the Incomparable Gardens, because the Gardens were the only part of the House likely to survive the onrush of Nothing that had already taken the Far Reaches, the Lower House and who knew what else by now.

All Arthur knew was that Lord Sunday was one of the original faithless Trustees who had not obeyed the Architect, and had broken and hidden the seven Parts of the Will instead of following the Will's instructions. As Arthur was effectively an agent of the Will, and the supposed Rightful Heir of the Architect, Lord Sunday was automatically his enemy.

But maybe we can work something out, he thought. *We both have to stop the tide of Nothing, to save the House and the rest of the Universe. Maybe I could confirm that he would stay in charge of the Incomparable Gardens and he'd be left alone, that seems to be what he wants...*

Arthur sighed as his thoughts continued into less optimistic regions.

Who am I kidding? Dame Primus would never agree. Besides, who knows what Sunday is really up to? I have to escape! But how?

He sighed again, the sigh turning into a grimace of pain as the dragonfly changed direction again, swinging Arthur out wide, scraping the manacles across the raw wounds on his wrists, no matter how tightly he held the chain above the manacles.

With the pain came an unexpected realisation. Since he'd taken the Fifth Key at least, any pain he felt had come with a burning desire to retaliate, to strike against whoever or whatever had caused him hurt. But he was not angry now and he felt no great store of rage waiting to explode within him.

I am weaker without my Keys, thought Arthur. *But I am also more myself.*

They were heading towards a new landmark, a tall green hill that was still several miles away. It looked a lot like Doorstop Hill in the Lower House, though it was significantly higher and the bottom slopes were terraced and dotted with trees. There was also something on the crest of the hill, a low building or construction of some kind, but it was too far for him to easily identify.

Directly below him, the variety of gardens continued, still divided and penned in by the tall green hedges. Arthur watched them flicker by as he desperately tried to think of some stratagem to gain his release. He let his eyes go out of focus, half-lidding them against the rushing wind, and the gardens below blurred into a patchwork of many shades of green and brown and blue.

Blue, thought Arthur.

He blinked and refocused. There was a lake and, about half a mile beyond, one of those strange, truncated oceans dumping its waves on to a two-hundred-yard-long stretch of cut-off beach.

Navigable waters, thought Arthur, swiftly followed by a single, piercing image of a tall, white-bearded sailor with deep-set eyes of the clearest blue, wielding a harpoon that glittered and shone with the most powerful sorcery.

This was the Mariner, second son of the Architect and the Old One, who had sworn to aid Arthur three times and had already done so twice. Wherever there were navigable waters, the Mariner could sail, and Arthur thought that if anything other than the Seventh Key could break his chains, it would be the Mariner's harpoon.

I have to call him straightaway, since he could take ages to get here. Which means I need my medal.

The Mariner's medal was in Arthur's belt pouch, near his hip, which presented a problem. Suspended as he was, with his wrists manacled together, he couldn't just reach down, undo the pouch and retrieve it. Nor, after a few attempts, could he pull himself up high enough to get his hands near the pouch, because when he did so he started to spin around violently.

Next, Arthur tried swinging his legs up so that he could hang upside down. But a few attempts showed him that even though he could manage to turn upside down and get his hands near his belt pouch without going into the same sort of spin, there was no way he could undo the pouch and get the medallion out, at least not without a very high chance of the medallion and his yellow elephant simply dropping out and being lost forever.

He was still trying to work out how he could get the medal when the dragonfly began to descend. It was still flying towards the terraced hill Arthur had seen, only it was no longer aiming for the top of the hill, but at a point about halfway up.

Arthur swung himself right way up again as he got lower, and tried to stop his spin. There was something on the terrace that had caught his eye and he wanted a better look.

He got it, and he felt a chill colder than the icy steel. On the terrace halfway up the hill, lying flat, was a twenty-foot-wide clock face, with vertical numbers of blue sorcerous metal. The clock had long, sharply pointed hands, and next to their central pivot was a small trapdoor.

It was a smaller replica of the Old One's prison, save that there was no one chained to the clock hands.

Or at least, Arthur thought, there was no one chained there *yet...*

CHAPTER NINE

The elevator fell faster than was usual, and the ride was far less smooth. Suzy and Giac were thrown against the walls, and Part Six of the Will had to constantly flap its wings to keep its balance, finally just latching on to Suzy's shoulder. It continued to flap there too, as Suzy tried to wedge herself into one corner to keep steady, with Giac in the opposite corner.

Even more alarming, every now and then a tiny globule of Nothing would explode through the floor and exit through the ceiling. This mostly happened near the back of the elevator and the three passengers kept well away. If the Nothing actually hit anyone, it would dissolve everything in its upward path. Even a glancing pass might destroy a hand or foot.

It was also a frightening indication that Nothing was continuing to impinge on the House. If there were globules and particles of Nothing loose in the elevator shafts, it was likely the Void had breached more defences.

"Are you sure you pressed the right button?" asked Suzy. "Cos you know half the House is just Nothing now, and if we're dropping into it—"

"The corroded buttons indicate high contamination by Nothing," said the Will, who had been studying the rows of bronze or formerly bronze buttons. "Those that are entirely black and crumbled show lost portions of the House."

"So the one for the Great Maze was still bright?" asked Suzy. "That's good."

"Not entirely," said the Will. "There are several elevator positions within the Maze. Some of them are black. The one I chose is a little tarnished, and the verdigris is spreading, even in this short time."

"The Maze is dissolving?" asked Suzy. "Nothing is spreading there as well?"

"It appears so," said the Will. "I think we had better hurry this elevator up."

It flew from Suzy's shoulder, up to the ceiling above the buttons and, using its beak like an ice pick, smashed through a small walnut-and-ivory veneered panel that was set into the plainer wood. There was a gold ring behind the panel.

The Will glanced back down and said, "Crouch and brace yourselves."

Suzy and Giac obeyed. The raven grabbed the ring, folded its wings and dropped back down to Suzy's shoulder, pulling a slender golden chain out of the ceiling by the ring. As the chain grew longer, the elevator's speed increased. By the time the Will arrived on Suzy's shoulder, she felt herself rising into the air, suddenly weightless as the elevator accelerated down.

"I'm floating!" she cried. "This is great!"

"Is it?" asked Giac worriedly. "Are you sure?"

"Hold on!" warned the Will. "We'll slow down just as fast. Or hit very hard. One, two, three, four, five, six—"

The raven released the ring on "six" and the chain shot back into the ceiling. As it did so, the elevator slowed suddenly, slamming Suzy and Giac to the floor. A few seconds later, there was a terrible impact. The elevator exploded around them, throwing them into the air again in a storm of splinters and broken floorboards. Before they could fall back down, everything tilted over on a sharp incline and all three of them slid down the wall and ended up in a confused tangle in the dangerous corner where the Nothing globules had turned the elevator into a sieve.

Finally a bell went *ping* and the inner door slid open to reveal a bent and buckled grille door that was hanging off its hinges. Beyond it lay a guard-room, where a dozen somewhat surprised Denizens uniformed in the buff coats and grey trousers of the Moderately Honourable Artillery Company were snatching up and readying their musketoons, pistols, sparkizan halberds and swords.

"Guess we're here," said Suzy as she crawled across Giac's legs and brushed the Will's wings away from her face, since it was perched on her head. "Wherever here is."

She stood up, brushed off the splinters and dust,

and held up her hands, which seemed a wise precaution given the number of Nothing-powder weapons that were now aimed at her, including a small, wheeled artillery piece that was being pushed over by another half dozen artillerists, its bronze barrel coming into alignment with the door of the elevator.

"I'm General Suzy Turquoise Blue, personal aide-de-camp to Lord Arthur," she called out. "Who's in command here?"

The weapons were not lowered and no one answered.

Suzy had a moment of doubt, which was unusual for her, as she wondered whether the artillerists had gone from being moderately honourable to dishonourable, joining the Piper or Saturday. Then a Gun-Sergeant, his sleeves resplendent with gold stripes and crossed cannons, gestured to the other Denizens, who lowered their weapons a little, though not so much that anyone in the elevator would have a chance to break out. The gunner with the slow match near the cannon also lifted this burning fuse away from the touchhole, but not enough for anyone to get comfortable.

"Stay there, ma'am, and you others," the Gun-Sergeant called out. "Marshal Dusk commands here and we are under orders to take no chances. I saw you at the Citadel fight, ma'am, but seeing ain't always believing, so if you've no objection, we'll send word to the Marshal."

He made a sign with his hand and one of the artillerists towards the rear slid out around the heavy ironbound door on the opposite side from the elevator.

"Good idea," said Suzy. "Um, where is here? We're not at the Citadel?"

"This here's the Cannon Arsenal," said the Gun-Sergeant. He was about to add something else when he was interrupted by three distant horn blasts from somewhere outside.

"You might want to block your ears," said the Gun-Sergeant, though neither he nor any of the other gunners made any move to do so.

Giac promptly obeyed, and the Will thrust its head under its wing. Suzy however was about to ask why when there was a sudden titanic blast outside. The stone walls of the guardroom shook and the elevator canted over even more, till it was almost horizontal, and Suzy was sitting on what used to be the wall.

The Gun-Sergeant said something, but Suzy couldn't hear it over the ringing in her ears. As the tinnitus subsided the Gun-Sergeant spoke again, and though Suzy couldn't really hear it she could work out what he was saying by watching his lips.

"Told you so," he said.

Suzy grinned and mimed cleaning her ears out with her fingers. It actually helped, so she kept at it and looked in surprise at her blackened fingertips. "Must be quite a while since the Bathroom Attendants washed between my ears," she said proudly. "I don't reckon they'll get another chance."

"I think it very unlikely," said Part Six of the Will. It hopped on to Suzy's shoulder and peered at the artillerists. "Tell me, Sergeant, why are you all wearing black armbands? And what was that explosion?"

The Gun-Sergeant narrowed his eyes. "I'm not answering questions from a bird of dubious background," he said. "You look like some kind of Nithling."

"I beg your pardon," said the Will. "I'll have you know that I am Part—"

"Shush," said Suzy, clasping the raven's beak shut. "The bird's all right. Marshal Dusk will vouch for it, as well as for me."

"What about him?" asked one of the other gunners, pointing at Giac. "He's one of Saturday's, isn't he?"

"Well, he was," said Suzy. "Only now 'e's not, orright? He works for Lord Arthur, same as the rest of us."

"If you say so," sniffed the gunner, but he maintained a ready stance with his sparkizan, and kept a thin blue spark sidling along the blade of the halberd-like weapon.

"So why the black armbands, then?" asked Suzy, repeating the Will's question. "And what was that boom? Someone smoking in the Nothing-powder store again?"

A chorus of irritated voices answered the last question first. It was a commonly held belief in the rest of the Army that the Moderately Honourable Artillery Company's artillerists and engineers were always on the verge of blowing themselves up by accident and that only good luck spared them. It was a completely unfounded belief, but that didn't make it any less irritating.

"Quiet!" roared the Gun-Sergeant. The ruckus died down, and the burly Denizen turned back to Suzy. "Now General, presuming you is who you say you are, you know that there ain't no artillerist who smokes, even if we could get the makings, which we can't since the fall of the Far Reaches. Likewise we don't play games with matches or fire-starters or flame-sprays or sparkizans or any of the things that them other units says we do. So we don't take kindly to jokes about our Nothing-powder stores blowing up or—"

He paused suddenly, and with the sixth sense of a long-serving sergeant, suddenly braced to attention and shouted, "Stand fast!"

The artillerists jerked fully upright to become frozen statues as the heavy door creaked fully open and a tall Denizen in a dark grey uniform with black epaulettes entered.

"Marshal Dusk!" Suzy called out.

"General Suzy Blue," Dusk answered gravely. He paused to offer an elegant salute, which Suzy returned with less elegance but considerable gusto.

"Your arrival is unlooked for," Dusk continued, with just the hint of a question. "As are your companions. Am I right in presuming that I address a Part of the Will?"

"You are," said the raven, preening. It liked to be recognised.

"And one of Saturday's sorcerers?"

"Oh no, sir," said Giac. "Just a Sorcerous Supernumerary, as I was, sir. But now I serve Lord Arthur."

"I am pleased to hear it," said Dusk. "I am sure there is much more to hear, but there is very little time to hear it. We must all be on the adjacent tile before it moves at sundown."

"Where are we going to go?" asked Suzy. She was familiar with the way the Great Maze was divided into thousands of mile-square tiles, that moved at the end of every day, often travelling great distances in a single minute. But she did not possess one of the almanacs that officers used to work out which tile to get on in order to move to their required destination.

She stepped out of the wreckage of the elevator as she spoke, and walked closer to Dusk, turning to one side for a moment so she could look out the narrow window in the thick stone wall.

"Too much of the Maze has been broken through by Nothing," said Dusk. "We are evacuating to the Middle House. Most of the Army has already gone over the course of the day. I command a rearguard that has been destroying our siege train and larger guns, since we cannot take them with us, and there is the slight chance the Piper or some other enemy might swoop in and retrieve some for later use against us, before Nothing completely destroys the Maze."

"That explains the explosion," said the Will. It flew to the window and peered out with its sharp black eyes. "Perhaps you might tell me why you wear funereal armbands?"

"For Sir Thursday," said Dusk after a moment's hesitation. "He was our commander in chief for millennia after all, though he broke his trust to the Architect."

"You mean he's dead too?" asked Suzy.

"Yes," said Dusk. "This morning, in his cell. The guards outside were also slain, and only Sir Thursday's boots remained."

"Sounds more like he escaped," Suzy said.

"His feet were still in the boots," said Dusk. "The rest of him had been dissolved by Nothing."

Suzy raised an eyebrow and scratched her head. "So they're all dead," she said. "Monday, Tuesday, Wednesday, Thursday... but who killed them?"

"What of Lady Friday?" asked the Will. "I understand she was also imprisoned in the Citadel?"

"She lives yet, for all I know," said Dusk. "But she was taken with the advance party to the Middle House some hours ago."

The Will mulled this over for a moment before cocking its head to ask, "And the other Parts of the Will? Where are they? Have they remade themselves as Dame Primus or are they still divided?"

"I believe they... ah... she... that is, Dame Primus has rejoined... herself... and is now at the Middle House, where she has established a command post," said Dusk. "In preparation for Lord Arthur, of course. You do not happen to know where Lord Arthur is, by the by?"

"We do not," said the Will with a look at Suzy. "But he gave me orders to prepare a force to assault the Upper House. If the Army has retreated to the Middle—"

Dusk interrupted him. "Not 'retreated', please," he said. "We have merely taken up an alternate position, in preparation for further offensive action."

"If the Army and Dame Primus are in the Middle House, we must go there," said the Will. "But we cannot do so from this elevator."

"Indeed," said Dusk. "I am surprised you arrived in it. Dr Scamandros judged that shaft to be too compromised by Nothing or we would have used it ourselves."

"Trust you to call a rotten elevator," said Suzy to the Will. It clacked its beak at her and flew to Giac's shoulder. He stiffened in alarm and looked away, as if he could ignore the presence of the sorcerous bird.

Marshal Dusk took a silver pocket watch out of his sleeve and flipped it open.

"Come! We have less than an hour. We must march to the next tile at once. It moves to the Citadel, and our last working elevator is at the Citadel."

"So the tiles are moving?" asked Suzy. "They haven't broken down?"

"Some still move," replied Dusk. "We must hope the one we need will take us. If it doesn't..."

"If it doesn't..." prompted Suzy when Marshal Dusk did not finish.

"We will be consumed by Nothing," concluded the Denizen.

CHAPTER TEN

Leaf was a step away from the Front Door, with her eyes averted, when the Reaper pushed her hard in the middle of her back. She stumbled forward, her arms outstretched to stop herself – and encountered no resistance. Instead she went straight through the Door and fell screaming into darkness.

She was still screaming when the Reaper caught up with her, his scythe casting a bright greenish light around him. Only then did Leaf realise that she wasn't actually falling, that her senses had betrayed her. She was more floating than anything else.

But if she looked away from the Reaper, or shut her eyes, the sensation of falling returned.

"Where are we?" she asked.

"Inside the Front Door," said the Reaper. "Where we should not linger. Climb upon my back, but do not essay any nonsense."

"Why should I trust you?" said Leaf. She was already thinking about trying to strangle the Reaper or something like that, with the vague idea that if she could stall her eventual arrival wherever the Reaper wanted to take her, it would be a victory of sorts.

"You had best obey. There are now many Nithlings within the Door," said the Reaper. "And I will need both hands to wield my scythe."

Leaf looked around. All she could see were the Reaper and herself within a globe of greenish light. All else was darkness.

"I have little patience for those who *choose* to die," said the Reaper. "Climb on my back. Now!"

Leaf looked around again. This time, she did see the hint of a shadow breaking the green light, a split-second warning before the sudden appearance of grasping legs that belonged to something that had the abdomen and legs of a spider, and the torso and head of a human. Before those spurred, hairy limbs could grasp her, Leaf dived for the Reaper's feet, even as the Denizen swung his scythe and the Nithling was parted in two. The different sections still scrabbled after Leaf, till the Reaper kicked them away and they spiralled off into the dark.

Leaf needed no more instruction. She climbed up the Reaper's back, like a monkey up a tree, and embraced his neck with shaking arms.

"Hold tighter," said the Reaper. Once he was satisfied she had obeyed, he jumped, extending his scythe ahead of him. Its green light shone around them as they moved through this strange darkness that was neither water nor air.

Like deep-sea creatures drawn to a glowing lure, the Nithlings came to the green light. The first one was a thing that was mostly a giant bird with a vicious beak and metallic feathers, though instead of talons it had vastly oversize human hands, each with eight fingers and no thumbs. It speared its beak at the Reaper, but he dived under it, sweeping up with his scythe, to burst through a sudden storm of blood and feathers and continue unslowed.

The next attack came from a dozen small Nithlings that had the general shape of crabs, though each had a human face upon the back of its shell, faces that cried and squealed and called out as they scuttled in from all directions — above, behind, below. But again the scythe moved and the Nithlings died, and the Reaper and his human burden moved on.

After the crabs with the human faces, there was silence. Leaf could not tell how swiftly they were moving, for she had no point of reference, nor was there any air moving past her face. She had a moment of panic as she wondered if in fact there simply was no air, and went as far as to lift off her gas mask, but even with it off she couldn't tell if she was actually breathing in anything or not. Still, she was alive, and if she couldn't breathe inside the Front Door, she'd already be dead, so there was no point worrying about it – particularly when there were plenty of other things to worry about, like where the Reaper might be taking her and for what reason. But even that paled into insignificance as Leaf suddenly saw that there was another glow up ahead, which looked like it was made by a whole lot of distant lights; these were not green, but a nasty black-tinted red, like the smoky flames from burning rubber.

"Hold on with one arm and hold out your hand," instructed the Reaper. He had not slowed at all, but was charging towards the red light. "You will also need to fight this time."

Leaf held out her hand and her fingers closed around the hilt of a sword that appeared from nowhere. It was a short sword with a slightly curved blade of blue steel that was broader near the tip than the hilt. Faint sparks ran along the blade. As Leaf raised the weapon, the sparks intensified and she heard a fierce crackling noise, rather like the hoarse whispering of an angry crowd.

"Strike at the glimmer in their chests," said the Reaper.

Leaf didn't know what he was talking about for a few seconds, till they got close enough for her to see what was making the red glow. Rather than coming from a fire or fires, the light was issuing from the chests of a hundred or more Nithlings who were arrayed ahead of them, both on the same plane and above and below. These Nithlings had rudimentary wings of leather that they were all flapping wildly, but more striking still was that, though they were basically humanoid, they appeared to have no heads. At least, they had no heads on their shoulders. Leaf saw that the red glow came from their eyes, which were in their chests and roughly level with their armpits, and that was where the rest of their heads were located as well. Horrible, malformed foreheads, noses and chins jutted out from their naked torsos, lit by the glow of their red eyes.

The Reaper seemed unperturbed by their numbers. Even as they flapped down, up and across to the point of his impact, he continued at full speed. Though he had no wings, Leaf saw that the scythe itself drew him forward, as if he were a diver hanging on to a propeller unit.

When they were only yards away, the Nithlings came to meet them, scores of them driving straight at their target from all angles. Leaf turned half around and swung about her with her sword, hacking and slicing in a desperate attempt to keep the Nithlings' horrible hands from latching on to her and dragging her away. The Reaper's scythe mowed all around them, and then Leaf was striking at air and the Nithlings fell behind, unable to keep up.

Leaf watched the red points of light fade into the distance, but held her sword ready, her gaze darting around in an attempt to keep every direction covered. She also realised that she was holding on even tighter to the Reaper and that if he had been human, she would have strangled him long since. But he made no complaint.

Leaf started to ask the Reaper a question, but stopped when no sound came out of her mouth. She gulped and took a few deep breaths before trying again.

"How... how long till we get out of here?" she asked, pleased to hear only a slight tremble in her voice.

"That depends," said the Reaper, "upon our foes."

"Right." Leaf shifted her grip on the sword and looked around again. As before, everything was dark. There was no light, save that of the scythe.

Then she saw something. A tiny, distant star, a pinprick of pure white light. They were heading straight towards it and it was growing larger by the second.

"Is that—"

"It is the other side of the Door," said the Reaper, though in fact Leaf had been about to ask if it was another enemy. She felt a surge of relief. Somehow, even though she knew the Reaper was not her friend, she feared him less than whatever unknown Nithlings might appear.

The relief was very short-lived, as the Reaper suddenly changed direction. At the same time, Leaf thought she heard the echo of a trumpet or another horn of some kind. Faint and distant, and so low that it might have just been some trick of her ears.

"Where... where are we going?" asked Leaf. Her voice was not as steady as she'd hoped.

"To assist a companion," said the Reaper. His voice, as always, was entirely devoid of emotion.

Leaf heard the trumpet call again as they flew through the strange atmosphere of the Door. It grew louder as they travelled, indicating that the Reaper was heading directly for whatever was creating the sound. It had to be an alarm call of some kind, though as usual Leaf couldn't see anything in the darkness. She kept looking though, craning her neck as she tried to cover all possible directions where Nithlings might suddenly appear and attack.

But no Nithlings did attack and after a little while the trumpet fell silent. Leaf wondered how the Reaper knew where to go, for he kept up their speed and made small changes of direction from time to time, so he clearly had a specific destination in mind.

Eventually Leaf saw something ahead: a single Denizen who at first she thought was standing strangely, till the Reaper turned sideways and she reoriented her notion of what was up and what was down. The Denizen was lying – or floating – on his back. He was wearing a swallow-tailed coat that looked turquoise-coloured in the green light, but Leaf knew it was actually blue and that the single epaulette on the shoulder was gold. His right arm trailed down at his side and his fingers barely held the hilt of a sword that had been fastened to his wrist. The braided cord was now loose, with one tassel falling down the blade and the other gone forever.

Leaf knew this Denizen was the Lieutenant Keeper of the Front Door, and even though dull blue blood was seeping through his coat and breeches in a dozen places, he was not yet dead. As the Reaper stooped over him, he raised his head.

"You come too late for the fight," he said weakly. "But I thank you."

"I have long thought it unwise you should fight alone in the Door," replied the Reaper. He transferred his scythe to his left hand and reached down to slide his right arm under the Lieutenant Keeper's shoulder. "Come, I will bear you away. My Master shall make you anew."

"Nay," said the Lieutenant Keeper, shaking his head. "I must not leave my post, and their blades were Nothing poisoned. I will soon pass a more mysterious door than this one."

Leaf, who was looking over the Reaper's shoulder, wiped a tear from her eye. It was as much a reaction to everything that had happened as it was sorrow at the death of a Denizen she didn't even know.

"Shed no tears, lass," said the Lieutenant Keeper. "In truth, I have long been weary of my unceasing work. But before I am released, perhaps you would take my sword."

"No!" the Reaper shouted as the Lieutenant

Keeper flicked the sword up to Leaf and fell back, slowly tumbling into a somersault, all strength and life gone, poured into his final act.

Leaf dropped her short sword and caught the hilt of the Lieutenant Keeper's weapon, as the Reaper shrugged her off his back and jumped away, twisting so that he had his scythe ready to strike against her.

As Leaf's fingers closed around the hilt, the golden braid fastened itself around her wrist. In that instant, she felt a new sense suddenly flower in her mind. She could feel the Front Door in all its vastness, could feel the thousands of entrances and exits, could almost taste the presence of intruders, sour and unwelcome... It was all too much, and she cried out and crouched down under the pressure of the sensory overload, not even noticing that her radiation suit was turning blue and softening, becoming a swallow-tailed coat just like the dead Lieutenant Keeper's, while the bottom half became white breeches and the suit's overboots became black top boots, the toe caps shiny as a mirror.

The Reaper raised his scythe, but did not strike. Instead he frowned and used the scythe to rise some ten feet above Leaf. He was still in striking distance, but did not make any further moves until the girl slowly uncurled and stood up.

"My Master will be displeased," said the Reaper.

"What?" asked Leaf. She was still trying to come to grips with her new ability to sense what was going on in the Door and it was hard to listen or talk at the same time.

"You are now the Lieutenant Keeper of the Front Door," said the Reaper. "As such, I cannot compel you to come with me. I could kill you, of course, but my instructions are otherwise."

"Whose instructions?" asked Leaf.

"Lord Sunday's, of course," said the Reaper. "As I'm sure you guessed."

"Yes," said Leaf. "What does he want with me?"

"I do not know," replied the Reaper. "My Master likes to gather all possible tools before embarking upon any work. In this case, he must forgo your possible use."

"What?" asked Leaf again, more sharply. She looked to one side, feeling the approach of a large group of Nithlings. "There are Nithlings coming—"

"That is not my concern," said the Reaper. "I will leave you now."

"But you can't!" said Leaf. There were *lots* of Nithlings inside the Door, and there were strange breaches where she knew there should only be closed portals into parts of the House or the Secondary Realms. "I need your help!"

"I answered the Lieutenant Keeper's call," said the Reaper. "A detour from my proper work that has cost me dear. Now I must report my failure."

"Wait a—" Leaf began, but the Reaper raised his scythe and it lifted him away. A moment later, he was accelerating into the dark.

"Farewell!" cried the Reaper, and he was gone.

Leaf hefted her sword, which shone with its own cold blue light, stark as a fluorescent tube, and looked to the direction from which the Nithling horde would come.

CHAPTER ELEVEN

The dragonfly swooped down to the third terrace that was cut into the hill, about halfway up, and Arthur was dragged over rough green turf for twenty feet before the flying creature came to a stop and went into a steady hover. The rope ladder tumbled down and the two tall green Denizens descended. They unhooked Arthur's chains from the dragonfly's tow rope and, as he had feared, dragged him over to the clock.

Lord Sunday followed close behind, directing the power of the Seventh Key against Arthur while

Arthur's own Keys struggled to break out of the silver net. The force of Sunday's power pushed Arthur's head down and made him feel weak and unable to resist the two Denizens. One of them held him while the other fastened the chains to the tips of the clock hands. Arthur felt the chains grow shorter, like elastic returning to its normal length, and they dragged him across the clock face till he had to sit on the central pivot, next to the trapdoor.

Arthur craned his neck to check the position of the hands. The hour hand was on the twelve and the minute hand just past it. Then he looked at the trapdoor. It was shut, but he could hear a faint whirring noise behind it and something like a low, unpleasant chuckle.

"This is like the Old One's clock prison," Arthur said to Lord Sunday, who stood by the number six, gazing down at his captive. He still held the Seventh Key close in his right hand and the silver net in his left. "Are there puppets within that will take out my eyes?"

"There are," confirmed Lord Sunday. "But you have almost twelve hours before they will emerge, and you will have a chance to be spared from their ministrations."

"How?" asked Arthur.

"You may surrender your Keys to me," said Lord Sunday. "And *A Compleat Atlas of the House*. If they are freely given, I will return you to your Earth."

"And my mother?"

"Yes, she shall go with you."

"And you'll leave us alone? I mean, leave the Earth alone? And you'll stop the Nothing from destroying the House and the Secondary Realms?"

"I do not interfere unnecessarily beyond these Gardens," said Lord Sunday. "It is unfortunate that events have so transpired that I must take a hand, to impose order where others have failed to do so."

"So you won't promise to leave us alone," said Arthur. "Or anything else."

"You have heard my offer," Lord Sunday replied coldly. "You and your mother will return to your world, if you give me the Keys and the Atlas."

Arthur slowly shook his head. "No. I don't trust you."

"Very well," said Lord Sunday. "Consider that allowing the puppets to take your eyes is only one of many things I can do to make you reconsider. While I will not stoop to menace mere mortals, I do hold your mother prisoner. Your friend Leaf has also been taken. If you wish to see either of them again, then you will give me the Keys and the Atlas."

Arthur shut his eyes for a moment. He was tempted by Lord Sunday's offer, but not because he was afraid for his mother or Leaf, or of the puppets that would tear out his eyes, but simply because it would mean he could lay down the impossible burden he had been given. Everything would just go back to the way it was before.

Except it's too late for that, Arthur thought as he opened his eyes. *I can't trust Sunday to do the right thing, for the House or the Universe... or for me. I don't even know what his plans really are, or why he has let Saturday destroy the House. There's no way he could leave me alone, not now. I have come too far, and I have changed too much to go back. I have to see this through. I'll use the medal to call the Mariner and hope he gets here before the clock strikes twelve...*

Arthur's hand fell to the pouch at his waist as he thought this and he saw Lord Sunday's eyes follow the movement. Instantly Arthur lifted his hand to scratch his nose, the chain clanking as he moved. But it was too late. Sunday's attention was on the pouch. The Trustee lifted his hand slightly and Arthur's belt broke apart, the pouch sailing across the intervening space to land at Sunday's feet. Waterless soap, a cleaning cloth and brush, several nuts and bolts, and the all-important silver bag fell out.

Sunday gestured again and the silver bag spewed out it contents: *A Compleat Atlas of the House*, the yellow elephant toy and the Mariner's medal. The Atlas disappeared as it touched the grass. Arthur jumped as it reappeared a moment later inside the front of his coveralls.

"Like the Keys, the Atlas must be given freely," said Sunday. "I hope you will do so before too much time passes. As for your sentimental possessions, I do not care to give you the comfort of them. Noon, take these things and throw them from the hill."

Arthur could only watch as the slightly taller of the two green Denizens scooped up the elephant and the medal and threw them away. The items separated as they flew through the air, the elephant on a high arc that ended suddenly as it landed in the high branches of a tree, the medal going lower and further, travelling several hundred yards before it disappeared below the level of the terrace.

Arthur watched every moment of the medal's fall and with it the loss of his only hope of escape.

"I have a garden to tend," said Lord Sunday. "I will return in a few hours when I trust you will have thought further about my offer."

He stepped off the horizontal clock face and walked away, but not to the dragonfly's rope ladder. Instead Arthur watched him cross to the rear of the terrace, where a line of steps wound up the hill. The two Denizens followed. All three were on the steps when a bright blue-and-red bird shot past Arthur and flew in front of Lord Sunday, hovering in place, its wings beating so fast they were a blur. Sunday held out a finger, the bird hopped on to it and was carried to his shoulder, where it spoke into his ear in a high-pitched voice that Arthur could almost hear, but not well enough to make out more than a few key words.

"Saturday... not... Drasils wilting... more..."

The bird finished talking. Sunday nodded once and it flew away, back down the hill. Sunday turned around and looked at Arthur.

"It seems you are not the only recalcitrant who cannot acknowledge the realities of their position," said Lord Sunday. "As always, it is left to me to personally take charge of matters."

With that, he handed the silver net to Sunday's Noon, who held it with both hands. It obviously took a lot of effort to keep it relatively still as the Keys jumped around inside, straining to reach Arthur.

"Distance will make them less restive," said Sunday. He placed his hand just above his breastbone, touching the Key that hung from a chain around his neck, hidden inside his shirt, and closed his eyes for a moment in concentration. "They will be completely quiescent when they are locked away. I have opened the cage, but it will soon close, so attend to that at once. Dawn, come with me."

Sunday retraced his steps back down to the clock terrace, with Sunday's Dawn following, and climbed back up the ladder to the dragonfly. But Arthur didn't watch Sunday climb and only saw the dragonfly

166

depart from the corner of his eye. He was intent upon Sunday's Noon, and watched him as he carefully carried the silver net and the Keys away up the steps that led to the next terrace and out of Arthur's sight.

A few minutes later, the dragonfly was away, turning to climb up and over the hill. Arthur was alone, chained to the clock. He could see only as far as the nearest hundred-foot-high hedge below the hill, and the slope of the terrace behind him.

The clock ticked – a sound like the sharp stroke of an axe on very hard wood. The minute hand swept forward and the chain on Arthur's left wrist rattled as it too moved.

Arthur bit his lip and tried to think. The medal was gone, but there had to be something else he could do. There was the chance that Dame Primus or Dr Scamandros might be able to rescue him, but even as he thought that, he dismissed it. His only real chance would be if he could do something himself. He had to regain the Keys, or free Part Seven of the Will, or somehow retrieve the Mariner's medal.

The clock ticked again, the hand moved and the

chain rattled. Arthur stood up and looked around. He couldn't see where the medal had landed. The only thing he could see was his yellow elephant, stuck in the upper branches of a tall tree that reached up from the next terrace further down the hill. The elephant looked like a strange fruit, the bright yellow a stark contrast against the tree's pale green leaves.

I wish you could help me, thought Arthur. *Elephant, you were always there to help me out when I was little, even if it was only in my imagination...*

Arthur looked away from Elephant, down at the clock face, and then at the green grass of the terrace.

The Old One conjured stuff out of Nothing when I first met him, Arthur thought. *He said I'd need a Key to do it, but that was ages ago, before my transformation. I might be able to make things from Nothing here.*

He laid his hand on the clock. He couldn't feel any interstices of Nothing lurking somewhere underneath, as was usual in other parts of the House, and it was likely the Incomparable Gardens were completely armoured against the Void, but it was worth a try. Anything was worth a try.

"A telephone, connected to the Citadel in the Great Maze," said Arthur firmly. At the same time he visualised the telephone Dame Primus had given him long ago, in the red box. He tried to picture it in his head as solidly as possible, but he felt none of the symptoms of House sorcery. Though these aches and pains were always unpleasant and sometimes extraordinarily intense, he would have welcomed them if it meant his attempts to make a telephone from Nothing were successful.

"A telephone, connected to other parts of the House!" he said again, snapping his words as if he spoke to some recalcitrant servant. But still he felt no sorcery and no telephone appeared.

Arthur tried to call up the rage he'd felt in his house, when he'd smashed the table, hoping that energy might somehow fuel his attempt to draw something out of Nothing. But he didn't feel angry and he couldn't recapture the emotion. He just felt drained and defeated and small. All of his triumphant, powerful feelings were completely gone, lost the moment he was chained by Lord Sunday and his servants.

"Maybe a telephone is too tricky," Arthur said to himself. "Or the connections are difficult... but what else could help now?"

He thought about bolt cutters, or a hacksaw, but they would be useless against the sorcerous metal of the manacles. In fact, apart from the Mariner's harpoon or the Keys, Arthur couldn't think of anything that would have any effect upon his bonds.

What I really need is some way to get the medal back. It's only down the slope. I need a retriever dog, or something... a smart animal who will do what it's told. I wish Elephant was real, just like I thought he was when I was four...

Arthur smiled to himself, remembering how real Elephant had been, and the conversations he'd had with Emily, recounting what Elephant had done that day, sometimes adopting Elephant's voice and manipulating his trunk to make him talk.

A sudden jab of pain ran through Arthur's joints from ankle to shoulder, and something touched his arm. He yelped and sprang to his feet, thinking of a puppet woodcutter and his axe or, even worse, the old woman puppet with her corkscrew. But the trapdoor was shut, and the touch, when it came again to his knee, was light, a gentle tap that came from the trunk of a small yellow elephant whose twinkling, jet-black eyes looked up at Arthur with wisdom and affection.

Arthur crouched down and cradled his lifelong friend, biting his lip to hold back the sobs that were so near to breaking out. Elephant waited patiently till Arthur had composed himself enough to sit back. The boy looked up at the tree where the toy had lodged. It was gone, and the elephant next to him was definitely a living, breathing version of his childhood companion.

I've made a Nithling, thought Arthur, and he supposed he should be afraid of what he'd done. But he wasn't. He was happy. He was no longer alone and, even better than that, now he had an ally.

"I'm so glad to see you, Elephant," he said. "I need your help really badly. There's a silver medal, about this big, somewhere down the slope of the hill in that direction. I need you to go and get it, please, and bring it back to me. But be careful. Even the plants can be dangerous – we have many enemies here."

Elephant nodded sagely and raised his trunk to blow a soft trumpet blast of affirmation. Then he jumped down from the clock face and strode off through the grass, towards the edge of the terrace.

CHAPTER TWELVE

Fortunately for all concerned, the tile did take Suzy, Dusk, Giac, Part Six of the Will and two score artillerists to a position adjacent to the Citadel. There they met one of the rearguard guides, who led them quickly past a gaping hole of Nothing that was slowly and inexorably spreading like ink across blotting paper, and on to the Citadel itself, through the abandoned trenches and firewash-blackened ground left by the Newniths' siege.

The great fortress was strangely quiet, its buildings abandoned. A winding column of black smoke rose from the lakeside bastion, which had been set on fire to destroy the last of the stores that could not be taken up to the Middle House.

The guide took them to the central keep by the shortest path, one that would normally be blocked by sealed gates, portcullises and heavy doors. But all the Citadel's portals and defences were open now, and the few sentries remaining left their posts to join the party as they passed, though they kept a wary eye out to the rear, watching for any of the old-fashioned type of free-willed Nithling that might try to follow, as many of these creatures were beginning to emerge from the pools and pockets of Nothing that were bubbling up all around the Citadel.

The soldiers who had already departed for the Middle House had left a lot of nonessential items behind, for there were packs, bags, chests and boxes pushed to the sides of many of the rooms and corridors. Along the way, Suzy snagged a Regimental Brigadier General's coat for herself, and a Horde staff officer's blue tunic with chain mail epaulettes and a curious hat called a shako for Giac, who adopted both with enthusiasm.

The elevator in Sir Thursday's study had been expanded to its maximum size, about a hundred feet wide and a hundred and twenty feet long, with a tall arched ceiling some sixteen feet high. Even before Dusk and Suzy and their troops arrived, it was packed with the rearguard, including a dozen Not-Horses, a wagon loaded with Nothing-powder and more than a hundred soldiers from the Legion, the Horde, the Borderers and the Regiment, with various officers and NCOs from the different units all trying to assert their authority in order to ensure their soldiers had the best and most comfortable placements.

This bickering ceased when Dusk arrived and took charge. Suzy left him to his organising and wove her way through the crush to join three Piper's children who were sitting on a barrel. They were wearing the peculiar mishmash of uniforms favoured by herself and adopted by the irregulars who'd now formed Suzy's Raiders. Suzy knew these three, though not well, since she hadn't had much time to meet all the other Piper's children in the Army.

"Have a biscuit, General," said one of the children,

reaching into the barrel, which was stuffed to the brim with biscuits. Since neither Denizens nor Piper's children needed to eat, but liked to do so anyway, it was surprising that the barrel was marked ESSENTIAL GOODS FOR EVACUATION.

Suzy took the raisin-filled biscuit with glee and, between mouthfuls, introduced everyone.

"Bren, Shan, Athan. This 'ere's Colonel Giac," she said. "He's my new aide-de-camp."

"Colonel?" Giac beamed, repeating his new rank to himself with great satisfaction.

"And the bird is Part Six of the Will," added Suzy. She swallowed and said, "Who'll be joining up with Dame Primus soon, I expect, so don't tell 'im nothing about you know what."

"What?" asked the raven.

"It don't concern you or Dame Primus," said Suzy. "Or anyone but us Piper's children."

Part Six of the Will looked at her with one beady eye. "I will be charitable and presume you have good intentions," it said. "But you be careful, Suzy Blue."

"Anyhow, what's the news?" asked Suzy.

Athan shrugged. "The Maze is falling apart, we're

all off to the Middle House, Sir Thursday's snuffed it. Don't know anything else."

Suzy was about to ask another question when the elevator juddered into movement and everybody stumbled into everyone else, which was very painful in the case of the Denizens who got trodden on by the Not-Horses' steel-clad toes.

"We're away," said an artillerist in the crowd as the elevator began to accelerate upward. She sounded relieved and there was a general lessening of tension among all the Denizens, and a sudden rise in the volume and extent of conversation.

Unlike Suzy's elevator descent from the Upper House, the ascent to the Middle House was quite a steady and civilised journey. It was much slower, taking several hours, but there were raisin-filled biscuits, and though the bandstand was empty to begin with, various soldiers produced instruments and soon there was a scratch quartet of musicians playing typically soothing elevator music not very well.

Suzy, in her usual fashion, did not dwell on the bad news or think much about what lay ahead. Instead she set her Piper's children to looking around the transported stores, to see if there was anything that they might want to "borrow", as she put it. But there was nothing of any great interest to Suzy, though she did procure a savage-sword for herself and got Giac a brassbound shooting stick that he said would be a fine replacement for his umbrella. He even thought it would be easier to cast spells with it and, in his newfound confidence, was going to give it a try before Part Six of the Will dissuaded him.

Their arrival was also smooth, with hardly a bump and the merest chime to announce the fact. The doors slid open and at once Marshal Dusk strode out, with Suzy, the raven, Giac and the Piper's children close behind. Suzy recognised the courtyard the elevator had appeared in. It was the central bailey in front of the main keep of Binding Junction, the fortress on the Top Shelf of the Middle House. Suzy shielded her eyes with her hand as she looked around. It was very hot and bright on the Top Shelf, a consequence of there being two suns in the sky above, one smaller than the other.

The courtyard had been empty when Suzy had

last passed through, but now it was full of Army wagons, all carefully lined up against the walls. The curious scaly-leaved trees were gone, not even their stumps visible. Soldiers were everywhere, moving about purposefully, either because they genuinely had work to do, or wanted to appear as if they did. There were a few High Guild Bookbinders wandering about as well in their velvet robes, carrying papers and pots of glue, or their long needle-like spears.

Marshal Dusk was met by several officers. After speaking briefly to them, he beckoned to Suzy.

"Dame Primus wishes to see you immediately, General Turquoise Blue," he said. "She is on the battlements, surveying the camp."

"Guess you'd better come too—" Suzy began to say to Part Six of the Will, but it was already in flight, flapping up to the top of the keep several hundred feet above them. Even at that distance, Suzy recognised the very tall and formidable figure who was looking down, straight at her.

Dame Primus raised her arm as the raven alighted on her hand. There was a flash of light, a disturbing sound like the hum of a giant cymbal lightly struck, and the raven disappeared.

"Pity," muttered Suzy. "It was the best part so far, if you ask me. 'Ope it has some effect on old grizzleguts."

"I beg your pardon?" asked Marshal Dusk.

"Nuffin'," said Suzy. "Just thinking aloud. Guess we'd better go up. Don't s'pose you've got a decent pair of spare wings? Or a couple of pairs? I've only got some mangy grease monkey pinions and I don't trust 'em."

"Wings are strictly rationed for the moment," said Dusk. "On the direct orders of Dame Primus. We will need every pair if we are to assault the Upper House, and the Incomparable Gardens thereafter. The stairs are over there."

"Fair enough," said Suzy. She looked back at Athan, winked and touched the side of her nose. The Piper's child grinned and he, Shan and Bren melted back into the crowd, towards the line of quartermaster's wagons.

"Come on, then, Giac," said Suzy. "Last one to the top is a rotten sorcerer."

She started off at a run, but paused after a few

steps when Giac didn't immediately follow. He was looking puzzled.

"Come on!"

"But I already *am* a rotten sorcerer," he said.

"No, it means… it's a joke," Suzy started to explain. "Oh, never mind. I'm just saying race you to the top. For fun, and also because it will annoy Dame Primus."

"Annoy Dame Primus?" asked Giac worriedly. "Is that a good idea?"

"Well, no," said Suzy. "It's a stupid idea, that's part of the…"

She stopped talking and took Giac by the hand.

"Never mind. We'll just walk fast. I can't expect you to take in everything at once. You remind me of Arthur."

"I do?" asked Giac. One of his rare smiles passed across his face.

"Yep," said Suzy. "I expect we'll have to go and get him out of trouble as well, soon as we see what Dame Primus wants."

The battlements were crowded. Marshal Noon, Marshal Dawn and Friday's Dawn were there, accompanied by numerous senior officers, their telescopes, aides and telephone operators. But even amid the throng, Dame Primus was easy to spot. She stood head and shoulders above even the tallest Denizen, and was now perhaps nine feet tall or even taller. She wore her armoured coat of gold scales, with its spiked pauldrons that threatened the safety of any neighbour when she turned around. In addition to her grey wings that were a legacy of Part Five of the Will, she now also had a plume of glossy raven feathers that appeared to grow directly from her head, testament to the recent absorption of Part Six.

She also had the First Key clock-hand sword thrust through her belt and the Second Key gauntlets on her hands. Interestingly, the Third and Fourth Keys had become a very large and ugly-looking pendant of a crossed trident and baton, hanging from a chain of golden esses around her neck.

Suzy slowed down as she got closer to Dame Primus, and she motioned to Giac to stay behind her. Though she wasn't scared precisely, for she prided herself on never being really scared, she had become increasingly wary of Dame Primus, particularly when others were concerned. Suzy thought she was protected by Arthur's orders to Dame Primus, but knew that didn't apply to Giac.

The embodiment of Parts One to Six of the Will of the Architect turned as Suzy approached, a flange of her armour slicing off the sleeve of an unwary Regimental Major who had been holding a field telephone for her. The Major winced and stepped back as Suzy saluted.

"Suzy Turquoise Blue," said Dame Primus. Suzy shivered as the Will spoke, for her voice was now even more powerful and laden with sorcery. "I am glad you survived the Upper House."

"So am I," said Suzy. "Uh, ma'am."

"You have learned some manners, I see," said Dame Primus. "Perhaps my lesson on the Border Sea was worthwhile."

Suzy didn't reply. She'd blithely forgotten that one of the things she actually was afraid of was being forced to behave like a lady again.

"Part Six is with me now, so I know much of what occurred in the Upper House and of the disposition of Saturday's forces, but I would like to know more. I have questions for you and this minion of Saturday's you have brought with you."

"Oh, to be a minion," muttered Giac to himself dreamily. "I was a *sub*-minion."

"You will speak when spoken to and not before, Colonel Giac," said Dame Primus sharply. Giac bowed deeply. When he straightened up, each of his epaulettes had sprouted a crown inside a woven wreath, Dame Primus perhaps unintentionally having confirmed Suzy's irregular grant of his rank.

"We have a great host here," continued Dame Primus. "The survivors of the Far Reaches, the Lower House and the Great Maze, combined with the forces of the Middle House. Our fleet from the Border Sea will soon arrive here on the Extremely Grand Canal, and the sailors, scavengers, merchants and marines will join the Land Army, as the Piper and the ships of his cursed Raised Rats have blockaded direct egress for ships into the Upper House.

"Due to the work of myself as Part Six, we have access to one elevator shaft into the Upper House," continued Dame Primus, pointedly ignoring Suzy's and Giac's contributions to that operation. "But that is not enough to land a sufficient force to engage both the Piper's troops and Saturday's. We need to open more elevator shafts. After we have discovered what additional information you may have to offer, Miss Turquoise Blue—"

"General," said Suzy, though it was difficult to get any words out against Dame Primus. "Lord Arthur made me a General."

Dame Primus bent her gaze down to the Piper's child. For a moment Suzy feared that she would blast her with words so potent they might as well be a death spell. Then the raven feathers on her head ruffled and the Will looked back up, above Suzy's head, to the bright sky above that was the underside of the Upper House.

"After we have spoken, *General* Blue," said Dame Primus, "I intend that you shall lead a strike force back to Floor 6879 of Saturday's tower, to open more elevator shafts. To secure our beachhead, as it were."

"Sure," said Suzy. "But I get to pick who comes along, right?"

Dame Primus narrowed her strange, luminous pink eyes in thought.

"You may, within reason. You will, of course, take Dr Scamandros, who will be needed to open the elevator shafts. There is also someone else I wish you to speak to, to enlist to our cause."

"Who's that, then?" asked Suzy.

"The Lieutenant Keeper of the Front Door."

"Well, he's right handy with a blade, but I never heard of him leaving the Door."

"I am speaking of the new Lieutenant Keeper of the Front Door," said Dame Primus. "Though she lacks the swordcraft, I suspect she may be of use. Certainly Lord Sunday thought so, enough to send his Dusk to fetch her."

"Exactly who is the new Lieutenant Keeper?" asked Suzy. She had never felt a need to suppress her curiosity.

"A mortal," said Dame Primus. "Arthur's friend Leaf."

"Leaf!" exclaimed Suzy. "I never!"

"It is a most peculiar and in many ways unfortunate circumstance. But if Lord Sunday wants her, then she must be secured. I believe we can get her out of the Front Door. What's left of the Door, that is. Now, do you have any idea where Lord Arthur may have gone?"

"Dunno," said Suzy with a shrug. "I didn't see

'im after he went down the plughole. Don't *you* know?"

"No." Dame Primus's mouth tightened and her lips became menacingly thin. "We do not. He and his Keys are sorely needed, both to stem the tide of Nothing that has risen alarmingly and to continue the campaign against the faithless Trustees and the aberration that is the Piper. I trust that you are not covering up for some mortal indiscretion of Arthur's, Suzy? Are you sure he has not gone back to his world?"

"I dunno." Suzy gulped. "Like I said, I 'aven't seen Arthur since he went down the gurgler and I got tied up."

Dame Primus's gaze bored into Suzy. The girl tried to meet the Will's eyes, but had to look away.

"Very well," said Dame Primus softly. "Now tell me about what you know of Saturday's assault upon the Incomparable Gardens."

"I don't know much," said Suzy. She coughed and added, "I never got to the top. Course I'll tell you what I know, only my throat's gone dry."

"Tea," ordered Dame Primus. Her long, elegant fingers snapped with a crack that was as loud as a small cannon, and several Denizens rushed forward bearing a samovar, an enamelled tea caddy, a silver teapot and fine porcelain cups.

Suzy eyed the samovar suspiciously. Dame Primus didn't normally respond well to hints.

She wants something, thought Suzy. *And that can't be good.*

CHAPTER THIRTEEN

Leaf let her incredibly weary sword arm fall, the Lieutenant Keeper's blade dangling from her limp fingers. She had been fighting almost nonstop for what felt like hours, though she had no means of measuring time, so perhaps it was only feverish, adrenaline-fuelled minutes. Her Nithling opponents lay dead, slowly drifting away from her, propelled by their final actions, or by the cuts and thrusts of the sword that had danced in her hand as if it had a life of its own.

Perhaps it does have a life of its own, thought Leaf

with distaste. After dispatching the first wave of Nithlings – a dozen slow-moving things that looked more like human-size turnips than anything else, though they had mouths with needle-sharp fangs – she had tried to drop the sword and run to the exit she knew led to her Earth. But try as she might, she could not lose the sword. If she let go, the gold-braided strap tightened on her wrist so she could not slip it off, and if she slipped the strap off first, her fingers became glued to the hilt.

Before she had been able to experiment further, another Nithling had attacked. It was alone, but far more trouble than the previous lot. It was rather like a bear with the horns of a bull, and it was fast and clever. It had scratched Leaf and would have taken her head off if she had jumped back any slower. Years of gymnastics when she was younger had finally paid off.

Leaf inspected the scratch. The blue swallow-tailed coat looked like it was made of wool, but was evidently made of much tougher stuff. The Nithling's horn had not even torn the cloth as it had scraped across, but the very tip had drawn blood from her unprotected throat. Leaf looked at the blood. It was hard to tell, since the only light came from the blue radiance of the sword, but she was relieved to see it still looked red and human.

From what had happened to Arthur, Leaf was well aware of the contamination caused by House sorcery and its transformative effects.

Which means I have to ditch this sword soon, she thought. *And get back home.*

There were lots more Nithlings inside the Front Door. Leaf could sense everything in the Door in a general kind of way, including intruders, entrances and exits, and if she concentrated on any particular aspect, she could work out more. Right now, there was only one group of Nithlings headed in her direction. Leaf decided not to wait for their arrival, but to check out the entrance she'd come in by, the one she knew led to Earth. There was something different about that one – it made a different sensation in her head when she thought about it, but she didn't know what that meant.

Apart from essentially fighting on its own, the Lieutenant Keeper's sword was also useful in other ways, Leaf found. When she lifted it and thought of heading towards the exit to Earth, it immediately oriented towards that point and began to pull Leaf along. It did so gently at first, but gradually accelerated until the girl had to hold on with both hands.

"Doesn't mean I'm going to keep you," said Leaf. She was thinking about how she might rid herself of the weapon and the unwanted post of being Lieutenant Keeper. If she could work out how to let go of the sword, she could just leave it behind. Or it might be as easy as finding someone to give the weapon to, just as she had received it from the previous wielder. Of course, she might need to be dying before she could give it up, which was a depressing thought.

Leaf supposed she also ought to think very carefully about who ended up as Lieutenant Keeper. Not that the job was as important as it once was, considering that large parts of the House weren't there any more. Leaf felt the dead ends like a toothache and immediately turned her mind away from thinking about them. There was nothing she could do about that anyway, and with any luck she'd soon be home and could hope everything would go back to normal.

As if that's going to happen, thought Leaf, but she repressed that thought too and returned to working out methods of losing the sword and the office that went with it. Getting Arthur's help, or the assistance of Dr Scamandros, would be the best bet. If she went to one of the exits into the Great Maze...

Leaf's train of thought derailed as she focused on the portals to the Great Maze and discovered that there no longer were any, though she was sure she'd felt some only minutes before.

"It's getting worse," Leaf said aloud. She was torn by indecision, unsure whether she should try to help in some way or just get out. If she could.

The just-getting-out part of her mind won for the moment, though she rationalised it as merely an attempt. She would try to ditch the sword and go home. If that didn't work she'd go and find Arthur and Dr Scamandros and the others... somewhere... the Middle House perhaps, since she could still feel exits there.

Soon after, she reached the exit to her world. It appeared as a normal-size doorway of pure white light that was always vertical whichever way Leaf approached it, rotating as she rotated, even corkscrewing around to match her movement, which she did just to see what it would do.

When she stopped up close to the shining portal, Leaf found she could see through it, out to the world beyond. She also sensed that the exit had a sort of frayed or fraying feel about it, as if it would soon collapse. The Reaper must have made it, she surmised, so it was only temporary.

The exit was still located in the same space as the front door of Friday's hospital. Leaf was momentarily puzzled when she looked outside, because everything looked almost exactly the same as when she'd left. The personnel carrier was there, smoke still trickling from the barrel of its machine gun. The front of it was bashed up and dented, the rear door was lying about twenty feet away, and she could see a masked and suited figure peeking cautiously around the right-hand track.

The caution was because the Reaper's creature – the beastwort – was also still there. Leaf had thought it would disappear with its master, but he'd just abandoned it. The huge tentacled thing was gently swaying on its many legs right in front of the doors.

Though Leaf had been gone for what seemed like hours, it appeared only a very few minutes had passed on Earth. She looked at the beastwort, its curious daisy-like head of questing tendrils and its very long and immensely strong tentacles. There was little chance of sprinting past it and, even with the Lieutenant Keeper's sword, she didn't fancy her chances fighting it.

In any case, Leaf knew she shouldn't take the sword out of the Door, and definitely not to Earth. It would create plagues and trouble, as all powers of the House did when brought to the Secondary Realms.

"OK, you have to go," Leaf said to the weapon. She unhooked the loop and tried to pry her fingers off the hilt with her left hand. But once again, she simply could not open her grip.

Leaf grimaced and put the loop back over her wrist. Then she let go, the sword dangling from the golden cord. Leaf let it hang for a moment, then swiftly pulled her hand back, to try to get it free of the loop in one motion.

It didn't work.

Leaf tried to throw the sword overhand and slip her hand away as the blade arced overhead, but all that did was nearly slice her own kneecap off.

She bit her knuckles in the hope that pain might help her move her fingers. That didn't work either.

Next she held the hilt with her left hand and slipped her right hand out of the loop, and was momentarily triumphant – till she couldn't let go with her left hand, and ended up having to transfer the sword back to her right hand again, out of nervousness that she might be attacked, for she sensed Nithlings getting closer.

Finally she gave in.

"All right! I'll just have to get help!" she said.

There was an exit to the Middle House not too far away, but before Leaf headed towards it, she took another wistful look at her own world. Nothing had changed. She could see movement and it was not in super slow motion, but evidently when she wasn't looking, time moved much more slowly out on Earth.

The soldier at the back of the carrier moved out a few paces while Leaf watched. She couldn't tell who it was, but thought from the size it was Major Penhaligon. He moved very carefully and kept his focus on the beastwort. It was observing him too, for several of its petal-like sensory organs aligned themselves in his direction.

The soldier took another step, and a tentacle suddenly lashed out and knocked him down. He rolled away and another soldier dragged him back into the carrier as the tentacle struck the ground where he'd been a moment before.

It's got them penned in, Leaf realised. *But it's not going over to get them. It's guarding the Door, I suppose – but that means no one can get in to help Aunt Mango and the sleepers. I have to do something.*

Leaf looked at the sword.

Maybe if I just run out and stab that flower thing it has for a head, that'll kill it. But to do that, I'd have to jump on its back.

Leaf looked again. The beastwort was the size of a small haystack. But most of its sensory petals were angled in front of it, and Leaf thought that if she jumped up to the handrail of the wheelchair ramp and took off from there, she could land on its back.

Suzy could do this, she thought, her mouth strangely dry. *Arthur could do it. Maybe I can. I kicked Feverfew's head pretty well, didn't I? Albert would tell me I could do it –* "Straight up the ratlines to the mast," *he always said.* "Don't look down..."

Leaf wiped her eyes, hefted her sword and took a deep breath.

"Go!" she shouted to encourage herself as she leaped out of the Door.

Or at least she tried to. The sword hit the brilliant white rectangle of the exit and bounced off, but the momentum of her jump carried the rest of Leaf on. Her arm twisted round horribly as she found herself falling down the wheelchair ramp.

Her right hand, and the sword, remained inside the Front Door, while the rest of her sprawled across the ramp.

Leaf groaned and tried to pull the sword through. But it wouldn't come out. She was anchored to the Door.

She looked up. The yellow petals of the beastwort's head were tilting towards her. Two tentacles, as thick as her arm, were rising in the air, as the creature swivelled round on its many, many legs.

Leaf concentrated all her willpower and pulled the sword halfway out through the glass door of the hospital.

"Come on!" she shouted, but she couldn't get the sword to budge, the last four inches firmly stuck in the Door. So she pushed it back and tried to follow it inside, only to be stopped by a tentacle gripping her around the ankles and dragging her back.

"No!" screamed Leaf. The beastwort was going to tear her apart, with her arm stuck in the Door!

Desperately she looked around for some other weapon, her left hand scrabbling about, searching in panic for anything that she could use as the first tentacle lifted her higher and the second tentacle whipped in and fastened itself around her middle, almost capturing her free arm. Leaf knew that this was it – she was going to be killed by a plant. Then her fingers found something – a rope or cord – and she grabbed it and tried to haul herself back towards the Door with it, but instead she went towards the body of the beastwort. Amid her panic, a sharp thought blossomed in Leaf's mind.

I've got the thing's lead!

CHAPTER FOURTEEN

Arthur waited anxiously for Elephant's return. The steady tick of the clock did nothing to help his nervousness, which increased as the time dragged on and his childhood friend did not come back. An hour passed, then two, and as the hour hand moved to the three, Arthur found his chains long enough for him to step a short distance away from the clock face. At six, he guessed they might be long enough for him to reach the edge of the terrace and look down. He tried not to think of what he might see, but he couldn't help visualising many images of his Elephant, dead or captured.

In any case, that was three hours away. Three more hours of waiting.

I need to think of another plan, Arthur told himself. But try as he might, he couldn't, and he found himself thinking again about Lord Sunday's offer. That made him remember *A Compleat Atlas of the House.* It had been blocked before, but there was always a slim chance...

Arthur took it out from inside his coveralls. The book had fallen down to his waistband and it was quite difficult to get it out, his manacled wrists clashing as he did so. He sat on the edge of the clock and rested the Atlas on his knees. As before, it opened and slowly grew to its full size.

"Tell me how I can get these manacles off," said Arthur. He thought for a second, and added, "Or undo the chains from the clock."

A blob of ink appeared, giving Arthur a moment's hope that the Atlas was going to write something. But it didn't. The blob spread and several more blotches materialised, none of them looking anything like a letter. Arthur watched them for a few seconds in case they formed a pattern, or a sketch or something that would help him, but they remained mere ink stains, devoid of meaning.

He was about to ask another question when he caught a faint sound on the wind – a kind of whirring noise that he instantly recognised as one of Sunday's dragonflies. Quickly Arthur shut the Atlas and as it shrank he stuffed it back down his front. Looking up, he saw a dragonfly commence its approach to once again end up hovering nearby. A rope ladder came clattering down and Lord Sunday descended.

The Trustee was alone this time. He looked around, satisfied himself that all was secure, then approached Arthur, making sure not to stand too close to the clock. Even from several paces away, and without Lord Sunday having to hold his Key, Arthur could feel the power of it pushing him down, making him feel like a servant or a beggar, or maybe, since they were in the Incomparable Gardens, some small worm to be stepped on and forgotten.

"Have you reconsidered?" asked Lord Sunday.

"I'm thinking about it," Arthur answered honestly. "Can I ask you some questions?"

"You may have fifteen minutes," said Lord

Sunday. He looked at the clock. "There are currently many matters that require my attention and I do not wish to waste my time."

"Why didn't you fulfil your duty as a Trustee?" asked Arthur. "Why break up and hide the Will?"

"So you do not know even that," said Lord Sunday. "I am surprised someone so ignorant has come so far."

Arthur shrugged. "That's not an answer."

"It is a matter of who will inherit the Architect's powers and authority, and the nature of the transfer," said Lord Sunday. "The Will specified a mortal heir, which was not, and is not, acceptable."

"Why?" asked Arthur. "I mean, if I'd just been *given* the Keys, I would have left you all alone, and the House would be all right and everything would be fine."

"And you think the Will itself would acquiesce to that?" asked Lord Sunday. "I believe it has already slain most of my fellow Trustees."

"The Will?!" asked Arthur. His chains clanked as he sat up straighter, shocked by Sunday's accusation. "You think Dame Primus killed Mister Monday and Grim Tuesday?"

"I am sure of it," said Sunday. "And you are

behind the times. Sir Thursday and Lady Friday have also been slain. The Will is an instrument of the Architect, with a single aim. The Trustees, in its view, are traitors and must be punished."

"I thought... I thought it was probably Superior Saturday... or you," said Arthur. But he did not protest more violently, because what Lord Sunday was saying sounded like the truth, and Arthur knew in his heart that murder was something that the Will was perfectly capable of doing.

"I have tried to simply tend my garden," said Lord Sunday. "That is all I have ever wanted. That is why I did not follow the Architect's instructions, and why I allowed the Will to be broken."

"But you're the Architect's son!"

"Yes," replied Lord Sunday, "but not as a mortal would understand it. It *is* true I am an offshoot of both the Architect and the Old One. In any case, a very, very long time ago we... disagreed, culminating in the Architect's imprisonment of the Old One. The Piper sulked in some hidden fastness, and the Mariner embarked on his journeying. I remained in my garden. The Architect herself withdrew completely and nothing was heard from her for a period of time you cannot even imagine. Then, completely unexpectedly, there came the Will."

"What happened to the Architect, then?" asked Arthur. "Is she dead?"

"No." A grim smile briefly curled across Lord Sunday's mouth, so swiftly Arthur wasn't even sure he'd seen it. "Not yet."

"So she's missing or has done that thing when kings resign."

"Abdicate," said Lord Sunday. "Yes. She has abdicated, and that is why there is a Will."

"A Will that chose *me* to be the Rightful Heir," said Arthur.

"Any mortal would have served the Will's purpose. Many would have done better, I suspect."

"So why don't you just give me *your* Key, and I'll let you keep looking after the Incomparable Gardens. Though you'd have to help me stop the Nothing first."

"And what of the Will?" asked Lord Sunday. "Would you take the Key and leave Part Seven of the Will captive in my care?"

"I..." Arthur stopped. He didn't know what to say.

"And if you did, would Dame Primus stand by your decision?" added Lord Sunday.

"She'd do as she was told," said Arthur weakly. His words didn't sound true, even to himself.

"You see," said Lord Sunday, "that is not a possible solution to our troubles. The only way out for you, Arthur, is to abdicate yourself. Give me the Keys you already hold. I will deal with the Will and the Nothing, and restore the House. You will be able to go back to your home and live a mortal life without the cares and woes that weigh so heavily upon you now."

"What about Superior Saturday and the Piper?" Arthur could feel himself weakening, the temptation growing. Everything Lord Sunday said seemed to make perfect sense. "They'll never leave me alone."

"I must confess I have underestimated Saturday's ambition and strength," said Lord Sunday. "But she is no more than a nuisance, and even without your Keys, I will soon defeat her. The Piper is a somewhat more significant threat, but not one that is beyond my powers."

"So if I give up my Keys—"

"And the Atlas."

"And the Atlas," Arthur continued, "you'll let me

go back to Earth with my mother... and Leaf... and you'll turn back the Nothing... and you promise not to interfere with my world. But what about my friends here? What will happen to the Denizens who've followed me?"

"Nothing," said Lord Sunday, but the way he said that word sounded more like *dissolution by Nothing*, rather than *nothing bad*. Arthur was about to ask him to answer in more detail when he caught a glimpse of a yellow elephant trunk waving at him from the edge of the terrace, behind a large, perfectly trimmed bush festooned with tall pink and violet flowers that were in turn surrounded by a shifting cloud of golden-winged butterflies.

"I... I need to think about it some more," said Arthur. The relief he felt at seeing Elephant made him almost stammer out the words. He hoped Lord Sunday thought it was just the stress of his situation.

"You have little time." Lord Sunday pointed at the trapdoor. "When the clock strikes twelve, your eyes will be taken. If they should grow back too quickly, I may reset the puppets to an older task, to take your liver. You should also be aware that with every hour, Nothing impinges further upon all other parts of the House. You mentioned 'friends' among the Denizens who follow you. Even as you waste time thinking, many of them will have met their final end. Think on that, as well as your own fate, Arthur."

This time, Lord Sunday did not ascend the ladder to the hovering dragonfly. He climbed the hill, disappearing over the edge of the next terrace above. Arthur watched him go, then looked up at the dragonfly. He couldn't see Sunday's Dawn or Noon, but there were Denizens aboard who were looking over the side, monitoring him.

Elephant must have seen them too, for he stayed back behind the pink and violet flowers. Arthur couldn't tell if he'd found the medal, because all he'd seen was Elephant's trunk.

An hour later, Lord Sunday came back down the hill. He stopped by the clock and looked at Arthur, who shook his head. Even that movement felt difficult, and a strong desire to agree with Lord Sunday washed over him, followed by a flash of fear.

He's using the Seventh Key's power on me, thought

Arthur. *Making me want to agree with him, to believe what he tells me. But it might be true. Maybe I shouldn't be trying to free the Will after all. Maybe it's all been a mistake. Maybe I should just give the Keys up...*

A clanking noise interrupted his thoughts. Arthur found his hand was inside his coverall, and he was about to remove the Atlas. Angrily, he pushed it back down and took his hand out.

"Everything I have told you is true, Arthur," said Lord Sunday, lifting his hand from the Seventh Key. "I will return before the clock strikes, to hear your answer. Do not disappoint me."

Arthur did not reply. His mind was awhirl, unable to decide on a clear path forward, unable to weigh everything Lord Sunday had told him against what he already knew, or thought he knew.

He heard the sound of the dragonfly depart and followed its swift passage till it was only a dark speck. As he lost sight of it, Elephant hurried out from the flower bush and strode towards him. Arthur blinked, for Elephant was larger than he had been before, and had grown imposing tusks. One of the tusks was stained with something green.

But more important, Elephant held an object in his trunk, a metal disc that glittered in the sunlight till it fell into the shadow of Arthur's palm.

It was the Mariner's medal. Arthur held it tight as he drew Elephant under his arm and hugged him, whispering thanks for yet another lifesaving mission performed so well.

Then he raised the medal and looked deeply into it, remembering what Sunscorch had said upon the Border Sea: if he spoke into the medal, the Mariner would hear.

"Captain!" said Arthur. "I need your aid. I am imprisoned by Lord Sunday upon a hill in the Incomparable Gardens, chained as the Old One is chained. I need you and your harpoon to break my bonds. Please come as quickly as you can!"

Chapter fifteen

"Put me down!" ordered Leaf, pulling on the beastwort's lead with all her strength. Either the creature didn't hear the quaver in her voice, or it didn't care as long as Leaf held the lead. The beastwort obeyed and its tentacles gently lowered the girl to the ground.

"Let me go," said Leaf, and the tentacles withdrew.

"Good girl," said Leaf. She lay on the ground, shut her eyes and felt her heart going at what seemed like a million beats a minute. She also clutched the lead with her left hand, as if the thin strap was the most precious thing in the world. Which at that moment it was, as far as Leaf was concerned. She tried not to think about the sword hilt that her right hand was stuck to, or the fact that the sword was stuck fast in the Front Door.

"Leaf!"

Leaf rolled over. Major Penhaligon was calling out to her from behind the armoured personnel carrier.

"Yeah, it's me," she answered weakly.

"Are you OK? I've got a flame-throwing tank en route, but it's still an hour away and we couldn't—"

"No, I... I think I'm all right." Leaf slowly stood up and tried to work out a position where she didn't feel so stupid with a sword stuck in one hand and a lead she couldn't let go of in the other. "Only I'm kind of going to have to go back through into... the... um... other dimension."

"What?" asked Major Penhaligon. Presumably they'd seen her go through the hospital door with the Reaper, not the House's Front Door, because most mortals couldn't see it. Though just going through the solid hospital door must have looked strange enough...

"It's kind of hard to explain," said Leaf. "Weird stuff, you know? I mean really weird—"

The sword suddenly interrupted her, dragging Leaf back till hilt and hand were inside the Front Door again. She felt the weapon buck and move around. It was fighting someone... or something... on the other side!

"I have to go!" said Leaf. "I'll take... Daisy... with me. Get help to the sleepers inside!"

"Where are you going? What happened to your suit?" shouted Major Penhaligon. "Wait!"

His voice was cut off as Leaf went back through the Front Door. She had braced herself to be ready to fight, and expected the disorientation, but even so she was surprised to find herself fighting a Nithling that was directly above her head and "standing" perpendicular to her.

This Nithling was humanoid, looked like a badly smudged photocopy of an uglified Denizen, and was wielding an oversize meat cleaver.

The Lieutenant Keeper's sword blocked a vicious chop, but was borne back, and Leaf felt the shock all the way from her wrist to her shoulder. The sword tried to come up again, but Leaf knew she was letting it down, that her muscles and reflexes simply weren't good enough, even with the sorcerous blade doing most of the work.

So she did a backflip and hauled hard on the beastwort's lead as the Nithling's chopper whisked past her heels. Leaf stumbled as she landed, because of the yielding nature of the Front Door's atmosphere, and spun down again. The Nithling gave out a grunting laugh and launched towards her, raising its chopper. Leaf lifted her sword to parry, even though she knew it wouldn't work. At the same time she cried out, "Daisy! Help!"

A tentacle lashed around the Nithling's wrist as the chopper fell, and arrested its descent six inches away from Leaf's chest. Another tentacle wrapped around the Nithling's neck and pulled its head off. But this had little effect, and Leaf shuddered as she saw that what she had thought were buttons on the thing's ragged coat were in fact eyes, and the coat its own hairy hide. The head was just camouflage, to make it look more like a Denizen.

Daisy was not discouraged by the Nithling's

persistence. Leaf looked away as the tentacles, strong as a demolition machine, ripped the Nithling apart and threw the pieces far away. Somewhere in the recess of her mind she knew this was a tactical move, because in the right circumstances such pieces could grow into small vicious Nithlings, combine with other new-formed Nithlings, or be transformed rather than destroyed if they met with patches of raw Nothing.

When it was quiet, Leaf let the sword pull her up.

"Well done, Daisy," she said. Overcoming her repugnance, she patted the thing's dimpled hide, which felt like the rough skin of a pineapple.

Daisy let out a noise that could possibly be considered a purr, though it sounded more like a drain being progressively unblocked.

Leaf wrapped her left hand around the lead a couple more times, just to make sure she'd keep control of the thing. Then she shut her eyes and concentrated on what was going on inside the Front Door. As before, she could sense that there were groups of Nithlings and a few single monsters roaming around, apparently aimlessly. Leaf wondered if they were either unable to see the exits or prevented from going through them. Possibly they were so newly formed from Nothing that they needed time for their brains to grow and become operational.

There were also large areas of Nothing within the Front Door. As Leaf focused her new sense upon them, she noted that the Nothing was slowly expanding, spreading in several different directions and moving on several different planes. It took her another moment to work out that this was because the Nothing was coming in through fifty or sixty different portals, and that the interior of the Front Door was a hemisphere, or dome, several miles wide and high, intersected on all sides by portals into the House and out to the Secondary Realms.

Some of the portals provided their own unique sensations when Leaf concentrated on them. The ones for the Upper House gave her an unpleasant tingling sensation on the end of her tongue, which she supposed meant they were guarded or closed against any traffic. She was now familiar with the toothache from the dead-end ones that went into Nothing, but there were also some into the Middle

House that, when she thought about them, made her smell baking bread, but it stopped as soon as she concentrated on a portal to somewhere else.

Someone's trying to get me to come to the Middle House portals, thought Leaf. *It has to be either Arthur, Dr Scamandros or an enemy.*

Leaf looked over at the beastwort.

If it is an enemy, they're going to get a very unpleasant surprise.

"We're going to the Middle House, Daisy," said Leaf. She jiggled the lead a couple of times, then launched herself in the direction of the closest Middle House portal, using the sword for propulsion. She'd been a bit worried that she'd have to somehow drag the beastwort after her, which would probably stretch her arms several inches longer, but its many feet adopted a swimming motion and it came along beside Leaf, so the lead was slack.

"You're a good girl," Leaf said absently. She was thinking ahead and wondering if she could leave the Front Door when it opened into the House. She'd only met the previous Lieutenant Keeper once before, but she clearly remembered him walking out on to Doorstop Hill in the Lower House.

Or did she? Now that she thought about it, Leaf couldn't recall how far he'd come out and where his sword had been. She had a sneaking and somewhat fearful half memory that the Lieutenant Keeper's sword had been in a scabbard, and the end of the scabbard had remained inside the Door.

Leaf frowned. She really couldn't remember and she told herself it was not the time to try. She should be keeping track of where the Nithlings were, to make sure she didn't get ambushed. So she concentrated on intruders and found that while there were still several hundred Nithlings within the Front Door, none of them were near her. In fact they were all moving away, to congregate around a particularly large pool of Nothing that was leaking in from what used to be a portal into the Great Maze.

I wonder what they're doing, thought Leaf, and she felt a strong compulsion to go and have an actual look. But it was a bit like being told to do something by a parent. Leaf ignored the feeling. Instead it merely hardened her determination to get rid of the sword and stop being the Lieutenant Keeper. As she'd told Arthur quite some time ago, Leaf did not want any more adventures. As far as she was concerned, she'd had enough.

A small point of light appeared up ahead. Leaf thought about going faster and straightened her wrist so the sword pointed directly at the portal. She sped up, the beastwort easily keeping pace. Together they accelerated towards the portal, which grew larger and became defined as a rectangular door of harsh white light.

A dozen feet away Leaf belatedly thought it might be a good idea to slow down rather than crash through into the Middle House with a three-ton creature on her heels.

But it was too late. Frantically Leaf swung the sword to the right, but that just meant she hit the side of the portal and was flung through it, wrenching her arm. She rolled across a thick carpet and collided with something wooden and fragile that broke.

The beastwort came through a second later, right on top of Leaf. She screamed, but the creature simply danced across her, its hundreds of legs exerting no more pressure than a small child, though that was enough to temporarily knock the wind out of Leaf.

The beastwort crashed into a wall just beyond Leaf, making the floor shudder and a large amount of dust fall from the ceiling. Leaf coughed and sneezed while she made sure she still held the beastwort's lead, then she slowly took stock of her surroundings. As she'd half expected, the sword was still stuck in the Door, though most of it was out.

The room she was in looked like a study or small library, as the walls were lined with book-laden shelves. The wooden thing she'd smashed was a chair, one of three that were standing in niches between the shelves. The portal from the Front Door was in the middle niche, which was why Leaf had landed right on top of it.

The beastwort had smashed a whole floor-to-ceiling shelf to pieces and was standing amid a pile of books, blocking Leaf's view of most of the room. She got up and twitched its lead.

"Over here, Daisy," she said, pointing to the opposite side of the room. The beastwort obeyed.

Now Leaf could see that there was a door at the other end – an extremely sturdy door for a library. It was studded with iron bolt-heads the size of small plates, and there was a heavily barred window near the top. As Leaf looked at it, she saw a hooded Denizen duck down and heard muffled shouting, quickly followed by the tolling of a bell and the clatter of armoured Denizens in the corridor outside, approaching at a run.

"Here we go again." Leaf sighed and tugged at the sword, which obstinately refused to come free.

CHAPTER SIXTEEN

"How you been, Doc?" asked Suzy as she led Giac into Dr Scamandros's temporary workroom, a former paper store. The sorcerer looked up from his bench, put down his peacock feather quill and doffed his latest hat to Suzy. It was an orange fez and when he took it off, several items fell out. Some of them scurried under the bench before Suzy could see what they were, but one rolled to her feet. She picked up the smooth metal ball cautiously and handed it back to Dr Scamandros. As he reached for it, it flicked out a dozen jointed metal legs and jumped clear, joining its brethren in the dark recesses under the furniture.

"I have been tolerably well," said Dr Scamandros, but the moving tattoos on his face told another story, with small furry animals sticking their heads into piles of sand while others covered themselves under piles of small rocks. "Given the circumstances."

"This 'ere's Colonel Giac, my aide," said Suzy. "He's a sorcerer too."

"Ah, I was a Sorcerous Supernumerary," said Giac carefully.

Dr Scamandros beamed and shook his hand. "As I would have been if I had stayed," he replied. "I expect it was political."

"Political?"

"Failing your exams!" exclaimed Scamandros. "Ah, it's a long time since I have spoken with a colleague. I wonder if you might give me your opinion on these spells I am preparing. They are reinforcing papers, to be pasted over small eruptions of Nothing, but I fear they are of such short duration that I doubt their worth. Of course, it is the Keys that are needed to properly contain the Nothing, so we can only hope—"

"Doc!" interrupted Suzy. "Dame Primus sent us over. We've got to go in the Front Door and get Leaf. She's the new Lieutenant Keeper. Then we have to get into the Upper House and open up a lot of elevator shafts."

"What? What!" said Dr Scamandros. The furry animal tattoos dug deeper, till only their feet were visible, waving furiously. "Leaf is the new Lieutenant Keeper?"

"That's what Old Primey reckons," said Suzy. Giac looked around nervously and crossed his fingers as Suzy said, "Primey."

"Apparently Sunday's Dusk went and got her from her world, but something 'appened in the Door and she ended up being the new Keeper."

"Oh dear," said Scamandros. "I fear this is another sign."

"Sign of what?" asked Suzy.

"The House is dissolving too fast," whispered Dr Scamandros. "We've lost the Far Reaches, the Lower House and the Great Maze, and the Border Sea is riddled with Nothing. If the old Lieutenant Keeper couldn't hold the Door, then the Nothing can spread through it into all parts of the House!"

"Arthur'll fix it up," said Suzy confidently.

The furry creature tattoos poked their heads out of their holes.

"Lord Arthur has returned!" exclaimed Dr Scamandros. "Perhaps there is hope after—"

"Uh, he's not exactly back," interrupted Suzy.

"Oh," said Dr Scamandros. The furry creatures turned into doors that shut themselves and dwindled into tiny squares.

"No one knows where he is," added Suzy. "So he's probably doing something important. Anyhow, what we have to do is get in the Front Door, find Leaf, bring her back, get a force together – I've got some of my Raiders working on that – get an elevator into the one shaft that's open, and attack the Upper House so's we can get more shafts working. Once the elevators are going, the main Army can come in and fight Saturday and the Piper's lot, and then open up the Incomparable Gardens and get in there to help Arthur, so he doesn't 'ave too much trouble."

"Uh, I'm not sure if I follow all that," said Dr Scamandros.

"Neither do I," said Giac.

Suzy sighed.

"Orright. One step at a time. We get in the Front Door and get Leaf. That's where you come in, Doc. Where's an entrance to the Front Door around here?"

"Ah, I shall have to undertake a lengthy divination," said Scamandros with a frown. He thought for a moment and his frown ebbed away. "Or possibly I can simply ask one of the Binders."

"Digby should know," said Suzy. "Let's track him down. Come on!"

"But my spells – I'm in the middle of a laborious procedure!" Dr Scamandros protested.

"No time," said Suzy. "You said it yourself. Let's go!"

Scamandros shrugged, his oversize greatcoat accentuating the movement. Then he reached across his bench, swept everything into one of the impossibly voluminous pockets on the inside of the coat, and followed Suzy and Giac to the door.

Suzy was already calling out to some unseen Denizen, "Hoy, mate! Where's Digby? Or Jakem?"

Shortly thereafter Digby was found in the Press Room. Drawing on a discarded proof with a pencil, he quickly sketched a map to show them the way to the nearest entry to the Front Door.

"It is heavily guarded, of course," he said. "And lies at the end of a corridor amply provided with murder holes, an oil trap and so forth. I shall write a note for the guards, to let you—"

As he spoke, a bell tolled in the keep, three times three. Digby cocked his head to one side.

"Hmmm, that's synchronistically curious," he said. "That is the alarm for an incursion from the Front Door. Perhaps I'd best show you over there myself. Jakem! Jakem!"

The former Pressmaster, who had been demoted by Arthur when Digby was raised up in his place, ran over and bowed deeply.

"Jakem, please inform Marshal Noon that there may be an attack through the Front Door portal located in the dungeon of the west wing. General Turquoise Blue, Colonel Giac, Dr Scamandros – please follow me."

Digby led the group at a quick pace down a stairway and into one of the auxiliary passages of the keep, which was largely occupied by a small rack-and-pinion railway – not much larger than an oversize toy train – that in normal times transported paper, ink and type throughout Binding Junction. Now the railway transported military stores, its fruit-box-size cars trundling steadily along loaded with savage-swords, Nothing-powder, binding spears and other such stuff.

"Quicker through here," explained Digby. "The main corridors are too full of soldiers."

At the next intersection they had to wait while another train crossed in front. The alarm bell continued to toll in the distance, repeating a refrain of three deep calls, a pause, then three again, a pause and three again. Every time it finished the ninth tolling, there was a longer silence and everyone cocked their ears to see if it would stop, indicating that the emergency was over.

But the bell continued to sound and Digby increased his pace as they crossed the tracks behind the guard's van of the train which carried an un-usually short Denizen guard dwarfed beneath her large leather cap. She waved her red lantern in greeting as they passed, but only Giac waved back. The others were too intent on what lay ahead.

When they reached the steps leading down to

the dungeon, it was crowded with a bristling hedgehog of Bookbinders and their long needle spears. Digby had to shout to get them to move to one side. As he led the way down, a platoon of musket-wielding Regimental soldiers marched up and began to file down behind Dr Scamandros, who was bringing up the rear of Suzy's party.

There were several thick iron-studded doors along the corridor, open to allow the spear-carriers passage. Suzy looked up and saw lots of murder holes in the ceiling, and caught a glimpse of the Denizens who waited above with cauldrons of hot oil.

The most massive door of all, at the end of the corridor, was shut fast and barred with four heavy beams. A Bookbinder was perched on one of the beams so he could see through the small grille window. As Digby and the others arrived, he jumped down and bowed.

"Press Turner First Class Horrybig, temporarily in charge of the Lower Ground Guard! Beg to report intruders from the Front Door!" he boomed in an authoritative voice. "A huge Nithling and a small mortal-shaped Nithling!"

"I told you already! I'm not a Nithling!" shouted someone on the other side of the Door.

"That's Leaf!" cried Suzy, and ran to the Door. But Dr Scamandros pulled at her sleeve and stopped her.

"Careful," he whispered. "It may be a trick. Perhaps even a Cocigrue of Leaf. Allow me to check."

The sorcerer rummaged in his pockets and pulled out his gold wire-framed spectacles, putting them on so that they sat on his forehead, above his eyes.

"Oh, I remember," said Giac. He sounded surprised at himself. "Inward seeing."

"Exactly, my dear colleague," replied Dr Scamandros. He carefully stepped up on to the lower bar and peered through the window.

"Hmmm..." he said. "The large creature was grown in the Incomparable Gardens and is not precisely a Nithling as such, but a sorcerously manipulated native of some Secondary Realm. The smaller being is a mortal... not a Cocigrue—"

"Dr Scamandros, it's me, Leaf! Is Arthur there?"

"Definitely a mortal," continued Dr Scamandros. "Probably Miss Leaf. I note the sorcerous weapon she holds maintains a connection with the Front Door, and the creature is retained under her command by the use of Grobbin's Commanding Leash—"

"I remember that too!" exclaimed Giac. "Old Grobbin was one of my tutors, but I'd forgotten everything he said until now. Fancy that. It was there all the time, but I couldn't think of it."

"Too much rain," said Suzy. "Got water on the brain probably. That'd hold you up."

"Suzy! Can you let me out?"

"Very interesting," said Dr Scamandros. "While the mortal – who I must say is almost definitely Miss Leaf – is an unaltered human, the uniform she is wearing is in fact a sorcerous construct of a very high order, as is the sword she wields. Both made by the Architect herself, I'd warrant. Colonel Giac, perhaps you would care to take a look?"

"I'd be delighted, um, honoured colleague," said Giac.

"Is anybody going to open this door?" shouted Leaf. "And help me get this sword unstuck?"

"In a moment, Miss Leaf," said Dr Scamandros through the window. "Please allow my colleague—"

He stopped talking as Suzy lifted one end of the bar, forcing him to step down, where he collided with Giac, who was waiting to step up.

"You can do your inward seeing thing just as well with the door open," said Suzy. She lifted the bar off completely and set it aside.

"Half a mo', Leaf," she called out as she lifted the second bar. "Got to get this all undone."

A wary murmur and shuffle behind Suzy reminded her that the passage was packed with armed bookbinders and soldiers. After she set the last bar down, she stood on it and addressed the crowd.

"Everything's sorted," she called out. "It's only Arthur's second right-hand... uh... mortal... ah... *Admiral* Leaf. So you lot can stand down. Who's got the key for this door?"

"I do," said Horrybig. He looked at Digby, who nodded. Horrybig looked surprised, but put the key in the lock and turned it before quickly stepping back.

Suzy opened the door and went in. She recognised Leaf, who was leaning out of an alcove and holding on to the hilt of a sword that as far as

Suzy could see was stuck in the wall. The creature Dr Scamandros had referred to was somewhat more imposing than Suzy had expected, occupying all the rear half of the room, its tentacles coiled up on the floor like strange, neck-high pots.

"Suzy! It *is* you," said Leaf. "Is Arthur here? I need him to get this sword out of the Front Door."

"Arthur's not here," replied Suzy. She advanced closer, keeping a wary eye on the beastwort. "Wot's that thing? And 'ow did you end up becoming the new Lieutenant Keeper?"

"That's Daisy," said Leaf. "She's a beastwort. The Reaper – that's one of Sunday's guys – brought her to Earth. Only he left her behind when he took me through. He was supposed to deliver me to Lord Sunday, but we stopped to help the old Lieutenant Keeper and... he was dying. He gave me his sword, and apparently now I'm the Lieutenant Keeper. But I don't want to be!"

"Bad job," Suzy agreed. "Too much work."

"You're telling me!" Leaf looked past Suzy. "Dr Scamandros! Maybe you can help?"

"I shall do my best," said Dr Scamandros. He stood next to Suzy and peered at Leaf's coat, apparently fascinated by her sleeve. Tattoos of small weaver's looms appeared on his face, shuttles flew across them and rolls of blue cloth cascaded across his nose. "How may I assist you?"

"First I want to get this sword out of the Front Door!" Leaf said as she tugged on it once again.

"Oh dear," said Dr Scamandros. "That is beyond my ability."

"But not, I think, beyond mine," said a cold and powerful voice behind him. Both Suzy and Scamandros jumped, and Daisy scuttled back on her many legs and emitted a high-pitched tone of fear or distress.

"Dame Primus," said Leaf warily. "Hello."

CHAPTER SEVENTEEN

It was half past eleven and the chains that bound Arthur to the clock had shrunk, dragging him back to the central boss. With each passing minute, they tightened further, pulling his hands behind his back.

There had been no sign or portent of the Mariner's arrival. Arthur tried not to think of how long it had taken the Captain to come to his – or Leaf's – aid in the past. He'd hoped that the Mariner might not be too far away, cosmically speaking.

Now he had to address the very real possibility that within forty minutes two horrendous puppets were going to take out his eyes. While he was pretty confident they would grow back, that didn't make him feel any better.

Elephant shifted at his side, sensing Arthur's fear. His friend had continued to grow for a while after bringing the medal back, but had stopped when he got to the size of a large dog. Or rather the height of one, for he was very round and would weigh much more than even the most heavyset dog.

"You'll have to go and hide soon," said Arthur. "Lord Sunday said he'd be back before twelve. And I don't want the puppets taking your eyes as well."

Elephant made a thrusting motion with his tusks. They were about a foot long now and very sharp.

Arthur shook his head. "No. You can't fight Sunday. Or the puppets. But thank you."

Elephant made a deep grumbling sound.

"No, I couldn't bear it if you were hurt or killed," said Arthur. He remembered when he'd lost Elephant all those years ago. It was an intense ache that had never really left him, though it had become smaller inside him as he had grown bigger. "You'd better go and hide now."

Elephant saluted with his trunk and rumbled off

to hide among a stand of tall, flowering shrubs. Arthur twisted round to look at the trapdoor in the clock face. He could hear rattling and scratching noises behind it now as the puppets came alive and readied their chopper and corkscrew.

"I'm going to kick the bark off your little wooden heads," warned Arthur, attempting to channel Suzy or the inner anger that had risen in him in the past. But his voice lacked conviction and he found no rage. He was going to try kicking them if it was possible, but he knew it probably wouldn't be. When the chains tightened up completely, he would be held down against the clock face and the puppets would come at him from behind his head. To kick them he'd have to be a contortionist.

"I'll bite too," added Arthur.

Not that my teeth would do much to those puppets, even if I could land a bite on them. I'd need much more serious teeth for that. Or I could just give up.

Arthur banished that thought. He wasn't going to give up.

I have to think outside the box, like Eric is always going on about. Maybe I could grow sharp teeth. Or extra arms. I could direct my power to change myself.

Arthur looked down at his manacled wrists and a new thought popped into his head.

Maybe I could make my hands really small and slip these manacles off!

He stared down at his wrists and concentrated on them, willing them to become thinner, to shrink down.

Nothing happened, save the tick of the clock and the rattle of the chain as another link crept into its neighbour and became one. Arthur kept concentrating for the next ten minutes, but it didn't work. His wrists and hands remained unchanged.

He was so intent on forcing his body to reshape itself that he didn't notice Lord Sunday till the Denizen was standing in front of him, on the rim of the clock face.

"It lacks but a quarter hour to twelve," said Lord Sunday. "Will you give me the Keys and the Atlas?"

Arthur looked up at him. Though many hours had passed, the sun in the Incomparable Gardens moved slowly and had barely shifted against the painted sky. Lord Sunday stood so the disc of the sun was behind his head, giving him a bright and blinding halo.

"No," said Arthur slowly. "I won't."

Lord Sunday frowned and turned away. Arthur blinked and looked up, but saw no dragonfly. Wherever Lord Sunday had come from, it was not on one of his winged creatures.

"I will wait," said Lord Sunday. "Perhaps you will reconsider *afterwards*."

Arthur craned his head around. Sunday had sat down just behind the clock, on a striped canvas chair that had not been there before. A Denizen in a butler's uniform who looked a bit like Sneezer, though he had green skin, was handing him a tall, pinkish drink. Beyond the butler, a tall-legged beetle the size of a van munched on the leaves of a tree. The beetle had a gilded throne on its back and several smaller cane chairs behind it, and was evidently Sunday's choice of ground transportation.

The clock ticked. Arthur watched the minute hand move to three minutes to twelve. The chain tightened again, and he lay back and stared at the sky.

It will only be a short pain, he thought. *Followed by an ache that will pass in an hour or two as my eyes grow back. It's not like when I was human...*

"Not like when I was human," he whispered.

"What?" asked Lord Sunday. "What did you say? Did you agree to my proposal?"

"No!" Arthur shouted. He shut his eyes. He wasn't sure he could stand the pain, but he was absolutely sure he didn't want to see it happen. "Do your worst!"

The last few minutes stretched out for a very long time. Arthur could see the red glare of the sun through his eyelids. He scrunched his eyes more tightly closed and tried to think of other, nicer things. Of Bob's music, and of his own songs. He tried to hum one, but he couldn't remember it, and there were other songs that he should be able to remember, but he couldn't think how they went either, not even classic songs he'd played a million times himself on the keyboard.

Bong! The clock began to strike. Arthur tensed as he heard the trapdoor fly open, his whole body taut as a bowstring. He ground his teeth together to keep his mouth shut as he heard the whirr and cackle of the clockwork puppets. A shadow eclipsed the red blur of the sun...

I will not scream, thought Arthur furiously. *I will not scream or cry or show any sign...*

The clock continued to strike, slowly counting to twelve.

Bong! Bong! Bong! Bong!

There was no pain. Arthur felt nothing, not the slightest touch on his eyelids or face.

Bong! Bong! Bong!

He gulped, unable to stop himself, and his eyes ever so slightly unscrunched.

Bong! Bong!

Only two strikes to go and still nothing had touched his eyes. Arthur took in a deep, racking breath...

Bong!

The last strike was taking forever and the puppets still hadn't attacked. They only had the time it took for the clock to sound the twelve chimes.

"Come on!" shouted Arthur.

Bong!

Arthur heard the whirr and the clatter of the puppets' wooden feet, and the slap of the trapdoor closing. Slowly, ever so slowly, he opened his eyes.

Lord Sunday was standing near him, sipping his drink.

"You are brave," he said. "Braver than I might

have expected, from a mortal. Yet I think you will not be so brave next time."

"Next time..." whispered Arthur.

"You must give me the Keys and the Atlas," said Lord Sunday. "It is the only hope for the House and the Secondary Realms."

Arthur stared up at him, his mind racing, fuelled by fear-induced adrenaline.

"You can't actually hurt me," he said with sudden realisation. "That would be like forcing me to hand over the Keys! You can try to scare me and that's it!"

Lord Sunday gave him a slight, unfriendly smile, and stepped off the clock face.

"I'm not scared!" shouted Arthur. He tried to shout it again, but he couldn't. Because he *was* scared. He didn't know if he was right about the Keys. Maybe the next time the clock struck twelve, the puppets *would* take his eyes.

There was a soft patter in the grass near the clock. Arthur lifted his head and watched the beetle race past, with Lord Sunday and several of his servants on board. The beetle went very close to the plants where Elephant was hiding. Arthur held his breath as it went by, brushing the shrubs aside before disappearing over the edge of the terrace.

Elephant emerged a minute later and crossed the grass. He gripped one of the clock's numerals with his trunk and used that to help lever himself up on to the clock face before trotting over to Arthur.

"I've still got my eyes, Elephant," said Arthur. "And twelve hours to figure out something else. I can't just wait for the Mariner. He took weeks to come to the Border Sea."

Elephant nodded.

"I didn't ask before," said Arthur. "Because I didn't think of it. But can you talk now?"

Elephant shook his head slowly and let out a soft, negative boom.

"I thought maybe I could send you to find a telephone," said Arthur. "To call Dame Primus. But if you can't talk... it's not that I want you to go anywhere..."

Elephant nodded and sat down next to Arthur with a loud thud.

Arthur kept staring at the sky, busy thinking.

"Maybe you could go up the hill behind us," he said slowly. "That's where Sunday's Noon took my

Keys. If you could find them and they're still in that net, you could bring them to me."

Elephant lumbered back upright and let out a short, eager trumpet.

"OK," said Arthur. "You go and take a look. But be very careful. Don't get into a fight or get hurt. Try to stay hidden. And remember you can't touch the Keys themselves. Only the net. Come back if it's too dangerous."

Elephant nodded, saluted with his trunk and headed off.

"I mean it!" Arthur called out. "Don't try to touch the Keys. Be careful!"

He waited until Elephant had left the clock before he let his head fall back. Quietly he added, "You're all I've got left. To remind me who I really am."

Chapter eighteen

Dame Primus bent down to Leaf and touched her sword hand with one gauntleted finger.

"*Ow!*" Leaf shrieked as a white-hot pain coursed through her fingers and up to her elbow, leaving her arm completely dead. Her nerveless fingers dropped the sword hilt and the loop fell from her wrist. The sword clattered to the ground, completely out of the Front Door.

"Oh," said Leaf, looking down at the fallen blade. "Does this mean I'm not the Lieutenant Keeper any more? Can I go home?"

"No and no," replied Dame Primus. "I have merely detached you from duty in the Door. I have another task for you."

"But I don't want any tasks!" Leaf protested. She massaged her arm as the feeling slowly returned, accompanied by ferocious pins and needles. "I want to go home!"

"I daresay you do," sniffed Dame Primus. "But like it or not, you will either do my bidding or you will return to the Door and resume your duties there."

Leaf clenched one fist. The fingers on her right hand still wouldn't close.

"I guess I don't have a choice," she said angrily. "What's this task?"

"You will take up your sword and go with General Suzy Blue to the Upper House to join with her in capturing sufficient elevator controls to enable our invasion to be launched. Should you survive that, then I expect you will join in our subsequent assault upon the Incomparable Gardens."

"I'll go along with that for now," said Leaf, crossing her fingers behind her back. "But as soon as I see Arthur, I'll just get him to send me home. So there."

Dame Primus smiled, a thin smile that had no good humour in it.

"As you wish," she said. "As we do not know where Lord Arthur is, and we cannot find him anywhere within our domains, within the House or out of it, I can only wish that you do find him, and quickly at that. Now tell me, did Sunday's Dusk say why he was taking you from your world?"

The sudden change of subject rattled Leaf for a second.

"No – he just said something about Lord Sunday liking to have all his tools ready before he did some work."

"Interesting," said Dame Primus. "I wonder..."

She looked up at the ceiling, her gaze distant, as if she looked far beyond the pressed plaster decorations of book fruits growing upon vines of words. Then she bent her head back down and snapped at Leaf.

"In any event, there is no time to waste. General Suzy Blue!"

"I'm here," said Suzy. She mouthed something under her breath, which Leaf thought might be "you old bat".

"Your force must strike within the hour, and at least twenty elevator shafts must be open into the Upper House within a further hour of your attack."

"*Twenty*, milady?" exclaimed Dr Scamandros. The tattoos on his face became tumbling Catherine wheels trailing sparks as they careened across his cheeks and crashed into each other. "In an *hour*? Even if they have been merely blocked, it will take me considerably more time to undo—"

"You have your colleague," said Dame Primus, pointing to Giac. "Put him to work."

"Even the two of us—"

"You will do it!" ordered Dame Primus. Her voice shredded the books in the shelf nearest her, their spine bindings falling to the floor like a nest of serpents suddenly all discarding their skins at once. "Don't you understand? There is no time! Without Arthur here, the Middle House will soon fall, and the Upper House after it. Only the Incomparable Gardens can survive, and we must all be in it just as soon as we can!"

Suzy blinked and wiped paper dust off her face. Then she saluted. "Right, then. Come on, Leaf! Let's go find our raiding party."

Leaf, partially stunned herself, bent and picked up the Lieutenant Keeper's sword. It practically leaped to her hand, instantly banishing the remaining deadness and pins and needles. But Leaf noticed at once she could no longer sense what was going on inside the Front Door.

"Dame Primus!" she called. The Will, who was already leaving, stopped and turned back. "The Front Door... there are lots of Nithlings in it and Nothing is leaking in everywhere. It needs to be defended."

"Yes," said Dame Primus. "It must be defended, for what little time remains. I shall dispatch Friday's Dawn and a force of Gilded Youths. It is unlikely the Piper would try to use the Door. He has no need for it, now that he is within the Upper House."

"That reminds me," said Suzy quietly, after Dame Primus had stalked out. "You get those things I was after, Doc?"

"What?" asked Dr Scamandros, who was already deep in a technical discussion of elevator sorcery with Giac, who once again seemed surprised at the return of his long-forgotten knowledge. "Oh, yes!"

He rummaged inside his coat and handed over

a large brown paper bag that looked like it was full of marbles. Or acorns. Suzy stuffed it in her own coat pocket, though like the doctor's, there didn't appear to be room for such a large bag.

"What's in that?" asked Leaf. "And what's with calling me 'Admiral'?"

"Earpluggers," said Suzy. "Make sure the Piper don't get us again. As for Admiral, I reckon you need to be a nob to get anything done 'round 'ere. Though I s'pose you *is* Lieutenant Keeper of the Door..."

"Only until Arthur can fix things," said Leaf. "And get me home."

"We got to do some fighting first," said Suzy with unconcealed relish.

Leaf shook her head and quietly followed Suzy as the Piper's child rushed past the lines of soldiers and bookbinders.

"Come on, Giac, Doc!" Suzy called at the next intersection. "Hurry up! We've got an elevator to catch!"

Scamandros and Giac caught up just as Suzy reached some stairs and bounded up them, with Leaf following less enthusiastically a few steps behind.

"But, General!" called out Giac. "Aren't there going to be more of us going?"

Suzy stopped at the top and tapped her pocket with the bag of earpluggers, as she called them.

"Of course!" she said. "Why do you think I need all these? And what do you think Bren, Shan and Athan have been up to? Gathering the Raiders, of course! Come on!"

Suzy's Raiders, threescore and six Piper's children arrayed in the most motley combination of weapons, uniforms and equipment that anyone had ever seen, were gathered in the courtyard, being watched suspiciously by a number of sergeants from the more regular units. The sergeants stood between the Raiders and the supply wagons, and whenever a Piper's child drifted too close, they grunted warnings and raised their swagger-sticks, bow staves or knuckle-duster knives.

A short, black-haired and very dark-skinned Piper's child in a uniform that was half Regiment and half Horde, with a savage-sword sheathed on his back rather than at his side, began to address the Raiders as Suzy and the others approached from behind.

"All right, you lot!" called out Fred Initial Numbers Gold. "Suzy'll be here any minute. Has everyone got everything they need?"

A chorus of "ayes" and "yes, sirs" with a "probably" and an "I hope so" answered him as Suzy tapped him on the shoulder. Fred spun round and smiled. "Wotcher, boss," he said. "Hello, Leaf."

"Hi, Fred." Leaf had only met him briefly at Friday's secret fastness in the Secondary Realms, but like everyone else, she'd liked him immediately.

"You got the message from Bren, Shan and Athan then?" asked Leaf.

"Yep," said Fred. "We've got sixty-six Raiders here. Almost all the Piper's children around Binding Junction, not counting the Gilded Youths. There's more coming in with the Fleet, but I'm told they won't be here for hours."

"Only sixty-six," said Suzy. "There should be a lot more survivors from the other demesnes."

"That's all that's here," said Fred. "I sent word to the camp at the canal-head, but no one's come in."

"I hope Old Primey isn't up to her tricks," said Suzy darkly.

"What do you mean?" asked Leaf.

"She wanted to kill us all off," said Suzy. "In case the Piper got a hold of us. Arthur stopped her, but I don't know... she's tricky."

"Yeah," said Leaf, unable to suppress a shiver. The embodiment of the Will had become much scarier, and certainly Leaf didn't feel Dame Primus could be trusted.

"Where are Bren, Shan and Athan?" asked Suzy, surveying the crowd.

"Uh, they got arrested," said Fred in a loud voice. "Something about a missing cannon and a Nothing-powder wagon. Marshal Noon caught them, or they'd have got out of it."

"Hmmph," Suzy sniffed. "They'll have to cool their heels till we get back. No time to sort things out for them now. 'Ere, hand these around."

She passed the bag of earplugs over, first taking a pair for herself and Leaf. Leaf sheathed her sword to take them, upon discovering that she had a scabbard at her side, and was relieved that she was able to let go of the sword.

The earplugs were balls of waxed paper that had tiny writing all over them. Suzy stuffed hers into her ears and, after a moment's hesitation, Leaf followed suit, as did the Piper's children, who were quickly taking their earplugs from Fred.

"I can still hear perfectly well," said Leaf. "They don't seem to do anything."

"They are not supposed to," said Dr Scamandros. "However, they should block most of the suggestive power of the Piper's pipe. Still, they will not last long in that circumstance and immediate removal from the vicinity of the Piper is advised. Particularly as... ah..."

"What?" asked Suzy.

"They may suffer spontaneous conflagration if subject to a concentration of the Piper's sorcery," said Dr Scamandros. "That is, if the sound is too close."

"You mean they'll catch fire?" asked Leaf. She felt the ball of paper in her left ear and frowned.

"More of an explosive burst of fire," said Dr Scamandros. "Nothing that would kill a Piper's child. If you do hear the Piper, keeping away would be advisable in any case."

"Great," muttered Leaf. "Do you know if I even need them? I'm not a Piper's child, and I certainly wouldn't survive an explosion in my ear hole."

Dr Scamandros peered at Leaf. "Hmmm. I believe the Piper's music has considerable power over mortals in general, given that is how he brought the children here in the first place," he said. "But since you are the Lieutenant Keeper, it would perhaps be a greater risk to wear the earplugs."

"Right," said Leaf. She took the earplugs out and put them in the stupidly small, tight pocket at the top of her white breeches.

"Is the elevator that's taking us up ready?" asked Suzy.

"Ah, I'm not sure," said Dr Scamandros. "I prepared one earlier to go to the Upper House, but Dame Primus didn't tell me who it was for, or how many. It will need a little expansion—"

"Orright, you nip off and expand it," said Suzy. "Giac, you go with 'im, give 'im a 'and."

"I beg your pardon?" asked Giac.

"A hand," said Suzy, forcing herself to pronounce the *h*.

Giac looked at his hands.

"It means help him," said Leaf.

"Oh, I knew that," said Giac. "Forgot!" He hurried off after Dr Scamandros.

"Where did you get Giac?" asked Leaf.

"Upper House," said Suzy. "'E's a good sort. Bit forgetful. Needs his self-confidence built up a bit."

"So, where is Arthur?" asked Leaf. "Last time I saw him was on Earth, but he was going back to the House."

"Tell you on the way to the elevator," said Suzy. She raised her voice and addressed the gathered Raiders. "Orright! We're going to zip up to the Upper House and help Doc Scamandros and Colonel Giac open some elevators for the Army to come through. Likely we'll be fighting Saturday's lot and the Piper's Newniths, but if we can make them fight each other, that'll be better. Any questions?"

A Piper's child near the front raised his hand. "What do ye call a Denizen with a sore foot?"

"I dunno," said Suzy. "What do you call a Denizen with a sore foot?"

"Well, I dunno either," said the Piper's child. "That's why I asked. I heard someone tell the first half of the joke in the elevator on the way up here but never the rest."

"Anyone?" asked Suzy as Leaf groaned and ran her hand through her hair, unable to believe she was about to go on an incredibly dangerous mission with a bunch of ancient lunatics, who looked like children and who all had the same sense of humour as a seven-year-old.

No one knew the actual punch line, though there were several suggestions, including "whatever you like, because they won't be able to run fast enough to catch you" and "an angler", which provoked questions about what fish had to do with sore feet, and not very well received explanations about double meanings and "not being able to walk straight".

"Best ask Dr Scamandros," Suzy concluded. "Any other questions? About what we're going to do, I mean?"

She waited for a few seconds, but there were no more questions.

"Let's go then," said Suzy with a negligent wave of her hand. The watching sergeants scowled as Suzy's Raiders ambled off after her, in no particular order and with no one purposefully in step with anyone else.

As the crowd opened up a little, Leaf saw that in addition to their many and varied personal armaments – and some of them were liberally festooned with weapons – a trio of hooded-and-cloaked Piper's children who'd come out from the shadow of the inner wall were pushing a small cannon and a wheelbarrow loaded with small Nothing-powder kegs and cannonballs. Suzy saw them too and looked at Fred, who winked.

"Guess they didn't *stay* arrested," he said quietly.

CHAPTER NINETEEN

The hour hand of the clock moved to the two as the minute hand passed twelve. Two hours had gone by since Elephant had left to climb the hill in search of the silver net and the Fifth and Sixth Keys.

Arthur sat cross-legged near the nine on the clock. He had been trying to distract himself by thinking of nice things, but had only become alarmed at how much of his own life had become hard to remember. Important memories – of his family life, his friends, the schools he'd been to – they were fading, and he could only remember them with great effort, tracking down scant threads of memory and binding them together.

He was afraid, but not of the puppets and the blinding that might be waiting in ten hours. Arthur was afraid because he felt his human life slipping away from him. Unless he really concentrated, he had difficulty even bringing an image of all his brothers and sisters into his head. Apart from Michaeli and Eric, whom he had seen most recently, he could not easily visualise the others, or recall such simple things as the exact colour of their hair.

He was concentrating on remembering his room in the old house, the one he'd lived in longest, when a very faint and distant noise distracted him. He stood up, the chains at their maximum extension, and listened.

The sound came again, and Arthur clenched his fists and strained against the chains. It was the trumpet call of Elephant coming from far, far away. He sounded distressed and in pain. It came again twice more, weaker each time, then there was silence, save for the ticking of the clock.

"Elephant!" Arthur screamed, throwing himself at the rim of the clock. Golden blood streamed from his wrists as he raged against the chains, the manacles cutting deep even into his toughened skin.

But it was no use. Arthur could not shift the manacles or the chains, and at last he fell down and lay sobbing in a pool of his own blood, oblivious to the pain.

"Elephant..." he whispered.

I never should have sent you, he thought bleakly. *I never should have brought you to life.*

Slowly he staggered to his feet and stared up at the next terrace, hoping against hope that he would see a small yellow elephant appear on the crest and come stomping down towards him.

Elephant did not appear. But Arthur heard a humming noise, like but not exactly the same as the sound of one of Sunday's dragonflies. He looked around urgently, but there was no dragonfly in sight.

The humming grew louder and louder, as if whatever made it was coming straight for him. Arthur turned wildly, chains clanking, as he tried to work out where and what it was.

Then he saw it. The silver net that Sunday had used to trap his Keys was zooming towards him, only a foot above the grass. Like some demented hovercraft it whooshed down the slope, jumped the number twelve on the clock and smashed into Arthur, knocking him to the ground.

Arthur grabbed it as it hit, but it flopped around in his grasp until it disgorged its contents – a mirror and a quill pen that leaped into his hands.

As Arthur touched the Fifth and Sixth Keys, he felt power flow into him, and all his self-doubts and fears were washed away. He stood up and, holding both Keys above his head, spoke in a deep and commanding voice that was only slightly reminiscent of his own.

"Release me!"

He felt resistance in the sorcerous steel, and from the clock under his feet. The manacles shrieked like train wheels locked and sliding on wet rails, and fought against him. Arthur focused all his will, concentrated all his power and spoke again.

"Release me!"

One manacle popped open and fell to the clock, but the other, though it spun around and writhed under his glare, did not open. Arthur howled in frustration and hit it with the Sixth Key, shouting for the third time.

"*Release me!*"

The manacle exploded into droplets of molten steel that sprayed the lawn beyond the clock. Arthur dropped to his knees, gasping for breath, totally exhausted by the struggle.

But he only had a second before the trapdoor suddenly sprang open and the woodchopper puppet vaulted out, swinging his axe at the boy.

Without thinking, Arthur blocked the blow by grabbing the puppet's forearm, in the process dropping the Fifth Key.

He tried to wrest the axe away, but the puppet was unnaturally strong, as strong as Arthur himself, and the axe was actually part of its arm. Its wooden teeth clattered in manic laughter as its mate came out of the trapdoor and lunged at Arthur with an oversize corkscrew. As always, it aimed for his eyes.

Arthur suddenly let go of the woodchopper and, as the creature stumbled forward, stabbed him in the head with the point of the Sixth Key.

"Drop dead!" he yelled, and he felt a savage pain flow through his body and out into the puppet.

The woodchopper didn't drop dead, but it fell back. Arthur kicked it into the corkscrew puppet and both fell over. Before they could get up, Arthur picked up the loose chain and whipped it around their legs, crossed it back on itself and then quickly wrote on a link with the Sixth Key.

"*Join*," Arthur said as he wrote the word.

The chain joined together as the puppets scrabbled desperately to get their entwined legs out of the loops of steel.

Tighten, wrote Arthur, and the chain shrank around the puppets' legs so that no matter how they pulled and struggled they could not get free.

"See how you like it," said Arthur wearily. He picked up the mirror and staggered off the clock. The puppets rattled the chain angrily and glared after him, their overlarge eyeballs rolling in their sockets and their teeth grinding.

Arthur took no more than a minute to get his breath and think, then he raised his head and shouted, careless of whoever might hear him.

"I'm coming, Elephant!"

Arthur broke into a run, taking great strides. He knew he had very little time before Lord Sunday found out his prisoner was free. He had to find Elephant and the Will.

Next time I meet Lord Sunday, things will be different, Arthur thought.

The next terrace was similar to the one below, a green expanse bordered by flowering shrubs and dotted here and there with stands of trees and other carefully arranged and unusually colourful plants. Arthur ran through a border of chest-high red and pink azaleas and across the well-tended lawn towards another set of steps cut into the slope that led to the next terrace beyond. But he was only halfway across when he heard the buzzing hum of a dragonfly.

He slowed and looked behind him. Even as he turned his head, he cried out in pain as he was struck by several arrows. One went through his right arm and another through his chest. The heads were glass, shattering as they went in, sending Nothing-poison into his bloodstream.

The archers were on the back of a dragonfly that was now hovering almost directly above him. Arthur roared in anger and pain, and raised the Fifth Key.

"Burn!" he shrieked, and a beam of intense light shot from the mirror. It hit the dragonfly, setting it on fire as it fell to the ground, the legs and wings still twitching. The Denizens aboard were crushed beneath the burning body of the huge dragonfly, and though they would probably survive, they'd be badly hurt for a long, long time.

Arthur only just managed to stop himself from firing more blasts. Instead he checked his wounds, ready to direct the Fifth Key to heal him. But he didn't need to do anything. Reinforced by the power of the two Keys in his hands, his own body was already fighting back against the poison. Arthur watched in fascination as the Nothing was expelled back out through the holes in his skin, falling to the ground and dissolving grass and earth as it sank out of sight. Then his bronzed skin closed over, leaving no scar or sign of any hurt.

Arthur scanned the sky, but saw no more dragonflies. Yet he felt something touch him, a sensation like a hand suddenly reaching out and lightly tapping the top of his head. It was Lord Sunday, he knew, using the Seventh Key to see what was happening.

This meant there was even less time than he'd hoped. Arthur started running again. As he leaped up the steps, he tried to remember how many terraces were cut into the hill, and which terrace the clock was on.

But he couldn't remember, and when he crested the slope to the next terrace, he saw that there was at least one more, and maybe another after that. Arthur increased his speed, crossing the slightly less wide lawn of this terrace at a speed that would have won him an Olympic gold medal in any sprint back home.

He was halfway up the rough stone steps on the other side when he ran into another one of Sunday's guards. Instead of his feet meeting a step, the step rose up to smash into him. As he fell back down the hill, Arthur saw that he'd been struck by a cunning camouflaged worm or serpent, one that had been disguised as the row of steps that extended up the next fifty feet of hill. The huge rough stones were in fact segments of its body. Now great coils of wormsnake were rolling down towards him, threatening to crush him where he lay.

Arthur flipped himself upright and jumped fifteen feet in the air, over the nearest coil, just as it smashed down where he'd been. The moment he landed, he looked around wildly, looking for the thing's head. He couldn't see it, and that alarmed him more than the huge coils of its body. They were relatively slow, but the head might be quick, with fangs roughly the same size as Arthur's body.

A coil rolled towards him. This time Arthur raised the Fifth Key and once more thought of fiery light. But when the focused light hit the wormsnake, it was reflected in all directions, the white-hot beam breaking into a scattering of rainbows. The creature was barely scathed.

"It's rock," Arthur said to himself as he once again had to jump away. "Or crystal!"

Whatever it was made of, the wormsnake was also clever. Though he still couldn't see its head or tail, the coils were gathering around Arthur, penning him in to a section of the lawn and doubling round so even with his prodigal strength he would not be able to jump past them.

Crystal reflects light, thought Arthur. *But it also shatters when frozen!*

He raised the Fifth Key and concentrated on it again, imagining incredible, intense cold, projected as a ray of particles that would instantly freeze the wormsnake.

"*Freeze!*" commanded Arthur, and the Fifth Key obeyed, sending a stream of cold against the wormsnake's flank. But this too splashed over the creature without doing any apparent harm.

For the first time since Arthur had regained his Keys, he suddenly felt afraid, even as he readied the Sixth Key to use against the creature. Surely that had to work!

The wormsnake is the Architect's creature, interrupted a voice inside his head – a voice that he instinctively knew must belong to Part Seven of the Will. Even though it was a mental communication, it sounded loud and close. *It is one of the first things She made and it is immune to the powers of all but the Seventh Key. But it is slow and stupid, so you—*

CHAPTER TWENTY

"This is the plan," Suzy announced as the elevator began to rise. "So pay attention."

Twenty-one Piper's children stopped playing seven very different games involving nine entirely different decks of cards. Four ceased juggling wax-sealed cheeses. Thirty-three looked up from checking their weapons. Five woke up. Three stopped arguing about the relative merits of tea from Earth versus that from other worlds, or the kind formerly made in the Far Reaches out of Nothing.

Leaf stopped scratching Daisy's pineapple-skin hide for a moment, but quickly resumed. It seemed to calm the huge creature, and in the limited space of the elevator, it was best if the beastwort remained still.

"You listening?" asked Suzy.

Everyone nodded.

"When the elevator goes *ping* and the doors open, we rush out."

"Sounds good," said someone. "Easy to remember."

Leaf shut her eyes and tried to remain calm.

"There's more to it than that," said Suzy. "Idiot." She looked over to Fred. "You and everyone from Elame will be one lot," she continued. "When the elevator goes *ping*, you go right. Leaf... *Leaf!*"

"Yes!" said Leaf, opening her eyes. "I'm listening."

"You take charge of everyone from Gowzer to Abidge. You go left."

"Right," said Leaf. "I mean OK, we go left. But shouldn't someone else be in charge?"

"You're an Admiral, aren't you?" said Suzy. "And you got Daisy and the special sword."

Leaf looked down at the sword and grimaced.

"Only until I can hand it over to someone better suited to being Lieutenant Keeper."

"Bren, Shan and Athan, you take the cannon out and set it up wherever looks good. I'll take everyone else and we'll go straight ahead. Doc and Giac, you come behind us and the first desks you get at, you start opening up elevators. The sooner they work, the sooner Old Primey can send up reinforcements."

"That's it?" asked Leaf. "Do we know exactly what we're up against? I don't even know what Saturday's tower is like!"

"Like I said before, we're facing Newniths wearing heavy armour and leather wings, and waving around big slow swords. Or if they're still Saturday's lot, there'll be a bunch of mid-level sorcerers. If it's sorcerers, get in close and go for their umbrellas. If it's Newniths, keep your distance from those swords. As for the tower, it's just a tower made up of lots of little office cubes. There's lots of desks on the floor we're going to. That's about it. Oh, except there's no outside walls, so don't fall out."

Suzy stopped talking. There was an expectant silence for a few seconds.

"That's it," she concluded. "Carry on."

The Piper's children resumed their previous activities. Leaf touched Suzy's elbow.

"What I don't understand," she said, "is why Dame Primus is sending us to capture the elevator controls. I mean, surely it would be better to send soldier Denizens. They're bigger and stronger and harder to kill—"

"We're sneakier and a lot smarter," said Suzy. "But that ain't the reason. Old Primey reckons we can do it, but if you ask me, she hopes most of us will get finished off as well."

"What?" gasped Leaf. Daisy, who had been quiescent next to her, rumbled and shifted her tentacles as she felt Leaf's shock.

"Maybe not you," said Suzy. "Though I ain't sure about that, neither, cos you're Arthur's friend and Old Primey don't want Arthur to 'ave any friends. Not ones he listens to. But she doesn't trust us Piper's children, cos she 'ates the Piper."

"I just want to go 'ome – I mean home," said Leaf. She looked at her sword. "I wonder if I can give this to someone without having to be practically dead first."

"We might need a little bit of your help," said Suzy. "But if you want to go after that, I ain't going to stand in the way."

"The portals to the Front Door in the Upper House are closed," said Leaf. "I don't know how else I could get back."

"Open 'em up again. Or there's Seven Dials. It's around somewhere. Might even have moved to the Upper House by now. Ask the Doc."

"Maybe I can open the portals from this side. But even then, the Door is full of Nithlings—"

"And there might not be anything to go back to," said Suzy cheerfully. "Depends where Arthur's got to, doesn't it? I mean, if the whole 'ouse falls down, then the Secondary Realms 'ave 'ad it. End of the whole picnic."

"Picnic?" Leaf shook her head again. "You're mad, Suzy."

"Nah," said Suzy, suddenly serious. "Just... just old, I guess. I mean, we've all 'ad a good run. Thousands of years, mucking around, taking nothing too serious—"

"Suzy! I'm *not* thousands of years old!" Leaf protested. "I'm not even thirteen yet! I don't want to die, and I don't want the whole world – the whole Universe – to end either!"

"Don't worry about it," said Suzy. She slapped Leaf heartily on the back. If it hadn't been for the Lieutenant Keeper's coat, it would have hurt. A lot. "I reckon Arthur'll save the day. We'll do our bit as well, of course."

"I really hope you're right," said Leaf quietly. She was about to add something else when Dr Scamandros edged between two juggling Piper's children and approached Suzy. He doffed his fez and said, "Eight minutes till we arrive, General!"

"Thanks, Doc," Suzy said. Then she raised her voice and added, "Get yer weapons ready!"

"Dr Scamandros," Leaf said, before the sorcerer could go back near the elevator door. "Do you know where Seven Dials is now?"

"Hmm, I'm afraid not," said Scamandros. "I believe it is likely it would move nearer to its controller. Formerly that was Monday, now it is Lord Arthur. So I expect it is somewhere in the Upper House."

At that moment, the elevator shuddered to a halt.

Dr Scamandros whipped a pocket watch out of his coat and peered at it.

"Six minutes early!"

Many decks of cards, several cheeses and a lot of other inessential equipment hit the floor as the Raiders belatedly readied their weapons. The door began to open and there was a very loud *ping*.

"Charge!" shouted Suzy. She had her savage-sword out and was already storming for the elevator door, closely followed by her central group.

Around twenty Piper's children looked at Leaf.

"Uh, come on!" she shouted. She fumbled at her sword and it leaped into her hand, twisting itself to avoid sticking one of her companions. Daisy rumbled up on her assembly of legs and her tentacles brushed against the ceiling, buckling it in several places. Leaf tugged on the beastwort's lead, tried to keep her sword up and joined the mad rush out of the elevator.

There were Newniths outside on the tower floor, but they were not ready for a surprise attack by Piper's children. They barely got to turn around before they were thrown to the ground by the rush and trussed up a moment later, the Piper's children chivalrously not using their weapons unless weapons were used against them first.

This happened some twenty seconds later. A rain of lightning-charged spears flew at the door as Leaf's group burst out. Without conscious direction, Leaf spun and danced, cutting down four spears with her sword, which essentially dragged her after it. The remaining dozen or so were caught or blocked by Daisy's tentacles, bouncing back to explode against desks or their unfortunate casters.

"Right!" shouted Leaf. "This way!"

She led a charge between a line of desks, but Daisy simply smashed through them, sending splinters of polished mahogany every where. Her tentacles ranged ahead, sweeping up Newniths and dashing them to the floor.

Leaf paused for a moment as she heard someone shouting her name.

It was Scamandros. "Leaf! Don't let Daisy break the desks!" Giac was hunched over an intact desk, writing something with a quill pen. Scamandros had evidently been about to do the same thing at one of the desks Daisy had just destroyed, because he was standing over a pile of matchwood.

Leaf tugged on the lead and Daisy swung back towards her, smashing a few more desks on the way.

"Sit!" commanded Leaf. It didn't look like Daisy would be needed any more anyway. There had only been thirty or so Newniths around the elevators and they had all been captured or slain. Looking out along the lines of desks, there were no more to be seen on the floor, though of course there could be thousands more on the floors above and below them, or even flying out around the tower.

"Keep a lookout for the counterattack!" shouted Suzy. "They'll be—"

Whatever she said was lost as the tower shook violently, knocking almost everyone to the floor, which was no longer level. Piper's children, tied-up Newniths and everything that wasn't bolted down started to slide towards the eastern edge. Then, just as suddenly, the tower leaned back the other way.

Leaf, holding on to Daisy's leash, was the only person who didn't go very far, since the beastwort gripped the upright columns of the nearer offices and planted herself very solidly in place.

The tower shuddered again and became still, leaning at a minor angle to the west.

"What was that?" Leaf called out.

Suzy was already on the move, checking on her Raiders and heading to the eastern edge. "Dunno," she said. "Everyone else! Keep looking out for the Newniths. Not you, Giac. You keep working on the elevators."

She jumped over some debris, grabbed hold of the outer column of an office, leaned into space and looked up. She looked up for quite a while, then across at the distant Drasil tree, a green smudge on the horizon.

After getting a full glimpse, she came back to Leaf. Fred hurried over too.

"I reckon something's 'appened to the Drasils," said Suzy. "The sky is lower than it used to be. Might be the Incomparable Gardens just fell down a bit and hit the tower. Could come in handy later."

She looked over at Scamandros and Giac. "'Ow yer going, you sorcerers?"

"Ah, we have three elevators open," called out Scamandros. "Without interruption, we may be able to open the requisite number in the time allowed."

"Sorry I asked," sniffed Suzy. She looked around. Several Raiders were playing cards again, and some had gone to look at the Big Chain.

"I said keep watching out!" she bellowed with uncharacteristic anger. Piper's children dropped their cards and the errant ones dashed back to their posts.

"I thought you weren't worried," said Leaf.

"I wasn't worried in the elevator. Now I am. You see these Newniths?"

She indicated a group of tied-up Newniths nearby, who smiled. One waved his little finger as well, because his hands were tied.

"They're second-raters," said Suzy. "They don't want to fight, unless the Piper is right behind them."

"That's good, isn't it?" asked Leaf. "Makes it easier."

"It's *bad*. It means the Piper's forces are already a lot higher up the tower, as well as below us. It means that we're surrounded, and it means the Piper 'imself is probably up above."

"Oh."

"Could be worse," said Suzy, reverting to her usual optimism.

"How?" asked Fred.

"It could be raining."

"True. There is a dark cloud over there," said Leaf, pointing out at the western sky. "Kind of low though, to rain on us."

"I don't think—" started Suzy.

"—that's a cloud," finished Fred. "It's winged Newniths. *A lot* of winged Newniths."

"They might not be coming here," said Leaf hopefully.

"They've launched out from up above and circled around," said Suzy, dashing that hope. "They'll hit us in minutes."

"Newniths at nine o'clock!" shouted Fred, quickly adding, "That's west!" as several Raiders got out their watches for the joke, since unlike Denizens, they knew what he was talking about.

"Get the cannon ready!" added Suzy. She took a step away, then turned back to Leaf. "If you've got to go home, go now," she said quickly and very quietly. "You may not be able to... after."

Then Suzy ran, vaulting over several desks before sprinting to join the cannon crew.

Leaf looked at the approaching horde of winged Newniths for a moment, then shut her eyes and reached out to feel for a portal to the Door. There was one somewhere nearby, though it was at least twenty floors higher up, and blocked. Leaf could sense a kind of tiny crack or flaw in the seal, and she felt sure that the Lieutenant Keeper's sword could open it up.

But if she ran away, what would happen to Suzy, Fred, Scamandros and everyone else?

CHAPTER TWENTY-ONE

The slight internal voice of Part Seven of the Will was suddenly cut off as the wormsnake's inner coil rolled closer, a ten-foot-high wall of stone-like snakeskin. Arthur jumped up and landed on top of the creature, jarring his knees. He balanced there for a moment, watching another coil as it rose towards him, and directed an anxious thought at Part Seven of the Will.

What am I supposed to do? How do I get away from this thing?

There was no answer.

Arthur jumped again as a length of the snake came crashing down. This time he landed badly and slid along the creature's back, almost falling into a thirty-foot-deep crevasse between three piled-up coils before he regained his balance.

That gave him a clue. Arthur stood up carefully, keeping his knees bent and his feet apart for better balance. He looked along the wormsnake's undulating body and across the coils. Then he began to run. He ran around the coil he was on, then jumped across to the next one that was slightly higher up and ran around that. Then he jumped not quite as far to another, till only a few minutes later he was at the top of the hill, and he slid down the narrowing end of the wormsnake and on to the welcoming grass of the next higher terrace.

The huge creature continued to coil and writhe down the slope, but not up it, and Arthur was none the wiser about whether he'd just jumped off its tail or its head. He was grateful that in this respect at least it was more worm and less snake.

Once again, this terrace was much the same as the last, though the flowering shrubs were a strange rusty colour and had almost perfectly round leaves that suggested these plants were not from Earth. Arthur kept away from them, just in case they were not exactly plants.

He was also wary of steps, but he couldn't see any on the slope ahead. It was just a grassy bank some hundred or so feet tall, steep enough that he would probably need to use his hands to help him climb it.

Arthur was halfway there, sprinting across the lawn, when the ground shook beneath him and then dropped away. The boy fell and rolled, bouncing around on the grass like a ping-pong ball on a table, as the hill continued to shake. When it finally stopped, Arthur was lying flat on his back and all the round flowers had fallen from the shrubs.

"What was that?" he said aloud as he got up and looked around. Everything looked the same at first, till he noticed there was a tall plume of smoke or dust in the far distance and that the sun had dropped significantly towards what he'd arbitrarily decided was west, making his shadow longer.

The Drasils have withered, said Part Seven of the Will. *The Gardens have dropped and Saturday's tower has broken through.*

Now you talk to me! thought Arthur. *Where are you? Do you know if Elephant is all right?*

I am in the Elysium, on the hill above you, came the reply. *However, I am locked in a cage and my ability to speak with you is constrained and erratic, unless you are very near. Come to me... no, wait!*

The Will's voice cut off again. Arthur stared at what he'd thought was a plume of smoke and narrowed his eyes against the glare of the lower sun. With the smoke or dust or whatever it was dissipating, he could see a little more clearly. What he'd thought was an insubstantial plume was clearly a solid object, several hundred feet high, overtopping the hedges and dominating the landscape of the Incomparable Gardens. It looked like it was at least the top fifty or so floors of Saturday's tower, poking through the underside of the Incomparable Gardens like a needle thrust through a cloth.

That'll give Sunday a headache, thought Arthur with satisfaction. *Thousands more of Saturday's sorcerers swarming into the Gardens.*

He turned to start up the slope to the top of the hill, but had only taken one step when he heard the distant buzz of a dragonfly. Instantly he changed direction and ran to the nearest tree. He crouched down under its lower branches and scanned the sky.

The dragonfly was flying straight towards him with lots of Denizens on its back. As it got closer, Arthur lifted the Fifth Key and began to build another blinding blast of intense heat. But just as he was about to unleash it, he felt the force of the Seventh Key emanating from the dragonfly. It was like a giant hand brushing the surface of the terrace, the fingers feeling for something hidden... unseen fingers searching for him.

Instantly Arthur stopped trying to focus on a heat blast and instead called on the powers of both Keys he held to hide him from Lord Sunday.

He felt no answer from the Fifth Key, but arthritic pain flashed through the knuckles of his right hand and, without his conscious direction, the Sixth Key suddenly began to sketch something in the air around Arthur, making his hand dart around like a swallow chasing flying insects. It left behind a spiderweb-thin trail of pale green ink that hung in the air and did not dissipate.

Within a few seconds, the Sixth Key had drawn a russet-coloured plant with broad sheltering leaves around the crouched-down Arthur, exactly like all the other ones along the border of the lawn. From inside, it looked to Arthur just like a three-dimensional open sketch that wouldn't fool anyone for a second, but he hoped that from the outside he was now effectively camouflaged as a plant and that it would resist at least the long-distance search of Lord Sunday.

The dragonfly flew overhead and hovered above the crest of the hill. Arthur watched, hardly daring to breathe as the ladder rolled down, and Sunday and his Noon and Dawn descended and disappeared from sight.

Stay hidden! said the Will, suddenly back in his head. *Stay—*

CHAPTER TWENTY-TWO

A thick cloud of Nothing-powder smoke blew across Leaf, making her cough and her eyes smart. A Newnith burst out of the smoke, her two-handed sword raised above her head. Leaf ducked aside and skewered her with the Lieutenant Keeper's sword, but the blade skittered across the Newnith's armour as she lumbered past and was gone into the smoke, with more of the enemy charging in behind her.

Leaf backed up against the beastwort, who was emitting high-pitched sonic squeaks of either excitement or anger as her tentacles lashed about, knocking the Newniths away from her mistress. But there were so many of the enemy, and the Piper's children now so spread out, that Leaf had to fight desperately herself, her wrist, elbow and shoulder burning with pain as the sword performed incredible manoeuvres that her joints and muscles simply couldn't cope with.

Not running away was possibly my dumbest move yet, thought Leaf as she was saved at the last instant by a combination of the sword and one of Daisy's tentacles, the former deflecting a thrown spear while the latter swept a Newnith off his feet into the remnants of a desk.

Maybe only slightly dumber than going to see Arthur in the hospital in the first place. If I'd stayed away, I might still be at home, and so might Aunt Mango, and I'd know the rest of my family was OK—

Leaf dodged another wild sword swing, fell to the floor, jabbed the attacking Newnith in the leg and sprang up again – right into the path of a flung spear.

It struck her in the right shoulder and exploded in a shower of white-hot sparks. Leaf was thrown to the ground, her breath and most of her senses knocked out of her. She didn't even know what had happened, except she couldn't get up and her left arm either wasn't working properly – or maybe it wasn't there at all.

Somehow she managed to raise and turn her head just enough to see that her arm was indeed still there, though she couldn't feel it. The Lieutenant Keeper's coat had turned the spear, but there were scorch marks all down the left side. Leaf tried to sit up a bit more, and as she did she felt something grating inside her shoulder, accompanied by the awful, nausea-inducing sensation of having broken bones.

Leaf lay back, gasping. A Newnith jumped over her and she flinched, the pain from that movement making her black out for a second, maybe more. She came swimming back to consciousness and looked at her arm again. She could feel her fingers now, but they wouldn't obey her. There was also something else wrong, something that it took her a long time to process.

I had something in my hand, thought Leaf woozily. *I had a hold of something important...*

There was only a broken piece of leather near

Leaf's hand. She no longer had Daisy's leash. She no longer controlled the beastwort.

That thought had barely registered when one of Daisy's tentacles suddenly appeared in Leaf's vision, heading straight for her. The tentacle hit the floor near her with a crack, slid back, curled around her and lifted her into the air.

Leaf screamed as her shoulder moved. Then, once again, she blacked out.

When Leaf came to, the tentacle was still wrapped round her, but there was also something else supporting her back so she couldn't move, and this made the pain in her shoulder almost bearable.

It was also quiet around her. The shouting and tumult of battle, the crash of Nothing-powder weapons and the sizzle of lightning-charged spears and swords had gone.

I've gone completely deaf, thought Leaf. *And Daisy's going to kill me as well.*

For some reason this made her laugh, a strange hysterical laugh that she cut off as soon as she realised she could hear it, though it was muffled and sounded like it came from far away.

So I'm not deaf. Leaf turned her head a little and saw that she was lying on Daisy's back, securely held down by a tentacle just near the beastwort's strange flower head. A petal twisted towards her, as if checking on her condition.

And I guess Daisy isn't going to kill me.

Leaf turned her head to the other side. In a dopey way she was surprised to see Suzy and Dr Scamandros, standing near a blazing fire made of wrecked desks, looking back at her. Some thirty or so Piper's children were sitting around the fire toasting marshmallows, a process that required constant movement as the smoke kept changing direction to blow horizontally towards different sides of the tower.

Beyond the fire, there were lots of Denizen soldiers. As Leaf watched them march out of numerous elevators, more sound slowly leaked back into her ears. She could hear their drums and fifes, bagpipes and rababs, and the bellowing orders of the NCOs.

Over the top of this background noise, and closer, there was something else. Leaf looked at Suzy and saw her mouth move. A few seconds later, she matched these movements to the sounds she was hearing.

"Leaf! Tell your pet to let Dr Scamandros come and fix you up! You're hurt."

Tell me something I don't know, thought Leaf.

"Leaf!"

Suzy stopped shouting and said something to Dr Scamandros, who shrugged. Leaf stared at them for some time, before it finally percolated through that she had to do something herself.

"Uh, Daisy," she began. Then she stopped, remembering that she no longer held the lead. Daisy wasn't under her control any more.

Two more petals tilted down towards her, paying attention.

"Um, Daisy, if you wouldn't mind," croaked Leaf, "could you put me down and let Dr Scamandros come and help me? I'm hurt."

The petals shivered and undulated, but Leaf didn't know what that meant.

"Please," she said wearily, and shut her eyes.

She opened them again a moment later and bit back a scream as Daisy lifted her up and gently deposited her thirty feet away, all three of her tentacles hovering nearby in a protective manner. Dr Scamandros rushed over and knelt by her side.

"Dear me, dear me," he said. The tattoos on his face were of a grovelling rabbit that got picked up, put in a pot and had the lid slammed down on it. The sorcerer was rummaging in his pockets anxiously as he spoke. "Lord Arthur will be extremely vexed—"

"I'm not... going to die... am I?" asked Leaf.

Dr Scamandros did not answer. He was busy writing something on Leaf's forehead with a long white feather quill. It tickled and Leaf wondered why she was unable to laugh. It was also deadening the pain, which was welcome, though at the same time, she was beginning to feel very sleepy.

"We held them off?" asked Leaf. "The Army arrived?"

"Yes, yes, all is well," soothed Scamandros. He had a scalpel out and was cutting Leaf's coat. She noticed idly that it was not the blue coat of the Lieutenant Keeper, but her radiation suit again, strangely bleached and tattered. That made her look at her right hand, and though her fingers were curled as if they still gripped a hilt, the Lieutenant Keeper's sword was not in her grasp.

"My sword," she whispered. The world was going blurry and sound was starting to become distant again, save for a single deep bass drum that was unaccountably becoming louder, even though its beat was very slow, and getting slower by the second.

Dr Scamandros didn't answer. He was busy with a large red tomato-soup can and a small silver funnel, which he had balanced without visible support on Leaf's chest.

"Giac!" he called urgently. He didn't turn around or look aside as he punctured the can in two places and began to pour the bright red liquid into the silver funnel. "Look in my left pocket! I need a magisterial watch!"

Suzy tried not to watch Scamandros and Giac as they worked on the mortally wounded Leaf. She kept one eye on the beastwort though, for there was no knowing what it would do if Leaf did die.

"I know I said I wanted to be a General," said Fred. "But I never wanted – it came to my hand. I didn't even know what it was—"

Suzy looked up at him. Fred had grown a foot since he'd picked up the Lieutenant Keeper's sword a scant few seconds after Leaf had fallen and been taken away by the beastwort to a far corner of the floor. Daisy's retreat had almost lost them the battle, but Fred's assumption of power and his sword-trained muscles had helped. Even so, Suzy's Raiders would have been overwhelmed if the advance elements of the Army had not arrived far sooner than expected.

Led by Thursday's Dawn, Noon and Dusk, they had made short work of the Newniths, who had quickly retreated. Upward, Suzy noted.

More than half of her force were dead. Thirty-nine Piper's children had been slain, and though Suzy talked about their very long, eventful lives having to come to an end sometime, even she found it hard to remain cheerful.

"Blue looks orright on you," she said now. "Got a bit of gold too. Appropriate."

"I don't know what I'm supposed to do," said Fred, his forehead creased in a deep frown. "I can sense the Door, and the sword... the sword wants to go back. Doc Scamandros says whatever Dame Primus did is wearing off. He said the sword is kind of a Denizen itself. The Architect made it."

"I knew that," said Suzy halfheartedly.

Dr Scamandros stood up, followed a moment later by Giac. Both took off their hats.

"No," whispered Suzy.

CHAPTER TWENTY-THREE

Dr Scamandros wiped his brow with a large silk handkerchief, and Giac wiped his with his sleeve. Then both turned and smiled.

"She will live," said Scamandros.

Suzy rushed over to them. "Don't you never take your 'at off like that again!" she scolded. "You sure she's orright?"

"It was a little delicate," said Scamandros. "Mortals are so fragile. But with adequate rest she will entirely recover."

He paused, and a dark tsunami reared up one

side of his face while on the other a tower was swallowed up by a dark hole in the ground. "Presuming we are not all destroyed," he added.

"We should get 'er 'ome," said Suzy. Her eyes looked very old as she gazed down at the unconscious girl. "She's not thirteen yet. I forget sometimes." She looked at Fred. "You reckon you could take her back to Earth?"

"Probably," said Fred. "Depends what those Nithlings are up to in the Door. You reckon Dame Primus'll let me though?"

"Don't ask," said Suzy. "She never said you 'ad to do anything, only Leaf while she 'ad the sword. And Old Primey ain't 'ere anyhow..."

"Yes, she is," said Giac. "Over there."

Suzy swivelled around like a spinning top. Sure enough, Dame Primus had emerged from one of the elevators at the head of a gaggle of superior Denizens.

"Pick 'er up and take 'er now," ordered Suzy.

Fred looked nervously over at the beastwort. "What about Daisy? She's not going to let me—"

"Ah, I believe that I may be of assistance there," said Dr Scamandros. He reached into his pocket and pulled something half out, before slipping it back in and walking behind Giac. He gestured for the others to crowd around and bend their heads to conceal what he had.

"Best not to let Daisy see it," he whispered, handing over a coiled leather lead to Fred. "I knew I had one of Grobbin's leads somewhere. As the beastwort is still collared, all you need do is walk up and throw one end of the lead. It will attach itself."

Fred took the lead and examined it carefully. "This is about twenty feet long," he whispered.

"It stretches, once attached," said Dr Scamandros.

"Daisy's tentacles are at least *thirty* feet long," said Fred.

"I believe the creature responds to kindness," said Dr Scamandros. "Look how it cared for Leaf even after she no longer commanded it by sorcery."

"I'll do it if you won't," said Suzy. She reached for the lead, but Fred snatched it away.

"I never said I wouldn't do it," he snapped.

"Do what?" asked a deep, powerful voice.

Suzy, Fred, Scamandros and Giac straightened up. Dame Primus looked down at them with her cold, cold eyes.

"Leash the beastwort, milady," stammered Fred.

"I see you have assumed a most important post," said Dame Primus.

"Uh, not intentionally. It was just that my savage-sword broke on a Newnith's helm and then I was knocked down, and I was crawling around looking for a weapon—"

"Enough," interrupted Dame Primus. "It does not matter. We must move onward and upward. The Drasils have wilted, and this tower now projects fully into the Incomparable Gardens, which has allowed Saturday to mass far more force there, with the Piper's army hot on her heels. We must capture both of them quickly, before they can interfere or, in some unlikely event, defeat Lord Sunday."

"That'd be orright, wouldn't it?" said Suzy. "I mean, if they off 'im, that's one less—"

"No, it would not be *orright*," said Dame Primus. "It is Lord Arthur who must release Part Seven of myself and claim the Seventh Key. If Saturday or the Piper do so... all will go astray."

"'Ows the 'ouse 'olding up, then?" asked Suzy.

"Pronounce your consonants and I may tell you,"

said Dame Primus. "For now, I desire all of you to stay close to me. That cursed Piper has got his army into the Gardens, so he's sabotaged the moving chains, or else Saturday has, and the elevators go no further, so wings will be issued. Somebody organise a transport sling for the beastwort and the girl."

A messenger corporal wrote *Transport Sling* on a slate and dashed away.

"We fly out and up in five minutes," concluded Dame Primus. Her own magnificent wings were already in place. The feathers looked like they were made of beaten gold and powdered with diamonds, so they glittered when she moved.

Suzy inclined her head, Fred saluted, and Scamandros and Giac both gave very deep bows.

Dame Primus did not so much as nod. She turned on her spiked heel and strode away, already barking out orders to the flock of officers and messengers that surrounded her.

"I liked her better when she was just a frog," said Suzy.

"So I definitely can't take Leaf home," said Fred.

"Nope. But you still 'ave to use the lead," Suzy

pointed out. "Ain't going to get Daisy into a transport sling by being nice to her."

"Yes, we will," said a weak voice from the ground. "I'll ask her. I need her to carry me anyway."

"Leaf!"

Suzy knelt by the girl's side, as Dr Scamandros and Giac hurried over.

"Gently, my dear, gently," instructed Scamandros. "You are held together by complex sorcery and must not move too quickly, or strain yourself, lest it all unravel."

"Daisy will pick me up," said Leaf weakly. "Did I hear you say something about me going home, Suzy?"

"Can't," said Suzy. "Old Primey gave a direct order. Got to bring you along."

Leaf nodded. "That's OK. I... I want to see it out now. I mean, however it goes. I might as well be there at the end."

"The end," whispered Giac. He shivered.

"Arthur will sort out Sunday," said Suzy. "Don't worry."

"But what happens then?" asked Leaf. "What happens when the Will is complete and Arthur has all seven Keys?"

"He fixes everything up," said Suzy quickly. Her consonant-dropping accent, always at its strongest when talking to Dame Primus, was almost completely gone and her voice had an urgency Leaf didn't remember hearing from Suzy before. "Come on, we'd better get moving. Wings to put on, which reminds me, I asked Bren, Shan and Athan to snaffle us a bunch of the good ones, officer grade. Leaf, you ask Daisy to pick you up, see if she will. The rest of us'd better get back to the marshmallow fire, have a few before it's too late."

She's really worried, thought Leaf. *And now I'm not, for I was almost dead, but here I am, still alive. And where there's life...*

"Daisy!" she called out. "Would you be very kind and pick me up carefully and carry me on your back again? Please?"

Daisy quivered and stood up taller on her hundreds of feet. One tentacle scooped up Leaf and very carefully laid her on its back, the tip curling around to make sure she couldn't fall off.

Fred smiled and dropped the lead back in Dr Scamandros's pocket.

* * *

The transport sling was rather like an enormous upside-down parachute, though one made of very heavy material. Following the directions of a Borderer Wingmaster, Leaf had Daisy go to the middle of the vast circle of canvas. Then a hundred winged Borderers picked up the ropes that ringed the cloth and began to hover as high as the ceiling would allow.

"This is the tricky part," called out the Wingmaster. "We can't go up, because we have to go out first, so the sling'll drop at first. Don't be concerned, Admiral. Uh, how much does your beastwort weigh?"

"I don't know," Leaf answered. "It – *she* – is very light on her feet."

"I'm sure there will be no problem," said the Wingmaster. She somewhat lessened this confident prediction by bellowing to her troops, "Keep it together, people! Synchronisation is the key to a successful sling! If anyone drops a corner or lets our *very valuable* and *important* passengers slide out, I will rip your wings from you and throw your miserable carcass straight down so the Nothing gets a head start on dissolving you! Is that understood?"

"Yes, Wingmaster!" chorused the Borderers.

"You need help, then, Wingie?" asked Suzy. She and her Raiders, all equipped with glowing golden wings of the highest quality, were also ready to fly, after the sling.

"No, thank you, *General*," replied the Wingmaster. "This is a very specialised operation, you understand."

She flew out the side of the tower and looked all around before shouting her next orders. The Borderers began to fly out, dragging the ropes and the canvas sling behind them. As it neared the edge, Leaf swallowed. If the Borderers flying out behind were too slow, she and the beastwort would slide out the back of the sling – and it was a very, very long way down.

But the Borderers knew their business. There was a frightening moment when the sling swung out and fell, but its downward movement was almost immediately arrested as the slack was taken up on the ropes. Very quickly the whole sling was rapidly ascending, the hundred Denizens flapping their wings furiously to lift their burden.

Leaf lay on Daisy's back and looked up at the

underside of the Incomparable Gardens. It was brown and dried-out looking, and there was an inverted forest of dead-looking roots or tendrils hanging down.

Above Leaf, stretching all the way to the hole in the Gardens around the tower's top, there were thousands and thousands of flying soldiers. There were so many of them she felt like she was part of a giant swarm, a tiny mote in a vast, ascending cloud of avenging Denizens.

It was comforting to be a part of such a huge force, and especially to not be at the forefront of it, since even several thousand feet below the entrance hole to the Incomparable Gardens, Leaf could hear the boom and crash of massed Nothing-powder weapons. Battle had been joined somewhere above.

Suzy swooped down inside the sling, ignoring the Wingmaster's shout to keep clear, and, flapping vigorously, landed near Leaf. Several of Daisy's petals rotated to point at her, but Leaf patted the beastwort and no tentacles struck the new passenger.

"'Ow are you?" asked Suzy.

"I'm all right," said Leaf. "I feel weak, but... I'm all right. Have you heard any news of Arthur?"

"Nope."

"What about everything else?"

Suzy looked around and scratched her head, then she said very quietly, "I just heard the lower two parts of the Middle House are gone and Nothing is bubbling up the Extremely Grand Canal. The Border Sea is so mixed up with Nothing, it's dangerous to sail. Luckily the Fleet got in and disembarked everyone just before we lost the Middle of the Middle. They're flying up behind us now."

"You said Arthur will fix everything up," said Leaf. "He's always come through before."

"True," said Suzy. She grinned. "Good point. I'd better go and check on the lads and lasses."

Suzy's wings beat down and she leaped into the air, climbing between the Borderers to the accompaniment of the Wingmaster's shouts telling her to stay clear of the ropes.

"Glad I could cheer you up," said Leaf to herself.

Pity I don't feel so cheerful, she thought. *Where are you, Arthur?*

CHAPTER TWENTY-FOUR

Arthur was crouched down, hidden inside the sorcerous illusion of a shrub. At least he hoped he was hidden because he thought there was still at least one superior Denizen on the hilltop above him and possibly even Lord Sunday himself.

The dragonfly had hovered for only five minutes, long enough for Sunday and his entourage to land, do whatever they did on the hilltop and then depart again. But Arthur was pretty certain six passengers had got off the dragonfly and only five had re-embarked, and since it was hard to see from the low angle inside the illusory shrub, Arthur wasn't sure if the Trustee was one of the five.

He couldn't feel the power emanating from the Seventh Key nearby, but perhaps Sunday was trying to hide his presence. Or, most likely, Lord Sunday *had* flown off again because he would need to use the Seventh Key against the invaders, particularly since Superior Saturday's army would have been greatly aided by the intrusion of the tower, allowing her reinforcements to come straight into the Incomparable Gardens.

There was certainly fierce fighting going on, because Arthur could hear the distant rumble of Nothing-powder explosions, and he'd seen several displays of something that was not quite chain lightning dance across the sky. The explosions or the lightning had also started a wildfire in the Gardens. There was a steadily growing column of grey and white smoke rising near where the tower had punched through, the smoke spreading as it hit the ceiling-sky to form a dark pall that would soon block the sun.

Are you there, Part Seven? thought Arthur.

There was no answer.

Arthur scratched his head. Very slowly, so as not to disrupt his camouflage.

Do I risk going up there?

Arthur made his decision and stood up. The illusory shrub grew taller, and then as Arthur moved, it moved too. Experimentally, Arthur raised his arm, and the branch that his arm was inside moved with it.

Arthur thought about using the Sixth Key to dismiss the illusion, but decided to keep it. A moving shrub probably wasn't that out of the ordinary in the Incomparable Gardens. It might help him surprise whoever was waiting on the hill, or at least give him a few seconds' advantage.

Carefully, he began to climb the grassy slope of the hill.

There was another decorative border near the top, only these were not earthly plants, but tall single stems of extruded metal that ended in crystalline blooms of translucent blue. Arthur's disguise would not help him when he was among those flowers, so he stopped a little short of the top and crawled the last few feet so he could see who – or what – lay ahead.

The hilltop was grassed, save for a small area no more than twenty feet square that was paved with pale golden stones. A spring bubbled up nearby, feeding a beautiful narrow stream that flowed around the paved area before winding its way down the other side of the hill. There were small wildflowers scattered around the grass, white and yellow and faded blue splashes of colour against the green.

There was a ten-foot-tall cage in the middle of the paved area, a domed cage of gilded bars that looked as if it should have a bird in it, but instead contained a gnarled and shrunken apple tree, its branches heavy with tiny red fruit. Next to the cage was a telescope on a tripod. A Denizen was using the telescope, pointing it at the distant fighting near the tower. He was green-skinned and wore a patchwork coat of russet and orange leaves. From the scythe that was propped close against the cage, Arthur guessed he must be Sunday's Dusk, otherwise known as the Reaper.

There was something else there too, something that made Arthur feel a pain somewhere deep inside. In front of the locked cage door there lay the body of a yellow elephant, shrunken back to its original size. But something about the way he lay told Arthur he had not just become a toy again, but had been killed.

"Elephant," Arthur whispered to himself. Then, without further thought, he charged, drawing his two Keys as he ran straight at the Reaper.

The Denizen, who had seemed so intent upon whatever he saw through the telescope, turned in a flash, his scythe in his hand. Arthur raised the Fifth Key and fired a blast of heat and light, but the Reaper ducked behind the cage and the Key's attack washed across the gilded bars and disappeared, like water soaked up by a sponge.

Next Arthur flicked the Sixth Key while thinking dire thoughts of retribution. A blob of Activated Ink spat out and shot towards the Reaper, but again he ran round the cage and the ink missile vanished when it hit the bars.

"I'll get you!" Arthur shouted. He could feel that familiar rage returning. How dare this green thing stand against him? He ran around to get a clear shot at the Denizen, but the Reaper was just as quick, keeping the cage between himself and Arthur.

"My Master will be here shortly," called the Reaper as he crouched behind the cage to avoid another blast from the mirror. "It would be best for you, your mother and your friend Leaf if you surrendered now."

Arthur stopped running and stood still, as if he was thinking about what the Reaper had said. But in fact he was thinking about how to get the Denizen. Obviously they could both run around the cage forever, which was evidently impervious to the Keys' powers. But that still left one direction.

"How do I know—" Arthur started to say, but instead of continuing, he jumped easily twelve feet in the air and directed another blast at the Reaper.

The Denizen was ready even for this. He dived to the ground, twisted round and though a little of the blast reached him, most was deflected by his scythe.

Arthur landed lightly and ran clockwise. The Reaper jumped up and ran the same way.

"What have you done to Elephant? And where is Leaf?" asked Arthur.

"Surrender and I'll tell you," said the Reaper.

Arthur looked at the cage.

If I jump on top of that, I'll be able to get him, he thought.

He had tensed to leap when the Will's voice suddenly burst into his head.

No, Arthur! The cage is death! You must not touch the bars! That is what happened to your elephant.

Arthur stumbled forward and only just managed to keep his balance. He landed awkwardly, his face close to the cage, and saw that the apple tree was no mere tree. Its bark and leaves and apples were all made up of tiny shifting letters, arranged in lines of minuscule type.

The tree was Part Seven of the Will.

Arthur stared at it for a moment too long, giving the Reaper his chance. The scythe came slicing down. Arthur saw its moving shadow and dodged, but not quite fast enough. The blade cut his arm from shoulder to wrist and he dropped the Sixth Key.

The pain was intense and would have incapacitated a normal boy, but Arthur had long since learned to cope with pain. He twisted around and fired a blast from the Fifth Key straight up at the Reaper.

This time, he didn't miss. The white-hot beam

went through the coat of autumn leaves and the green waistcoat behind, right through the Denizen's chest, carving out a hole as wide as a dinner plate.

"Ouch," said the Reaper. He staggered back a few feet and sat down.

"What have you done with Leaf?" asked Arthur again. He tried to pick up the Sixth Key, but his arm was useless.

Impatiently he focused on the Fifth Key, ordering it to heal him. Even more pain lashed through his body, but he gritted his teeth as the flesh rippled and reformed, and in a few seconds his arm was whole. Arthur grunted and picked up the quill pen.

The Reaper's scythe lay near the Denizen. Arthur picked that up too, and threw it off the hill. It went several hundred yards, and for a moment Arthur watched it and wished that he could have once thrown a ball like that. But he never had, and he knew he never would.

"I do not have the heart to fight you now," said the Reaper, indicating his hollow, cauterised chest. "In truth, it was a foregone conclusion. But I have played my part. My Master will deal with you now."

He pointed to something in the sky.

Arthur followed his gaze. There was a dragonfly approaching. It was distant now, coming back from the tower and the smoke, but it would arrive in a matter of minutes.

"Not if I have the Will he won't," said Arthur. He turned back to the cage and knelt down by Elephant.

Bending his head, he whispered something no one else would ever know and picked up his oldest friend, taking extra care when he drew the animal's trunk out from between the bars of the cage. Then, walking very slowly, he took him to the spring, and laid him down on the fresh green grass, next to the clear water.

The Reaper watched him, but made no move to interfere.

Arthur returned to the cage and looked at the rectangular door in the front. It had a lock plate the size of a postage stamp, with a very small keyhole.

So how do I open the cage and release you? thought Arthur to the Will. *The Sixth Key writing on the lock?*

No, replied the Will. *Only the Seventh Key can turn that lock.*

"What!?" exclaimed Arthur aloud. "But I can't get the Key unless you help me!"

Indeed, said the Will. *And I cannot help you obtain the Key from inside this cage. However—*

I don't believe this, thought Arthur furiously. He looked out at the approaching dragonfly. He could almost feel those sorcerous shackles again and his eyes were burning...

There is always hope, said the Will. *As I said, only the Seventh Key can turn the lock, but—*

An incredibly loud boom interrupted the Will. Arthur was knocked to the ground by a shock wave that sent flowers and leaves flying, bowled the telescope and tripod over, and tumbled the Reaper almost to the edge of the hill.

Lying on his back, Arthur saw a huge fireball scream across the sky. A second later, there was another deafening boom and the earth shook as the fireball hit the ground about half a mile away and smashed its way through a dozen or more tall hedges and garden beds, starting even more fires.

"What was that?!" he exclaimed.

The Mariner's sunship, said the Will. *You must go to him and bring him back. Quickly! There is little time.*

Arthur swung around. The dragonfly was getting

close. But there were other dots in the sky behind it. A great number of them.

You'd better hurry, said the Will. *This is our chance!*

Arthur ignored it. He picked up the telescope. It was very long and heavy, but he lined it up and held it steady.

The dragonfly had Lord Sunday aboard, and some of the dots behind were dragonflies too, but many more of them were Newniths with leather wings, and winged sorcerers of every rank and department. The Newniths and the Denizens were not fighting each other, but were attacking Sunday's dragonflies together.

"Saturday's joined the Piper," said Arthur. "Or the other way around."

Of course, said the Will. *Without her Key, Saturday would be easily swayed to the Piper's service.*

As Arthur watched, Sunday's rearguard was driven from the sky, the dragonflies overwhelmed by the sheer numbers of their enemies. But as the Newniths and sorcerers flew on, Sunday's dragonfly suddenly turned back to face them. The Trustee gestured and great arcs of lightning played across the sky, striking down hundreds of his enemies. But there were thousands, perhaps even tens of thousands more.

Sunday will soon realise that battle is not the most important thing, said the Will. *Arthur! Pay attention!*

Arthur kept watching. Sunday's lightning was the most spectacular, but there were other things going on as well, too much to see in the limited field of view of the telescope. Thousands of the huge beetles with snapping jaws were scuttling in towards the action, and in the front ranks their carapaces were open to show bejewelled wings. They hadn't yet launched into the air, but had the capacity to do so.

There were also lots of Nothing-powder explosions around the tower. Arthur shifted the telescope and grinned. Even as the Piper's and Saturday's forces harried Sunday's rearguard, their own rearguard was under attack from Denizen soldiers in bright scarlet uniforms.

"Go, the Regiment!" shouted Arthur.

Arthur!

The Will's shout was deafening.

The Mariner can open the cage! You must bring him before Lord Sunday returns or all will be lost!

As the Will shouted in his head, Arthur saw the

beetles take flight and Lord Sunday's dragonfly turned again. It was headed straight for the hill, and flying faster than Arthur had seen any dragonfly go before.

Arthur dropped the telescope and ran down the hill in great leaps and strides, easily clearing a dozen feet each time, landing and springing off again in the same motion.

Even the wormsnake didn't slow him down. He jumped straight on to it, raced lightly down its back and continued springing from coil to coil. At the end, he even bent down to pat its strange, stony hide, before jumping clear.

Arthur crossed the next terrace in a blur and was halfway down the steps to the one with the clock when he saw figures hurrying across the lawn below, clouds of billowing smoke at their heels. They all looked a bit singed, especially the leader. He was an old man with a white beard, very tall, wearing a blue naval coat and carrying a tall harpoon of curdled light. He was followed by a score or more of Denizens wearing blue pom-pom berets, blue-and-white-striped shirts and nankeen breeches, all of them armed to the teeth with sparking cutlasses or fiery boarding pikes and quadruple-barrelled Nothing-powder pistols of imposing bore.

"Captain!" shouted Arthur as he tried to stop himself, his legs continuing to carry him down the steps. He waved and pointed at the approaching dragonfly. "Hurry! We have to get to the top of the hill before Lord Sunday! I need you to open a cage!"

CHAPTER TWENTY-FIVE

Leaf looked around in wonder as she and Daisy were carried up through the hole in the underside of the Incomparable Gardens. The impact of the tower had greatly enlarged the initial hole made by the assault ram, creating a circular gap at least half a mile in diameter. As they flew up through this, Leaf could see a cross section of the materials that made up the floor of the Gardens. There were stratified bands of several different shining metals, four varieties of crystal and, near the top, lots of what looked like just plain old dirt. There were also secret tunnels exposed, and the cutoff roots of the hanging plants that had once plucked fliers from the sky below.

Saturday's tower had been damaged too, of course. The top floors were bent and missing office cubes around the edges. They were occupied by Borderers now, who hung out the sides and kept watch with their muscle-fibre bows, occasionally shooting a winged sorcerer or Newnith who tried to come back down the hole.

Leaf hadn't known what to expect when they emerged into the Incomparable Gardens itself, but she hadn't thought it would be into a vast and only loosely organised horde of flying Denizens, heavily mixed with smoke that reminded her very much of the bushfires at home. She coughed and wiped her eyes as she tried to look around. There were Denizens hovering about all over the place, getting organised into massed formations that were stacking up above her and for miles on either side of the tower.

In the distance, through the swirling smoke, Leaf could see the flashes of Nothing-powder muskets and carbines, and several times amazing lightning flickered across the sky.

The Borderers carrying the transport sling flew across and up to find their place in the line between a battalion from the Regiment on the left, a detached cohort of the Legion above and a squadron of the Horde to the right. The Horde troopers were riding winged Not-Horses, which Leaf hadn't even known existed. The Not-Horses' wings were easily thirty feet across and made of a silver, pearly metal, and clattered like Venetian blinds. The troopers on their backs carried very long lances made entirely of bright steel, with small pennons hanging near the needle-like points.

It all looked amazing, and even as exhausted and sick as she felt, Leaf still felt a small thrill to be part of this great enterprise.

She wished she knew what was going on. She couldn't see Dame Primus or Suzy because there were just too many Denizens in the sky, too much colour and sound and movement.

"What are we doing?" she called up to the Wingmaster circling above, one hand idly conducting, making sure her troops beat their wings together.

"Waiting for orders!" the Wingmaster called

back. "Hurry up and wait... hurry up and wait... just like always. Could be hours."

But the Wingmaster was wrong. Only a few minutes passed, with Leaf scanning the throng to see if she could find Suzy, before Dame Primus spoke, her voice amplified by the Keys she bore, so that everyone in the Army could hear her, even though most of them, like Leaf, couldn't see her.

"Glorious Army of the Architect!" came the booming words, so loud they made Leaf wince and Daisy's tentacles shiver. "All our enemies lie before us! Though Saturday has joined forces with the Piper, both contend with Sunday. We shall spare none of them, but fly forward to our final victory!"

The great voice stopped for a moment then. Soldiers looked at one another, waiting for more, till some smart Sergeant-Major twigged what was required. A ragged cheer broke out, slowly building as more and more Denizens joined in, till it became a roar as loud as a crashing wave.

"There is only one order!" shouted Dame Primus. "We charge for the Elysium, where Lord Sunday makes his stand! For the Architect and Lord Arthur!"

"For the Architect and Lord Arthur!" bellowed

the soldiers. Leaf found herself shouting it too, and even Daisy roared out something that had the emotion of the battle cry, if not the words.

"Forward!"

Wings beat down, so many in unison that they caused a great rush of air that made the fires flare beneath them. Tens of thousands of Denizens flew forward, shouting the battle cry, clashing their weapons, sounding their trumpets and cymbals and horns.

The Borderers carrying the transport sling picked up the faster beat, their wings spreading wider, drawing more air. The Wingmaster called the time and slowly they picked up speed, though not so fast as the Legionaries above them, who began to forge ahead, but only until the Not-Horses settled into their full wing stride, and all the different squadrons of the Horde flew out of the line and joined up into a massive wedge formation a half a mile ahead.

Leaf was watching them in admiration when Suzy suddenly plummeted down next to her, braking so hard in the last minute that she lost a bunch of tip feathers from her wings.

"Wotcher," said Suzy.

"Hi," said Leaf. She was still intent on the marvellous cavalcade of flying Not-Horses.

"It's all show, you know," said Suzy. "Sunday could knock us all off if 'e's got a mind to."

"What?" asked Leaf.

"Only reason he hasn't is he's busy with the Piper," said Suzy. "But as soon as 'e's done with him…"

"And Saturday," said Leaf.

"Saturday don't count now," said Suzy scornfully. "Anyhow, that ain't why I dropped in. I got some of my Raiders to stick 'emselves to the ceiling with a telescope, and one just dropped down to say they reckon they've seen Arthur—"

"Arthur's here!"

"And the old Captain, wot came down in that big fireball—"

"What big fireball?"

"You might 'ave missed it. Anyhow, they're heading to the same place where we're all going, this Highlisium or whatever it's called, though Jonty says it don't look like much—"

"Suzy! Why are you telling me this? Is there something I need to do?"

"Wot? Nah," said Suzy with a slightly amazed look. "I thought you'd want to know. Course, it might not be Arthur and the Mariner, but if it is them, we've at least got a fighting chance."

"Does Dame Primus know Arthur is here?" asked Leaf. "You should tell her straightaway!"

"She knows," said Leaf. "Fred went to tell her. I'd better get back to the lads and lasses. Here's hoping Arthur can sort out Sunday before he sorts out all of us."

"Suzy! Wait!" Leaf called out. But it was too late. Suzy was already gone, straight up like a rocket, with only one beat of her wings.

Leaf looked ahead again. If only she could see what was happening! The sky ahead was full of Legionaries and Regimental soldiers now, as well as the Horde. Try as they might, the Borderers couldn't keep the transport sling up with the forward line and they were falling behind.

"Arrgh," Leaf groaned in frustration. Everything was happening up ahead and she was going to miss out!

Daisy made a strange noise. Leaf looked down

at her unusual steed. The beastwort suddenly lashed out with a tentacle, cutting a massive gash in the material of the sling.

"No, Daisy! Don't!"

A human-size insect looked in through the rent. It was spiked all over and had very, very long limbs that were lined with hooks or burrs. It began to climb into the sling, till Daisy lashed out again, smashing it off into space.

"'Ware attack from below!" shouted the Wingmaster. "Escorts ahoy! Hold her steady!"

Borderers not holding ropes dived down from above, bows and savage-swords ready. But even as they descended, they met an inverted rain of the spiky insects, which had no wings, but were being shot up from below. As the insects passed through the ranks of flying Denizens, they stuck out their hooked legs, and whenever they hit someone, they pulled themselves into them and made both fall.

Falling seemed very likely to happen to Leaf and Daisy as well. Even though the beastwort kept batting away any insects that got inside the sling, the material was slowly tearing. Soon Leaf and her companion would fall through the hole.

"Put us down!" shouted Leaf. "You have to get us on the ground!"

Chapter twenty-six

"Well met, Arthur," said the Mariner gravely as he strode over to meet the just-stopped boy. "I see you do not need my aid to be freed from that cursed clock."

"No," gabbled Arthur. "I need you to open the cage that's got Part Seven of the Will in it. Before Lord Sunday gets back."

"Aye," said the Mariner. "I thought it might come to this. But then all journeys must end somewhere, sometime. Lead on."

He gestured with the harpoon, and his sailors

marched forward, following close behind the Captain. Arthur thought two of them looked familiar, but he had no time to waste figuring out who they were. He turned around and began to run again.

But the Mariner did not run. He lengthened his stride, but even so, Arthur was a dozen yards ahead when the boy looked back and halted.

"Come on! There's no time!"

"There will be time enough," said the Mariner with a well-gauged look out at the distant aerial battle, the smoke and the nearing dragonfly. "Provided we do not stop to gossip. I'd best let that old wormsnake know we're coming up."

He lifted the harpoon above his head. Arthur heard its crackling paper noise and tensed for the toothache and joint pain that would strike when it flew. But as the shaft of light leaped from the Mariner's hand to flash up the hillside, Arthur experienced no more than a passing twinge.

Within a second, the harpoon, moving too fast to see clearly, slapped back into the Mariner's open hand.

"Did you kill it?" asked Arthur. He had to force himself to only walk fast, rather than run.

"Nay," chuckled the Mariner. "It is one of the first things, not readily slain. I have encouraged it to become steps on the hill again, and make the way easy, lest my companion touch its stony hide in earnest."

"You've been here before?"

"Of course. We climb to the Elysium, the beginning of All. The very point where Mother emerged from the primordial Nothing."

"Part Seven of the Will is trapped there inside a gilded cage," said Arthur. He had to keep turning his head to talk to the Mariner, because try as he might to slow down he was always ending up yards ahead. "I think your harpoon will break the lock, and then I can get the Will to make Sunday give me the Key and then—"

"Indeed," said the Mariner. He looked up again. Sunday's dragonfly was less than half a mile away. "I said we'd not need to run—"

"Yes?"

"I was wrong. Swiftly now!"

The Mariner broke into a sprint, taking the wormsnake steps three at a time. Arthur outpaced him, running fast ahead.

They were both on the next terrace when Sunday's lightning lashed down behind them. Arthur was blinded for a moment, and deafened by the crash of thunder that drowned out the screams of the sailor Denizens. He looked back, but could only see the Mariner, who was himself looking back, though only for a second, before he began to run again.

"Use your Keys to shield us!" commanded the Captain. He ran close to Arthur, so close their shoulders touched.

Arthur raised his Keys above his head as he ran, and thought of shields. He remembered illustrations of Roman testudos, the tortoise formation, and that made him think of tortoises themselves and their thick shells. He felt the mirror and the pen twitch in his hands, and the now familiar pain of sorcery. Then the lightning came again and he was briefly blinded, catching the fading afterimages of the great arc of electricity as it bounced off him and into the hill.

Three times the lightning came as they climbed the last slope, and three times Arthur's shield deflected it. But it was not without cost. Arthur felt like he'd been carrying a vast weight above his head and he could barely make the last ten feet to the Elysium and the paved area with its gilded cage. He staggered and would have fallen, but the Mariner held him under the arm.

"Sunday will not strike from the air against us in this place," said the Mariner after a swift look upward. "But here he comes! Now, is it truly your wish that I should break this lock and open this cage?"

Arthur lowered his arms. He looked up too. The dragonfly was coming in to hover and he could see Sunday running towards its tail.

"Yes," he said.

"This is the third of three times that I swore to aid you," said the Mariner. "There will be no more."

"Please! Open it!"

Sunday didn't wait for the ladder. He jumped from the dragonfly, fifty feet up, without wings, as the Mariner touched the very tip of his harpoon to the lock of the cage.

Arthur put his arm in front of his face, expecting an explosion, or at the very least a cascade of white-hot sparks. But there was only a gentle click.

The door sprang open. The Mariner took a step back and let the harpoon fall from his hand. The weapon turned into water as it fell, becoming a dark, white-crested wave that broke on Arthur's feet, the smell of salt strong in the air as the wash sank into the ground.

"All journeys end," said the Mariner. He inclined his head to Arthur, then turned to his left and nodded. "Farewell, brother."

Lord Sunday caught the Mariner as he fell and laid him down. Then the Trustee clapped his hand to his chest, his fingers reaching for the gap between the top two buttons of his shirt, just above his waistcoat, where something gold gleamed against his skin.

But before Lord Sunday could touch whatever was inside, one of the branches of the tree snapped out through the open door and finger-twigs gripped his arm. At the same time a root exploded out of the ground and wound around Sunday's legs. Tiny words and letters thronged and wriggled on the branch and root, flowing off the tree and on to Sunday. These words multiplied, becoming more branches and roots, all of them spreading across the Trustee's body, all struggling to keep his hand away from the Seventh Key.

Arthur! You must act now! came the urgent voice of the Will. *Now!*

The voice seemed distant and far away to Arthur – as in fact did everything else. He knew he was speaking, but even his own voice felt as if it came from some distant, faraway place.

"I, Arthur, anointed Heir to the Kingdom, claim the Seventh Key and with it sovereignty over the Incomparable Gardens, the House and the Secondary Realms. I claim it by blood... and bone... and contest. Out of truth, in testament and against all trouble."

There was silence when Arthur spoke the last word. The sounds of battle were muffled and far away. Arthur felt like he was alone with the tree-wrapped Lord Sunday, just the two of them on the hill.

The silence stretched into long seconds, before Sunday finally spoke.

"You have doomed us all."

The tree retreated from Lord Sunday, words slipping back to branch and root, these limbs shrinking back to the tree inside the cage.

Lord Sunday reached behind his neck.

Where is the Key? Arthur thought frantically. He looked at the tree in the cage. It wasn't doing anything now.

Is Lord Sunday reaching for a weapon? What does he mean that I've doomed us all?

Sunday lifted a chain from around his neck, pulling it over his head to reveal a small, shining object on the end of the chain, the object that had been hidden under his shirt.

It was a key. A tiny golden key, the length of the smallest joint on Arthur's little finger.

Lord Sunday let the chain fall. It hung in the air for a moment. Then, with the jangling noise of a falling harp, the Seventh Key flew to Arthur.

The chain briefly rested around his head like a crown before it slipped down to lie about his neck, the Key itself coming to rest upon his chest. As it settled there, Arthur felt a titanic infusion of certainty and confidence.

I've done it, thought Arthur. *I am the Master now!*

The tree inside the cage shook its branches, rustled its leaves and, one by one, began to draw its roots out of the earth. Lord Sunday turned away from Arthur, as if by not seeing him he could deny his existence.

Arthur let him. Sunday was of no account now. He simply didn't matter. Arthur could feel the glorious power of the Seventh Key filling him up, a power that would soon be augmented by all his other Keys, as soon as Dame Primus could get there and deliver them.

"You must stop the fighting," said the Will, speaking aloud. "It is delaying matters, which is annoying after so long a wait."

It turned its trunk sideways and leaned through the door, reaching out with several branches and some of its taproots, like a contortionist coming out of a box.

"How?" asked Arthur. He had the power, he knew, but he wasn't sure how to use it.

"Why not slay them all, myself included?" suggested Lord Sunday bitterly, without turning around. "You hold three Keys directly, and all by acclaim; you have the power."

"Yes," said Arthur. He knew that he could. "I suppose I could kill you all."

It seemed like a reasonable suggestion for a

moment, perhaps even a useful exercise of his newfound power. Arthur's hand crept to hold the Seventh Key, but even as his fingers closed around it, he was distracted by something. The lingering scent of sea spray; a glimpse of the body of a small yellow elephant; an old man dead on the ground with a far-travelled smile still on his face...

"No... what..." said Arthur. He groaned and snatched his hand away. "I am Arthur Penhaligon! I'm not killing anyone!"

He let his arms rest at his side, and reached past the anger and the pride, past the arrogance of power, to that small inner core of his being, where he was still a quiet, thoughtful boy who had been brought up in kindness and peace.

"Whatever else I may have become, I am also Arthur Penhaligon," he repeated. "I am not going to kill anyone."

"It would be a mercy, in many ways," said Lord Sunday. "I still find it hard to comprehend that I have failed. How could a mortal have defeated me?"

Arthur didn't answer, which made Lord Sunday look even haughtier, and at the same time more defeated.

Instead Arthur gazed out at the battle that was being fought across the Incomparable Gardens. He didn't need a telescope now, for if he wanted to he simply focused his attention and saw as closely as he wished. His mind worked faster too, processing the images, taking in everything almost instantaneously.

He saw the Horde charging home against a flying hedgehog of umbrella-armed sorcerers; the Legion locked in vertical combat with Newniths in a battle two miles high; jewel-winged insects and Border Sea sailors in a confused, circling melee that moved like a tornado, sucking in combatants and spitting out the wounded and the dead; he saw Suzy's Raiders, though without Suzy, the Piper's children valiantly attacking the most powerful foes; and finally he saw Leaf and Daisy, falling through the torn-apart sling, still a thousand feet above the ground.

CHAPTER TWENTY-SEVEN

Suzy lifted Leaf off Daisy's back just as the sling finally tore apart, holding the slighter girl under the arms. The beastwort flung its tentacles up and Borderers grabbed hold of them, but with the barbed insects still being fired against them, and confusion everywhere, there were not enough Denizens to keep the creature airborne.

"Try for that lake!" shouted Leaf wildly. She pointed down at a large body of water, still some distance away. "Drop her in the lake! Hold on, Daisy!"

The beastwort let out a long, high-pitched cry and fell away, with too few Borderers holding on. Leaf took a breath to shout for more of them to chase and grab hold, but could not get the breath she needed, instead getting a stabbing pain in her chest. She coughed it out, but could not speak. The Gardens below went blurry, and for a moment she didn't know where she was or what she was doing.

"Daisy?" she whispered.

"I reckon she'll hit the lake," said Suzy. She was flying upward as fast as she could, trying to get out of range of the spiked insects. The living missiles were being propelled upward out of strange bulbous flowers full of a pink gas, but the flowers could not send them higher than three thousand feet. "Very tough critter, that Daisy. Like as not, she'll pick 'erself up."

Leaf nodded and pressed her hands into her eyes, to try to refocus them and get her head together. "Where did you come from?" she asked.

"Saw your sling coming undone," said Suzy. "So I doubled back."

"Are we winning?" Leaf asked. She couldn't

concentrate, couldn't look out. It was easier just to hang in Suzy's arms and ask the question.

"Dunno," said Suzy. "But we're making ground. Or air. Only a few miles from the Elysium now. But the Piper's ahead of us."

"Keep lots of soldiers in between us then," said Leaf. She was having trouble staying conscious and the world kept slipping away, darkness alternating with flashes of confused light and sound.

"Do my best," muttered Suzy. She was looking for her Raiders, but couldn't see them. There was fighting everywhere and it was difficult to work out where to go. The Elysium did lie ahead, the hill one of the few landmarks Suzy could easily spot. But the battle was especially heavy around it... though Suzy frowned as she realised that there were no longer any insects or dragonflies defending the place. Instead the air above the hill was packed with Newniths and sorcerers, who were desperately holding back multiple assaults by different units of the Glorious Army of the Architect.

"The Piper must be there already," Suzy said to herself. "And it looks like something's happened to Sunday. 'Oo would have thought? I hope you're there too, Arthur!"

She tapped her ears, to check the plugs were in, and swooped down behind a cohort of Legionaries who were about to descend against the defenders of the Elysium hill.

Arthur had just decided how to make the fighting stop when the Piper and Saturday landed by the stream, their respective bodyguards flying back up to join the rearguard that was slowly being pressed back and down by the forces of Dame Primus.

Both of Arthur's enemies wore black-lacquered leather wings, which looked odd against the Piper's yellow greatcoat and fashionable with Superior Saturday's new armour of reddish plates. But Saturday was no longer as tall as she had been, nor as astonishingly beautiful, and she remained a step behind her new Master, with her head bent.

The Piper lifted his gold-masked face to Arthur and spoke, his voice as mellifluous and charming as it had been before Part Four of the Will spat poison in his mouth, before the battle for the Citadel, which felt to Arthur so long ago.

"So you have claimed the Seventh Key, Arthur. What now?"

"That is my business," said Arthur shortly. "I give you permission to remove yourself and your army, and Saturday as well."

"To where?" asked the Piper. He spoke as if to an old friend. "The House has been eaten up by Nothing, Arthur. Only the Gardens remain, and perhaps not even that, at least not for very long. Not unless you let me take matters in hand."

"*I* will force the Nothing back," said Arthur. "You have your worldlet. Return there."

"It too is gone," said the Piper mournfully. "Lost, all will be lost. Unless you give me your Keys. They are too great a burden for a mortal. Better I take them, and put everything to—"

"It is too late for your tricks," interrupted Lord Sunday. "He is too strong. Submit and let us finish this."

"Too proud to fight to the last, are you?" snapped the Piper. "None of this would have happened if you had not been too haughty to raise your hand. But I, bested by a mortal? I think not!"

He shook his sleeve and a pipe appeared in his hand. He had it at the mouth-hole of his mask, his fingers over the holes, when Arthur spoke.

"No," he said, and touched the Seventh Key. "I would like to hear you play, Piper, but not dance to your tune. I think there has been enough fighting."

The Piper's hand clenched into a useless claw and the pipe fell to the ground. Saturday bent to pick it up and returned it to her Master. He took it slowly, then suddenly tried to put it to his mouth again.

"No," said Arthur even more firmly. The pipe blazed with a sudden fire that ran from end to end. The instrument became a stick of ashes, and then the ashes blew away.

The Piper's shoulders sagged.

"So," said the Piper. "I would have liked mortals less if I knew what they might become."

He reached up and removed his mask. Arthur watched intently, ready for some trick or sneak attack. But he wasn't prepared for what he saw. There was only the ghost of a face behind the mask, faint traces of light sketching out someone who once would have looked a little like Lord Sunday.

"I see no reason to continue the struggle to hold myself together just to share *your* company for these last few minutes," said the Piper to Arthur. He turned to Sunday. "But tell me, brother – was it you who cast me into Nothing, some seven centuries ago?"

"Not I," said Sunday. "Would I stoop to such a thing?"

The Piper looked at Saturday. She cringed before his gaze. "My Rats told me it was you. I should have believed them."

Saturday cried out as the Piper suddenly lunged, a knife with a blade as dark as night appearing in his hand. He plunged it deep into Saturday's chest and twisted the hilt.

An instant too late, Arthur directed the power of the Key against him, throwing the Piper back a dozen feet. He landed on his feet, but did not move.

"In this at least, I command my destiny," the Piper said. "Enjoy your triumph while it lasts, mortal."

He dropped the mask he held in his left hand. As it hit the paving stones, his lightly sketched face suddenly winked out like a hologram turned off, and his yellow coat fell to the ground. There was no body inside. All that remained of the Piper was the golden mask.

"I deserved better," croaked Saturday. "If I had been made Sunday—"

She fell face down. The Nothing from the Piper's blade continued to dissolve the greater part of her body, including her head. It would have spread further, but Arthur stopped it, forcing the Nothing to become the blade of a knife once more.

"Stop the fighting, please, Arthur," said the Will. "My other Parts need to join me as soon as is possible."

Arthur nodded and held the Seventh Key tighter as he straightened to his full height. He overtopped Lord Sunday now, he saw, which meant he was around ten feet tall. He also had wings, though he had no memory of putting them on, or indeed of ever procuring wings that shed such brilliant light.

"Seventh Key," said Arthur. "Magnify my voice and let the light of my wings be cast upon all within these Gardens."

The Key felt warm under his hand. Arthur looked out at all the warring creatures, so tiny and small, and spoke.

"I am Arthur, Rightful Heir of the Architect, Wielder of the Seven Keys! I command that all fighting must now stop. Let Dame Primus come to the Elysium and I shall claim my Kingdom!"

His words echoed out all across the Incomparable Gardens and beyond, and with them came a blinding flash of light that emanated from the Seventh Key, a light that was caught up and echoed by all the other Keys, those borne by Dame Primus and by Arthur. Wherever the light fell, weapons ceased to function, sword-arms tired, and all the fury and hatred were washed away.

CHAPTER TWENTY-EIGHT

Leaf regained consciousness with a start. It took her a while to work out that she was still flying, carried along by Suzy, and that Dr Scamandros and Giac were flying next to them, with Fred a little further along the line.

"Did I hear Arthur?" Leaf asked muzzily.

"Yep," said Suzy.

"What's happening?" asked Leaf. "Why is everyone cheering?"

"Dunno exactly," Suzy replied. "But Arthur's got

the Seventh Key. The fighting's over. We're going in to see him now. Hang on!"

She swooped down towards the Elysium, swerving between the ranks and ranks of hovering soldiers, Newniths, sorcerers and insects. All save the insects were cheering. The idea of peace was equally attractive to all participants, though perhaps this was only because the power of the Seventh Key had taken away the madness of battle.

Suzy and Leaf saw Arthur first. He had become very tall, and even more impossibly good-looking. He was a head taller than Lord Sunday, who stood behind him, next to a stunted apple tree that was swaying on exposed roots, as if it stood on tiptoe. Arthur himself was leaning on a tall cage made of gilded bars and staring into the distance.

Dame Primus was a dozen yards ahead of Suzy. She landed next to the cage and folded her wings. Suzy landed behind her, but not too close, and let go of Leaf, who took a few shaky steps forward. Dr Scamandros and Giac at once went to either side and took her arms to keep her steady.

"Thanks," whispered Leaf. She whispered because she suddenly felt like she shouldn't be there. It was like dropping in unannounced on the inauguration of the president or the coronation of the queen or something, made somehow worse and more terrifying because Arthur didn't look like Arthur any more. He was too dazzling, too bright and obviously too far beyond human for Leaf to even think of him as the boy he had once been.

"You have done well, Arthur," boomed Dame Primus. "You are in truth the Rightful Heir."

"I am," said Arthur. "I would have my Keys, so that I may turn back the Nothing and rebuild my Kingdom."

Dame Primus inclined her head graciously. With that movement, the clock-hand sword that was the First Key flew to Arthur's belt. The gauntlets of the Second Key disappeared from the Will's hands and reappeared on Arthur's. The trident and baton brooch split into the Third and Fourth Keys and grew somewhat, before flipping end over end to join the sword at Arthur's belt. The Fifth Key, which Arthur already had, joined the Seventh Key on the chain around his neck, and the quill pen that was the Sixth Key slid into position above his left ear.

Arthur smiled and raised his hands, letting the power of all seven Keys infuse his being.

I can do anything now, he thought. *Anything at all...*

Dame Primus picked one of the tiny, wizened apples from the Part Seven tree and bit into it with her perfect teeth. The sound was sharp and incredibly loud, redolent with the snap of something breaking that isn't meant to break.

Arthur felt that sound like a blow to the stomach. He dropped his hands and stared as the tree and Dame Primus stepped into each other. For a moment they were mighty Denizen and stunted tree, then both joined to become a column of swirling words. Words of fire, so hot and bright they could be seen through closed eyelids, seen even if you looked away. There were millions of words, but one phrase was repeated over and over again, clear not only to Arthur with his newfound mental powers, but to everyone else as well.

I am the Will of the Architect, said the burning words. *Let the Will be done.*

Arthur read this phrase and, to his horror, found that he had spoken it aloud, unknowing, without conscious direction. His mighty voice, and the power of the Keys, had been conscripted to the Will's purpose, the execution of long-delayed intent.

What that intent was became immediately apparent.

Beyond the hill of the Elysium, with a roar like a thousand planes taking off, a great gout of Nothing burst from the ground, continuing upward to cut through the ceiling of the sky. A second later, through the great gash in the fabric of the House above, an answering torrent of Nothing came cascading back down.

Thousands of Denizens, insects, Newniths and others were destroyed in this first assault from the Void. A few seconds later, before anyone could react, another fountain of Nothing burst up, and another. Nothing spread everywhere, annihilating the Gardens as quickly as someone might wipe a table clean.

"Stop it, Arthur!" cried Leaf. "Stop it!"

Arthur tried to turn to her, his face contorted with the useless effort. He tried to speak, but could not. He tried to use the Keys against the Nothing that was pouring in on all sides, but he couldn't do that either. He had become a mere channel, a conduit for the Will.

The others were also fixed in place. The tendons

on the back of Suzy's hand were taut, her sword drawn a mere half inch from its sheath. Dr Scamandros's fingers had only touched his pocket. Both Giac and Fred had just managed to shut their eyes.

Nothing spread to the edge of the lawn, and high waves of it crested together above Arthur's head. But the waves did not come crashing down. The Nothing stopped, as if an invisible dome covered the small paved area of the Elysium.

It had only taken a few seconds, but the Incomparable Gardens were destroyed, and with them, nearly all the Denizens, Newniths and other inhabitants of the House. Only Arthur, Suzy, Leaf, Dr Scamandros, Giac, Fred, Lord Sunday and the Will survived.

A word inside the column of burning letters flashed, and Arthur and his friends found their mouths at least unfrozen, though they still could not move.

"I regret to say..." began Dr Scamandros, whose face was for once completely clear of tattoos. But whatever he regretted was not heard, for he suddenly stopped talking in order to gasp as someone stepped out of the Nothing that surrounded them.

It was a man, unbowed and vigorous despite his obvious age. He wore only a plain white robe, a little like a toga.

"The Old One," said Arthur. "Free from the clock!"

"Freed by your hand, Arthur," said the Old One. "For which I give you thanks."

"But... what is happening?" asked Arthur. "Why is the Will... we have to stop the Nothing! Won't everything be destroyed if this last part of the Garden goes? The whole Universe? Everything!?"

"Yes," said the Old One.

He walked over to the column of words that was the Will and stepped into it.

As he did so, Nothing crashed in.

The Elysium was annihilated in that final wave of Nothing, and with its destruction, so too the Secondary Realms were destroyed: every galaxy, star and planet, including Earth and all its people, life and wonders.

The Architect's Creation was no more.

The Universe had returned to the Nothing from which it had been made.

CHAPTER TWENTY-NINE

Arthur was alone in total darkness. In shock, he was unable to comprehend what had happened, so it took him some time to work out that he was still alive. Or something. He was still aware of himself, at least. And he still had the Keys.

"Light," he whispered, and there was light. A pale radiance surrounded him, though all else remained in darkness.

I am surrounded by Nothing, thought Arthur. *Yet it has not destroyed me.*

No, came an unexpected answer.

It was the voice of the Will, inside his head again.

You are too strong for Nothing to destroy you, save by your own desire.

Arthur turned round. There, surrounded by a light similar to his own, was Dame Primus. Or not Dame Primus. She... or he... flickered between two forms that were sometimes rather like Dame Primus and sometimes rather like the Old One.

"You are the Architect," said Arthur.

We are the Architect, at least for a little time longer. Soon we will return to the Nothing from which we came, so long ago.

"Why... why did you destroy the House? Why destroy everything?" burst out Arthur.

More than fifteen billion years ago, as mortals count time, I made the stars and waited while planets were born. I watched as life began. But it was slow, so slow, even for such as I... I thought to intervene, and chose to separate part of my nature, to create a related entity who would oversee this work. So it was I made the Old One from myself. More time passed, and the work went well, most particularly with the advent of you mortals, something I did not anticipate... as I did not anticipate that the Old One would grow apart from me and disagree.

We fought, and my anger grew, till at last I chained him and made him suffer. Yet it was also I who suffered.

"But what has this got to do with why... why you destroyed everything?" whispered Arthur. He still couldn't believe what had happened. He could still see Leaf's face and hear her calling out.

Billions of years, mused the Architect. *Billions of years... You cannot yet comprehend how tired I became, despite all efforts to amuse and distract myself. The House was one such entertainment, inspired by mortals. Our children were another, and they did distract me for a time. But time is a weighty burden and all distractions fade. I grew to wonder what might lie beyond time, what might be found beyond my own existence.*

Ten thousand years ago, my anger with the Old One finally cooled and I found that this rage alone had sustained me for that time. I was weary, so weary, and I wished to go beyond.

I decided to give myself to Nothing... but I could not. I was held back, because I was not whole. The Old One anchored me in this Universe, for in my rage I had made his bonds eternal, to last as long as my Creation.

I could not release the Old One and so free myself, without destroying everything I had made, the House and all the Universe beyond. So I began that process of destruction with the fracture of myself and the making of the Will. It should have been quickly executed, but the Trustees had grown disobedient and they would not perform the actions that would lead to their own demise.

Yet they could not entirely resist the powers of my Will. In time it twisted their natures... and so unwittingly they came to work to my desired end.

"But why me?" asked Arthur. "Why choose me? Couldn't you just have got a Denizen to do your dirty work?"

No. It had to be a mortal, someone who can create. Denizens were made directly by me and can only copy. I made the basic stuff from which you mortals evolved, Arthur, with some tinkering here and there, but I did not make you directly... and you mortals surpass even Us with your ideas.

"Why do I need to be creative?" asked Arthur bitterly. "I've done what you needed, haven't I? I guess we can both just dissolve into Nothing now!"

Surely you know, said the Architect. *You are the New Architect.*

"What!?" exclaimed Arthur, though it was not really a surprise.

As the old Universe is destroyed, a new one is made.
You will make it.

"What if I don't want to?" asked Arthur quietly. He felt very much a boy again, alone and lost. "I liked the old Universe!"

That is your choice, said the Architect. *Farewell.*

The Architect shut her eyes and lay back, as if settling down to sleep. Nothing spread across her like a blanket. She smiled and pulled it up over her head, and then there was only Arthur's light, the only light anywhere in existence.

Arthur looked at his hands.

"How do I make a... a *Universe?*" he shouted.

The Keys answered him. Not in words. He felt their power coursing within him, and something changed in his head.

The boy who had been Arthur, and had become something more, finally completed his transformation.

He was no longer Arthur. He was the New Architect, and now he knew how to use his power, how to shape the stuff of Nothing, how to direct it on a cosmic scale.

He just had to decide *what* he wanted to make. The easiest thing would be to create a raw, new

Universe of simple matter, mostly hydrogen, and set some basic reactions going. In a few billion years there would be suns and planets and perhaps, billions of years after that, the beginnings of organic life.

The New Architect was tempted by this. He could make that Universe, but accelerate things. He wouldn't make the mistake of the Architect in separating a part of himself to speed things up. He would do it himself. It would be like tending a garden, with steady work in most of it, with special parts that got concentrated attention. It would be fascinating to see what grew, and he could direct it in particular ways...

Deep inside the New Architect, the part of him that was Arthur cried out, a cry of such savage pain and loss that it halted the New Architect's thoughts of a raw young Universe begun from the beginning.

"No," said the New Architect to himself, to the Arthur that he had been. "No... you are quite right."

As he understood everything now, the New Architect knew what the Architect had meant when she had said, "That is your choice."

He gestured, and a stone formed beside him. A small boulder of pleasantly weathered granite. It was exactly like the one that had stood near the spring in the Elysium.

The New Architect sat on the stone, reached into his coat and drew out *A Compleat Atlas of the House and Immediate Environs*. He did not open it, but simply knew its contents as soon as he held it in his hand. It contained a complete snapshot of the former Universe, taken a moment before the destruction of the Elysium of the Incomparable Gardens, when the Will had frozen everyone. All the records of the Secondary Realms slavishly made by thousands upon thousands of Denizens were just a small and largely irrelevant part of the true record.

The Old Universe in all its fine detail lay in the palm of his hand.

The New Architect sighed as he thought about the work ahead. He had planned to tweak things here or there, particularly on Earth, but now he knew he could not for that would endlessly complicate his task. If he was to remake the Universe, he would have to do so exactly as it was recorded in the Atlas. That meant the Secondary Realms would be no different, and all that would remain of the House would be the Elysium.

But there was one difference he *would* make. He had dismissed the notion when thinking of a new Universe, but on reflection he had come to decide it would be a good idea. At least it would give him some personal satisfaction, a little counterweight to the sadness that lingered inside him, a legacy of his mortal past.

The New Architect rested his chin on his hand, his elbow on his knee, and began to think.

CHAPTER THIRTY

Arthur blinked and choked back a surge of nausea. The sun was too bright and his legs felt weak... so weak that they began to crumple underneath him. He quickly sat down on the grass and noticed that not only were his legs not holding him up, they were back to being normal boy-size, and he was wearing jeans. He had a T-shirt on too, a vintage Ratz band T-shirt, and his chest and arms were certainly back to normal as well, and when he ran his hands through his hair, it felt... human.

But a moment ago he had been the New Architect and was recreating the cosmos. Now he was – Arthur looked around – now he was back in the Elysium. An Elysium surrounded by Nothing.

"Arthur," said a somewhat familiar voice behind him.

Arthur turned round and had to shield his face with his hand. There was a twelve-foot-tall shining winged figure there, a figure almost too bright to look at. But Arthur could make out the shining one's features – which were a stylised and improved version of his own.

"Are... are you me?" asked Arthur.

"After a fashion," said the New Architect.

"But... what am I, then?" asked Arthur. Apart from the actual creation of the new Universe, he could still remember everything he'd done, and what he'd become, from that first moment when he'd met Mister Monday and Sneezer.

"You are yourself," said the New Architect. "As the Old One was a part of the Architect, so you are part of the greater being that we became."

"But I'm back to being a boy again," said Arthur, wonderingly. "The real me."

"Yes," said the New Architect quietly. "I knew that was what I wanted."

"Am I mortal?" asked Arthur.

"Yes," lied the New Architect, for his own good. "But you will not get sick, ever again."

"I can go back to Earth," whispered Arthur. He blinked again and casually wiped a tear from his eye, as if it were the New Architect's brilliance that was making his eyes water. "Uh, I mean... you did remake Earth?"

"Exactly as it was, unfortunately," said the New Architect. "Arthur... I was not able to remake everything as I... or you... would wish. The Atlas recorded the House only minutes before the end..."

"Yes..." said Arthur. "But Leaf and Suzy, and Fred and Dr Scamandros, they were here, they'll be—"

"Leaf is here," said the New Architect. He gestured, and Leaf *was* there, asleep on the grass nearby. "I have not yet decided about the Denizens and the Piper's children. But all those lost in the greater part of the Gardens, I cannot—"

"Oh," said Arthur.

Bed 27. Pot 5. A house from Earth, with a woman in it...

Tears streamed down his face now and he made no pretence that it was from the fierceness of the light. "Mother."

"Yes," said the New Architect. He hesitated, then said, "I could make her again, solely from our memory, but she would not be exactly right—"

"No!" shuddered Arthur. He took in a deep breath and choked back the tears. "No."

"I will return you and Leaf to a friendly house, a safe distance from the bombed hospital," said the New Architect. "It belongs to an old woman called Sylvie. Leaf knows her. She will look after you until Bob comes home."

Arthur nodded. The notion that someone would be looking after him felt so utterly strange and at the same time so comforting that he almost burst into tears again.

"Bob will need your help too," said the New Architect. "And our brothers and sisters. It will be difficult."

"Yes," whispered Arthur.

"If you want to talk to me," said the New Architect, "there will be a red lacquer box in your room. A small one. I don't care for that old phone stuff."

"Thanks," said Arthur. He wiped his eyes and nose and took a deep breath. "I guess I'd better get going, then. Um, how..."

The New Architect pointed. Arthur was sure there had been nothing there, or more precisely that there had been Nothing there, but now Seven Dials stood waiting, the grandfather clocks arranged in a circle on the grass.

As he walked over to the clocks, Leaf woke. She sat up and touched her shoulder, seeming surprised by something she felt – or didn't feel – there. Then she saw Arthur.

"Arthur! Is that really you?"

She ran over and hugged him, before stepping back awkwardly.

"It is me," said Arthur.

"But how?" asked Leaf. "What happened? One minute the Nothing was coming in, and then I just woke up here, and... Where is everyone else?"

Arthur looked at the New Architect, who was standing in clear view. He inclined his head slightly and pointed at the clocks, which began to strike.

"I'll explain when we get back," said Arthur. He took Leaf's hand and hurried to the centre of the circle of clocks. "Seven Dials will take us to a friend of yours. Someone called Sylvie."

"All right!" said Leaf. "Isn't it amazing, Arthur? You won!"

"Yes," said Arthur quietly. "I guess we did."

Epilogue

"I ain't calling you sir all the time or nothing like that," said Suzy.

"No," said the New Architect. His radiance had considerably dimmed. He had also adopted a shorter, more human size, and looked quite like how Arthur would look when he was about twenty-one. He was dressed comfortably in twenty-first-century clothes and had cool sunglasses on.

"And I reckon it's time I grew up," continued Suzy. "I mean, I'm at least a couple of thousand years old!"

The New Architect handed over a mirror. Suzy took it suspiciously then looked into it.

"Blimey!" she crowed. "That ain't half bad."

"Indeed," said the New Architect.

"Orright," said Suzy. "I'll take the job. What'll we do first?"

"I think we will rebuild the House," said the New Architect. "Then populate it with Denizens. They can keep watch upon the Secondary Realms, particularly Earth, of course. Though we must ensure there is an absolute minimum of interference, given our pernicious influence upon the environment there. I shall look into that though."

"Watching, but no interference," agreed Suzy. "I bags being Lady Sunday. 'Ere, when are you bringing back the Doc, Fred and Giac?"

"Soon," said the New Architect. "They can help design the new Denizens."

"Time for a cup of tea, I reckon, Art," said Suzy.

The New Architect, known to his friends as Art, smiled and nodded.

"And a biscuit, I think," he said. "Or three."

ACKNOWLEDGMENTS

According to my notebook, I started writing down some ideas for *Mister Monday* early in the year 2000. It is now May 2009, and over the last nine years I have had incredible support, encouragement and assistance from many people, all of which has helped me write the seven books of *The Keys to the Kingdom*.

As a regular life is inextricably mixed up with a writing life, I couldn't have written these books without the unstinting support and encouragement of my wife, Anna McFarlane; our sons, Thomas and Edward (who weren't even born when I started); my parents, Henry and Katharine; my brothers, Simon and Jonathan, and their families; my parents-in-law, Beverlie McFarlane, Peter McFarlane and Jill McLaughlin; many other members of my extended family; and, of course, my friends, who couldn't stop themselves from asking, "Are you finished yet?"

At the actual coalface of writing and publishing, my heartfelt thanks go to Editorial Supremo David Levithan and everyone at Scholastic Inc. in the USA; to Erica Wagner and Rosalind Price and their crew at Allen & Unwin in Australia; to Stella Paskins, Gillie Russell and the team at HarperCollins in the UK; and to all the publishers around the world who have put *The Keys to the Kingdom* into many different languages and many different hands.

My agents have also been instrumental in these books seeing the light of day, and for much else besides. I am extremely grateful to Jill Grinberg of Grinberg Literary Management LLC in New York; Fiona Inglis of Curtis Brown Australia in Sydney; Ant Harwood of Antony Harwood Literary Management in the UK; and the translation specialists of Gillon Aitken.

Finally, I am perhaps most grateful of all to the readers who allow me to keep doing what I love most: making up stories.

Thank you, everyone.

Garth Nix
15th May 2009, Sydney